RUINED

A Breathless Novel

SAVANNAH KADE

GRIFFYN INK

T icks—*there's a little bit of Satan in each of them.*

LENNON SAT BACK ON HER HEELS AND SURVEYED THE DAMAGE she'd done to the ground in front of her. She felt a lone bead of sweat run down her spine, and she pressed at her shirt to make it stop. She hated the feeling of sweat rolling along her skin. But the work she liked.

She'd dug small holes at various points on her patch of ground. None of the holes was wide but each was several feet deep. Before she abandoned one, she would look down in to see if she could spot changes in the soil pattern, maybe see layers where dirt had been moved in recent centuries, or even find human bones or pieces of ancient clay. She'd already spent weeks getting a ground penetrating radar specialist out here to mark her spots and then gridding the area with stakes and string. It felt good to finally be digging.

Some people didn't realize how much of getting your degree was about navigating the bureaucracy. Her last year had involved getting her thesis approved by her committee at school and then getting the town council of Breathless to approve her digging on some of the public lands.

Three years earlier, Lennon had found a good-size piece of pottery while out for a walk on this patch of ground. That's how long it had taken to get far enough in her degree to propose a thesis, to get that idea approved by the research board, contact the local native tribes, and get them to agree to what she had suspected all along—that the piece of clay pot and the design on it were definitely not theirs. Then, she'd had to get the Breathless town council to write up extensive paperwork, saying it was okay for her to come out and dig up some random test spots.

She'd kept that piece of clay pot to herself. She could have told one of her professors what she'd found. It was an interesting discovery. But being who she was, she'd wanted to do the research herself. She was pursuing a joint anthropology/archeology degree. And handing over the discovery would have meant the dig would fall into the hands of a professor and she'd be lucky if she was even allowed on the student team.

Keeping it to herself had been a gamble. She'd had to both downplay the find enough that no one stole the research from her, but make it clear enough what it was to justify doing the dig.

But here she was—*finally!*—with her fingers in the soil.

Her back hurt and her gloves were sticking to her hands. She didn't take them off; the alternative was blisters. Still, if she got lucky, this would possibly become an important dig showing roots of North American human history right in her hometown.

The other possibility was that the piece she had found had traveled some distance from its origination point, and—for whatever reason—gotten lodged in the soil here in Breathless, Georgia. Lennon did not like to entertain that possibility.

The good news for her was that there existed evidence of ancient cultures having migrated through here. They could have come north, through Central America, and passed through this section of Georgia even before the known natives. It was a hotly-contested issue since the vast majority of names of the

Native American tribes literally translated to "First People." But there was a growing body of evidence that others had come through and died out maybe even long before that.

If she already had her doctorate, if she was running her own dig, she would have a bevy of graduate students doing this work for her. Instead, she was on her knees and troweling the dirt herself. To be fair, her thesis was only about the preliminary research to determine whether or not more digging was required. It was still a lot of work.

So far, she'd found nothing. Exactly jack squat. Day three of truly digging and she was out here again, sweating into her uniform of work boots, tank top, and old cargo pants. The pants themselves were lightweight but she'd filled all the pockets until she looked lumpy. The outfit was practical and not much else.

She'd come home every evening, peeled all of her clothing, and stuck it directly in the washer. Then she'd stuck herself directly in the shower. She'd do the same tonight, though *home* wasn't even *her home*.

While her Mama and Daddy lived in town, Lennon couldn't quite face moving back in and settling into her old room and the old rules. She loved her parents, but they were a bit on the strict side.

Instead, she'd moved in with her cousin. She'd been excited to have a roommate. She and Bailey Ann were nearly a decade apart in age. But as they'd become adults, she'd realized what an amazing person Bailey Ann was. They had lived together for almost two months while Lennon finished up all the paperwork and started her planning phases.

However, over the course of the past several weeks, Bailey Ann had moved out. She'd moved in with her boyfriend, now fiancé, Finn Malloy. Those two had begun dating in high school and broken up in college. But whatever they'd worked out this time was jealousy-inducingly solid. So Lennon now had the house to herself.

She'd once again offered to pay rent, but her cousin refused.

She told herself to enjoy having her own home, and at least she tried. It was strange being an adult back in Breathless. Luckily, all her cousins were turning into good friends, even if the youngest Mayfair sister, her best friend Emma Kate, was still at UCLA finishing up her own degree. Lennon and Bailey Ann were establishing a new relationship as adults now. And she was trying to establish one with her older brother Jackson, who also lived in town.

Though none of it had turned out the way she expected, Lennon was still doing her best to enjoy it. Though she was rattling around in a house by herself, it was good not to be in her parents' home. She would always be her mother's daughter, but it was harder to be herself at home.

Leaning back over the hole she'd been working on, she stuck the trowel in and widened it. Her lack of finding anything for three days was not discouraging. In any other job, it probably would be, but in this one, she knew she could dig for months and not find what she needed. What she was looking for was likely broken, tiny, and muddy enough to not be seen until she was directly on top of it. So with plenty of enthusiasm still in place, Lennon went back with her little hand shovel, carefully scraping the edges of the hole.

She couldn't even really dig. If she did, she might break something and damage the very artifacts she was looking for. But twenty minutes later, she heard the first telltale clink.

Her heart soared. She knew that was odd. Who got excited about pot sherds? She and her archeology friends did—the same people who liked to explain that they were, in fact, "sherds" and not "shards." That's who.

Setting the trowel aside, Lennon shone her flashlight into the hole as she leaned over. She couldn't quite make out what she'd hit. So she reminded herself it could be a lost dog tag, a bottle cap, a scrap of an old wooden sign...anything really.

After a few more minutes of work, she identified it. It was a broken bit of a baked clay pot!

As she smiled and stared at the small piece in her hand like a long-lost lover, she heard a noise off to her right. Turning her head, she spotted a pair of expensive and too-clean-to-be-used hiking boots. When her gaze lifted, following long, lean legs, a cut torso and striking brown eyes, her heart plummeted.

Of course.

Who else would possibly be standing there but Gabriel Zemp?

2

Lennon felt every muscle in her body clench. She had just found the first piece! And here was Gabe Zemp, right on time to ruin it.

She'd carefully dug around the tiny sherd, plucked it out, and used her water bottle to rinse it off enough to see what it was. She'd held it up to the light, and just as she'd spotted the zig-zagging black lines, she'd also noticed those damned boots.

"What are you doing, Lennon Mayfair?" Gabe asked her, his tone nonchalant, as though it wasn't obvious what she was doing.

She paused, staring at him, uncertain how to answer. She almost blurted out, "My thesis."

Was that the right thing to say? She didn't want to open up a conversation with him. She didn't want him to know that this meant something to her and saying "My thesis" would tell him it was certainly important.

Lennon mostly wanted to not answer at all, to go back to her work and ignore him, but it wasn't an option. She could list every anthropological and archeological portion of her research. . . "I'm digging for sherds or possible pieces of human bone from an indigenous South American tribe that may have immigrated through Central America well before the first peoples of the

Native Americans arrived." But she didn't say that either. It would just be snotty. Though she felt like being snotty, her Mama would have her hide if she'd heard about Lennon saying that. Never mind that she was twenty-six years old.

So she looked him in the eye and responded sweetly with just one word. "Digging."

Why not go with the obvious? And she was pissed. Despite the sweat and the heat and the days without any reward, she'd finally found one thing that looked like an actual artifact. Then Gabe Zemp showed up.

She'd managed to successfully avoid him for over a month now. She hadn't even seen him.

Damn Zemp boys ruined everything, she thought. Then she thought, *what an understatement that was.*

When he didn't respond to her ridiculous answer, Lennon went back to ignoring him. She focused her gaze down into the spot, slowly digging into the hole again. She'd gingerly set the piece of clay aside, the sharp edges long since worn down and not a danger to her.

Though she would never admit it out loud, she did not want to give him any clue that her find was precious. He'd likely seen her pull it out of the ground—she had no idea how long he'd been standing there, watching. But she set it on the ground beside her as though it were nothing. Let him think it was value-less and then walk away.

But he didn't leave. He still stood there, just watching.

Was "digging" not a good enough explanation for him? she wondered and went back to the task of ignoring him. It didn't work, but she faked it. The fact of the matter was any member of the Zemp family would have made her this tense. Maybe she was lucky that Gabe was the only one left.

It didn't help that Gabriel Zemp reserved a special, mean, little knot in his heart for her. He seemed to think she had something to do with his brother's death. All he really knew was that she and Brodie had been dating for the year before Brodie's car had gone into a tree. That was not on her. Hell, so much of that entire year was not on her, but it wasn't her job to explain that to Gabe. Besides, sometimes he was just an asshole.

Given what had gone down, Lennon was relatively confident she could explain it, and he still wouldn't believe her. No one would.

Lennon had grown up and stopped begging people to believe her or like her or agree with her quite a while ago. So she focused her eyes back into the space where she had been digging and almost hoped she didn't pull anything out while he stood there.

When he didn't move and it was time to start digging the next test hole, she looked up at him. Though she was on the ground and dirty and he was standing and clean and pressed, she hoped she could convey a princess looking down on her peasant. She tried. "What are you doing?"

"Watching," he said. Just when she thought he was going to give her as stupid an answer as she'd given him, he gestured with a tilt of his head and added, "I'm curious why you're digging all these little holes."

This time, she did launch into the full snobby explanation of her thesis. In fact, she tacked on every individual piece of information she could think of, hoping to bore him to tears. Instead, he merely nodded as she went along, and when she ran out of things to say—comments about the migration routes and time frames, possibilities about how the pottery had been made or even carried to the area, and the interesting piece about how it had wound up here, nestled outside of Atlanta on Georgia soil— she shut up abruptly. She'd said enough. She'd said too much. She'd made her work important, and that meant he would know he could hurt her with it.

"So, if you found something. . ." he asked.

Lennon fought a sigh. Good Lord, he just kept speaking to her. Why wouldn't he just go away? But, like a true Zemp, he needed to insert himself into every situation. He had to be prince of the manor. He also needed to be a bit of a dick, she thought.

"If you found something," he asked again, "who would it belong to?"

She didn't even look up this time. "It belongs to the city. The ability to do the research on it, to take it for testing, determine what tests are needed and clear the piece with the National and Global Archeological, Anthropological, and First Nations is mine."

Next, he asked, "Do you have any paperwork for that?"

"Oh, good Lord!" she spouted before thinking. She hated to let him know that he'd riled her up, for it seemed to be his only goal. She and Bailey Ann had run into him when they'd been out at dinner a while ago, and that had just been a staring standoff, icicles forming in the restaurant lobby, but *this*?

"I'm digging on city land, you dipshit. Of course, I have the paperwork."

He calmly ignored the part about being called a *dipshit*. "Can I see them?"

"My hands are dirty," she growled, holding them up.

"Take off your gloves and show me the papers," he returned, ice in response to her fire.

"No. You go talk to the city council. Feel free to ask them directly. I'm in the middle of something," she told him and turned back again to her work, hoping this might finally make him go away. Where the hell did he get off like this?

"What if the land didn't belong to the city?" he asked.

"It does," she replied.

"Oh, but whatever you just dug up, it doesn't belong to the city. It belongs to me," he said, his hands clasped behind his back, head tilted as though he were judging her. "You're on my land."

3

Gabe watched the irritation flare in Lennon's large, bright eyes.

She leaned back on her heels, her hands resting on her thighs, leaving more dirt on the already filthy cargo pants. Clearly, that didn't matter to her.

He knew she'd been raised as a belle, but what would her mama say if she could see her daughter out here digging in the dirt like a common child? Then again, he knew her mama, and who knew what Gigi Mayfair would say about anything?

Today Lennon had scraped her hair back into a poofy pony-tail. She would have been cute had she not been glaring at him the way she was. Now it looked as severe as her expression, despite all the tight, dark curls bursting like fireworks behind her head.

"This," she said, "is city land."

"Show me the papers," Gabe demanded again, his tone soft but firm.

It wasn't city land. It was his. He knew.

He watched as she pulled off the gloves, slapping them onto the ground as though ready to demand a duel. Instead, she stood and walked a good distance away, clearly irritated, and Gabe fought the urge to gloat.

She didn't know it, but she'd been digging on his land, and he'd seen her pull up two little pieces of...something. Whatever they were, they looked like trash to him. But the one he'd watched her find, just before she spotted him, had seemed to make her excited. Though she had clearly fought the urge once she did see him, Lennon seemed absorbed in the piece when she'd first found it.

She also didn't appear to have noticed that he'd stood back from the tree line and watched her earlier. He'd been out wandering, a mostly consumed bottle of Gentleman Jack hanging from one hand. The only thing he could say in his defense was that he'd been out in the woods for hours. So he wasn't completely drunk or anything.

But on today, of all days, he wanted to be.

So he'd stood back and watched her. It would just figure that Lennon Mayfair would show up now. He knew she was back in town, but he didn't know why and the one time he'd run into her they'd had a standoff. It was the best he could do where she was concerned. He'd sipped from the bottle and thought about Karma and how Lennon Mayfair would get hers.

Finally, he'd set the bottle down—it was still back there in the grass—and he'd come out a little ways and been standing at the periphery of her work. He waited for her to see that he was there, but she didn't even notice him.

There was something about her. She was beautiful—it was easy to see why his brother had fallen so hard for her. Her skin was dark, like her mother's. Her nose straight and strong, like her father's. She had her mother's brains and her Daddy's connections, her father's ability to calculate and manipulate and her mother's ability to hide it from the people who most needed to see it.

She was smart, too. No one was surprised that she was out here running her own experiments already, before she even had her degree. He wasn't sure why she was getting some archeological degree. He expected her to go into business and try to take over the town. But other people didn't see her the way he did. She was sweet and kind to old people, but to him she always looked like she could use her tongue like a knife at any moment, and he hated her.

She was gathering the papers and heading back toward him before slapping them against his chest. She let the envelope go, silently demanding that he catch it if he wanted it. He smacked his own hand against his chest to stop it from falling, but he was looking at her.

Her hands were remarkably clean despite the dirt on the rest of her. The envelope the paperwork was in was pristine, in stark contrast to its owner. She hadn't pulled the correct papers out, just slapped the whole thing at him and walked back to the space where she'd been digging.

One then the other, she slid her gloves on and ignored him. Only this time she headed over to a different spot and began digging a brand new hole on his property. He let her have at it. What did he really care about a few little holes?

It wasn't like he came out here much, and God forbid the worst that could happen he, or some wandering fox, might turn an ankle. Once he shut her little research project down, he'd fill them back in. Better yet, he'd make her do it. In the meantime, he rifled through the papers, many of them outlining her thesis.

The crap she'd been mumbling at him before had not been incorrect. She was not making any of that "ancient cities buried under Breathless" crap up. Clearly, a large number of people believed that there was a reasonable possibility some group originally from South America had migrated through Central America and made it all the way up into Georgia. According to the papers, Lennon already had a solid piece of evidence, and that was why she'd been granted permission to dig.

He told himself to turn the pages and get to the part he needed—the map of her approved dig site. The thesis itself was not interesting to him. Or it shouldn't be. Getting her off his property was, so he didn't read more, just forced himself to flip through.

"Here," he said, holding up the map.

"Yes," she said as blandly as she probably could. "That's the map of city property, and I'm aware that it abuts your property, however—" She sat back on her heels again, gloves once again in place, and pointed with the trowel. "This isn't yours. Those big trees over there, that's your line, Bud."

He almost grinned. He could see she wanted to tell him to get out of her space, but since she was on city property, that wasn't anything she could threaten.

Also, he thought, *she just thinks its city property.* It wasn't. Though she was digging for something much, much older, the town of Breathless itself was relatively old in American terms. It had once been named "Mayfair" after her ancestors, bearing the surname that she herself still bore. But it had gone through a period where almost everyone had disappeared except for a handful of families, and after the Civil War they had renamed it "Breathless."

Gabe's family had not been here as long as hers. The town was not named "Zemp," but the Zemps had come in three generations ago and taken Breathless, Georgia, by storm, amassing wealth and a big house high on the hill.

So while she might be one of the Mayfair princesses, he still had plenty of power. One of the things he'd learned going through his father's holdings after his death, was that the property records in Breathless were as old as the town itself. They often referenced trees, rocks, and things that may no longer exist or were possibly turned under by encroaching society. Even the oldest of trees eventually died, and those were often the line markers when your property records were sometimes four hundred years old.

Pointing to the same place she had gestured earlier, Gabe tried to get her attention, though she was once again deftly ignoring him. "The tree line you think is back there is not back there," he said. "It's over here."

"No, it's not."

"Yes, it is. Look at me, Lennon!" *Dammit*. Why did he have to work so hard to even get her to pay attention to him? "Do you see that over there, that big boulder?"

She offered a small nod. It said she clearly understood what he was saying, but what he was discussing bored her.

"Well, that's this one." He pointed to the photocopy of the map hand-drawn by some Breathless city record-keeper from long ago. "See? This rock over here..." He pointed the other way, "is this one." He pointed back to the map, talking to her as though to a child.

She raised an eyebrow.

He repeated his earlier words. "This is my property. And whatever you find belongs to me."

4

"That boulder," Gabe pointed again, and then again to the map, "is sitting on this mark on this line. Therefore, you have approximately five hundred yards from that boulder heading due east before you run out of city property. You're well over that mark, Lennon," he said it with confidence. It might be the Gentleman Jack talking, but he didn't think so.

He could see the slight twist in her lips, the furrow of her brow. She did not like him calling her by her first name, but he hadn't heard her calling him "Mr. Zemp" either, so he went with it. Every little dig he could get on this woman should have made him feel better, as though he were getting some kind of revenge. Only it didn't. Still, he did it anyway.

"I'm not." Her confidence rivaled his, and he didn't think she'd been drinking. She'd always been a bit of a prude in that regard.

Finally letting his frustration show, he argued, "Look, I get it, you're a woman and you just don't understand things like measurements and math." He didn't really think that, but it was such a good insult he couldn't resist. He watched as her middle finger flipped up. But she didn't rise to anger other than that.

"I'm an archeologist," she said it with one of those sugary-sweet smiles he remembered from high school. "I can estimate distance within an inch up to sixty feet, and I can handle a good estimate of five hundred yards. I'm telling you, you're wrong."

"You're well on to my property right here." He pointed to the ground where she was digging holes.

"Nope," she said, and continued putting her trowel into the ground, carefully scraping the walls of the new hole she'd dug. Whatever she was looking for it must be delicate. Made sense, he thought. If only *she* did.

Then he frowned at her as she worked, once again ignoring him. She looked like she was digging, but she wasn't. She seemed to be lovingly rubbing the dirt instead. Shouldn't she scoop it out and sift it? Wasn't that what they did on National Geographic shows? It would be faster. Then again, what did he know? Other than that he needed to get Lennon off of his property. The last thing he needed was any kind of interaction with her.

"Regardless," he said, "and you will be proven wrong in the end. It is my property. We have a dispute. Thus, you must stop digging until it's resolved."

"Proved."

"What?" He was confused.

"It's *proved*. Not *proven*. And no, I don't have to stop digging," she said. "It's city property. Please go away."

Shit. She was just dismissing him. She wasn't even going to stop, and it was his property! He'd had enough of this. While it didn't necessarily matter if she dug holes, he would get the city council to make her stop, but he wanted to tell her now, and he wanted her—just for once—to do what he said. She'd never listened to Brodie either and look what had happened to him.

The "year of Lennon Mayfair" had been the year before Brodie died and everything went to hell. Gabe wanted her gone. He pulled his cell phone out of his pocket, grateful that he still had service. "I'm going to call the councilman right now. I'll get a temporary stay and you'll have to stop digging."

Gabe was not above using any of his connections or his

money to get what he wanted. It was a decent threat, he knew. Normally, people would call the councilman and it would take several weeks, but the Zemp family owned so many of the businesses in town—a whole chain of pizza shops as well as the nice restaurant up on the hill. And they were looking to open more. Before he died, Gabe's father had invested in strip malls and other buildings around town. There almost wasn't a neighborhood in Breathless where he didn't have a Zemp property.

He'd been considering moving some of the business money into rental homes. He would own not only places where people had businesses, but also where they lived. So he could call the councilman, and the councilman could—right now, over the phone—talk to Lennon Mayfair and insist that she stop digging.

However, Lennon Mayfair, true to form, did not seem the slightest bit threatened by this.

"Oh," she said, "good point, why don't you call the councilman? I'll call the mayor." She peeled just one glove as though he didn't bother her enough to take off both and reached into one of the pockets on her pants. She pulled out her phone as he had, only instead of just threatening, she began dialing.

Right then, Gabe understood his mistake. The mayor, the new one anyway, was her uncle. *Fuck*, he thought to himself. He'd had too much Jack. He should have thought ahead.

The Mayfairs had never had money the way the Zemps did. In fact, it never seemed they'd pursued it. As far as he could tell, the families had nice homes and retirement savings. He thought Bailey Mayfair and her sisters were doing pretty well after their father Con died earlier that year. At least as far as Gabe could tell, none of the Mayfairs had ever been out to build an empire the way his father had. But he'd been remiss thinking that she couldn't play in the big leagues with him just because she didn't have the money or pockets as deep as his.

She had connections, and they were genetic. He was going to be hard pressed to beat that one. He figured he could make the councilman still do what he wanted, and so as he listened to her talking to her uncle on the phone about how Gabriel Zemp was harassing her on city property, he filed his own complaint with the councilman. Unfortunately, he was stuck leaving a message, and he tried to make it sound like a conversation as much as he could because Lennon was smiling when she hung up.

He put the phone back in his pocket. "The council will shut you down shortly," he said.

"Cool story. Uncle Jeff says he's got me covered," and she turned back to her work. He walked over and dropped the papers beside her into the dirt, trying to show as little respect as he could for what was clearly photocopies. He'd done no real damage.

Lennon leaned back as he came in close. "Jesus, Zemp, you smell like a distillery."

Crap, he thought, he shouldn't have gotten near her, and she was probably right. He'd likely also just screwed his entire case of getting her off his land by letting her smell that.

He didn't say anything. What could he say? That it was the eight-year anniversary of his brother's death. And why didn't she know that? Or did she, and like had always been the case, she just didn't care? Did she know his father had killed himself three years ago on this same day?

Hence the bottle of Gentleman Jack.

This day needed to go fuck itself, Gabe thought as he turned and walked away. He headed back into the woods—on his property—and walked the ten or so yards back to where he'd left his bottle.

Luckily, he'd been too out of it to open it before he left the house and he'd thus had the cap in his pocket. So it sat there, closed, and for that he was grateful. None of the ants climbing on it had gotten in.

Gabe wiped them off and opened the bottle for the second time that day. Only now, he wasn't just going for a walk. He was heading home, and he was going to get roaring drunk.

5

Lennon ate her dinner alone at Bailey Ann's lovely dining room table. She'd come home and as usual, peeled all of her clothing and stuffed it into the laundry, along with yesterday's. She had five nearly identical versions of this outfit. She needed them when she was going to dig sites every day.

But she was happier at the site than here. Here had grown lonely. She'd pulled back the cardboard top on a microwave container and nuked it for the several minutes the instructions said. The required turning of the container and the stirring of the ingredients inside at the midway point was about as much as she could muster as a chef on a regular basis. Also, she couldn't afford to eat what she knew how to make, not money-wise nor health-wise.

She remembered being a child and her Mama teaching her how to make biscuits at the kitchen counter. Unfortunately, most of what she was able to cook did not qualify as healthy food, but she made a mean waffle, an excellent pancake, and a light fluffy biscuit. They would taste great, if she ever decided she wanted to cook that long in order to eat it.

These days, it seemed she never did. Unable to stand the thought of eating from cardboard, she'd plated everything and taken it into the dining room, at least hoping her glass of ice water and her dishes would look nice. She was grateful that Bailey Ann had left the house wares behind, though she and Finn had moved Bailey Ann's bed from the master bedroom. They'd packed all her clothing and several of the larger pieces of furniture. At least Lennon still had dishes and silverware.

She was close to convinced that Bailey Ann had left them behind simply because she'd told Lennon she could stay in the house and not warned her that it would be stripped bare. To be fair to her cousin, moving out wasn't anything she'd been planning for but when you found the right guy, you held on tight, even if that meant moving to a house you were remodeling half a town away.

After five minutes of eating her boxed Indian food at the dinner table, Lennon found she was staring at the wall. The sideboard was only a little more interesting. Now cleared of all of Aunt Della's knickknacks, it sported family pictures, recently added by Bailey Ann. There were old black and white prints from grandparents as well as several new ones of Bailey Ann and Finn together, and a recent one of Lennon with her cousin just a few days after she'd arrived. Right now, looking at family pictures by herself was a little on the depressing side.

Though she loved the pictures—and she loved that Bailey Ann either had somehow found the time and the drive to take those pictures, get them into frames that, apparently, she had lying around, and get them placed around the house—it only highlighted what Lennon couldn't or didn't do. It did make Lennon feel a little more like she lived here. But staring at pictures during a meal wasn't quite what she had intended.

She'd also found herself thinking about her encounter with Gabe Zemp that day. Though she was confident she'd been digging only on city property and she was also relatively confident he'd been drunk, she didn't doubt his ability to make trouble for her. She'd actually found it a little embarrassing at the time to hear that uncle Jeff had been elected Mayor, but now she was grateful. When he'd run for office, Bailey Ann had even gone out and campaigned for him. Apparently, she'd been bored out of her skull a lot of the time when she'd been home caring first for her mother and then her father. Her cousin had even volunteered at a local elementary.

So had their other cousin, Christian. Lennon was thinking she needed to do something besides digging. Get out more. But she didn't want to run into Gabe Zemp, and she had work to do. So she was stuck with dinner alone.

Both Lennon's aunt and uncle had died in this house, but it didn't feel haunted in any way. That, at least, felt warm. If there were ghosts, they were friendly. They were family, and they would take good care of her. For a moment she thought the Zemp home must also be filled with ghosts, but they would be nothing of the sort.

Those thoughts were the last straw. She was letting Gabe Zemp interfere with the dinner she was eating alone. Picking up the plate and her glass, the napkins and the silverware, she headed downstairs. There were TV trays tucked discretely around behind the couch because that's how Bailey Ann rolled. Lennon pulled one out and turned on the television and ate her Indian food while watching a medical drama. When her food was gone, she sat back and watched the show in a bit of a daze. Until the house phone rang.

She wondered for a moment why Bailey Ann even still had a landline, but she picked it up just as she'd been trained as a kid. She thought she recognized the number, but then a name popped up along with it and she frowned as she said the words, "Hello, Mayfair residence."

"Bailey Ann?" The voice asked cautiously, clearly having dialed the right number, and that's when it clicked in Lennon's head.

"Harper Rose!" she exclaimed. "It's me, Lennon."

They went through a few moments of catching up. Lennon asked how the girls were doing and Harper Rose made her tell all about the dig. Lennon didn't mention Gabe Zemp and the new contention over property lines. She went on to explain that Bailey Ann had moved out of the house.

"Did she now?" Harper Rose asked.

It was a bit of a family taboo to move in with a man you weren't yet married to. But Bailey Ann had been breaking all the rules lately, and Lennon wished she could be as brave.

"So, you're in the house by yourself?"

"Yes," Lennon said. "Honestly, I kind of hoped for a roommate."

"How would you like one?" Harper Rose asked, the sound tentative.

"What?" That didn't make sense, unless Harper Rose knew someone...

Her cousin went on to explain how they'd been bumped out of their own home with her late husband's bad financial dealings. Though she'd hoped to be granted the house in court, it had originally been bought by a shell corporation. Given the shady history of the money, the court had taken a while to make a ruling. Unfortunately, they'd ruled against her. She was not going to be allowed to sell the place and keep the money, and she now desperately needed a home for herself and her girls.

"When?" Lennon asked, suddenly excited. She would not have thought she'd be glad to live with several children under the age of six.

There was a deep sigh on the other end. Though elegant, it was long suffering. Lennon understood. She'd only been partly following the drama that had trailed Thad Bass's funeral like an oil slick. Only after he'd died suddenly had Harper Rose learned that her husband was a financial fraud. His life insurance had been a lie, as had his job. The money she'd always believed was "theirs" was moved around too many times to trace—which meant Harper Rose and the girls had nothing. Lennon knew her cousin had stayed home to raise the girls—so she didn't have a career or even a work history to fall back on.

She was going to have to pack up everything she had left and bring the girls to Breathless. "I guess the good news is I don't have much. I have a couch and some clothes and most of a kitchen."

Lennon laughed. "That's perfect. Talk to Bailey Ann. She left her linens and her china here, but I think she did it for me. Whenever you're ready, bring the girls. This house belongs to your family, Harper Rose. I'm the guest."

"No, you're family, too. We'll make it work!"

"Always."

Lennon watched the rest of the show with a smile on her face at least. She might stare at the walls now, but she wouldn't have to for long.

Then the phone rang again. This time it was her cell phone in the other room. She went running back upstairs to catch it just before it went to voicemail. "Uncle Jeff?" she answered on a huff.

"Hey, sweetie. I'm sorry to call so late but I think I have some bad news."

Her heart sank.

"I'll just say it. Gabriel Zemp talked the council into shutting you down until you meet with him about the property lines. We can all aim for Friday, I think."

Friday! "But that's two days I can't dig. It will put me behind schedule." She was trying not to lose it.

"I know, sweetie, but it's the council. I can't just go against them. And he's a Zemp."

Didn't she just know it?

❦ 6 ❧

A*belle knows when to hold her tongue and when to use it to flay.*

IT WAS TWO DAYS LATER THAT LENNON WAS FINALLY ALLOWED back at her site. *Her site*, she thought angrily. And she still wasn't digging; she was standing there, not in her work clothes but in her best pair of slacks, flats, and her nicest blouse. Though it was an informal gathering by all accounts, she was there with the mayor, several council members, and, of course, the new bane of her existence, Gabriel Zemp.

Gabe had once again walked through the woods. Apparently, his status spoke for itself. He had not seen the need to dress up for any of these people, or at least that's how Lennon read it. He probably did dress like this most days. He wore jeans that fit him as though they'd been made to hug his ass, sneakers, and a button-down white shirt. This time he didn't smell like a distillery, nor did he have a bit of a glaze to his eyes.

Now, the glare that lodged there was clear, and it was aimed right at her. It was a shame the man was so good looking, she thought. He and his brother both, but she had learned early on with Brodie that good looks amassed a multitude of sins many times. Brodie had hidden behind his looks, but he'd become the asshole he was in large part because he played on those looks. He'd played Lennon, too.

Mostly, she was grateful that Gabriel looked different from his older brother. Where Brodie had dark hair and blue eyes, Gabe was blonde-haired and brown-eyed. It helped a lot, but still she could see the family resemblance. No doubt about it. A Zemp was a Zemp.

She needed to stop staring at him, or at least glancing out the side of her vision, and start paying attention to what the councilman was saying. It was an odd little meeting, with way too much politics involved for something that should have been scientific.

The councilman was standing next to Gabe and saying, "You can see from the property records, that this is Mr. Zemp's land here that's she's been digging her little holes on."

Lennon held back an unladylike snort and clasped her hands in front of her to keep from flipping the man off. Aside from the rude comment about "digging her little holes" as though she was a toddler in a sandbox, it was clear neither of them actually understood how to read property records. She desperately wanted to say exactly that, but it would probably net her more trouble than help.

Luckily, her uncle Jeff kept his head and calmly refuted the ridiculous idea. "I'm sorry. I know the records are old, and I understand that the graphs reference as landmarks a couple of trees that don't exist here anymore. However, the boulders are in the original placements, and if you draw a line between them," he pointed from one to the other, though Lennon figured it was just for effect, before he continued talking, "we'll see that Lennon has stayed on the city side of the property."

He shouldn't have called her "Lennon," she thought. He

should have said "Miss Mayfair." Then at least it would be clear she had a different last name than he did. Still, it wasn't like their familial relationship was going to go unnoticed. Gabe hadn't yet jumped in. He'd said a curt hello and shook her uncle's hand, probably only because he was the mayor. He'd not said anything to her.

After his greeting, he then promptly closed his mouth and let the councilman make his argument for him. Lennon again tried to calculate what he was worth as the last Zemp standing. She wondered how much money it had taken to put a councilman in his pocket. But she never doubted that's what had happened.

There was a time when she, too, had been in a Zemp's pocket. A time she regretted and had learned far too much from.

The councilman blustered on, basically saying the same thing he'd said the first time. He finished up his statement with a grand gesture as though he were a lawyer and he had just presented some damning piece of evidence on a TV courtroom show.

Her Uncle Jeff, *bless him*, turned abruptly as though he spotted something. Following his line of sight, Lennon did too. Another man walked up. He wore jeans and a chambray shirt along with hiking boots. Several pieces of equipment and a clipboard were tucked under his arm. He was the only one of them who looked like he might be here to do any work. Even so, the clipboard and the mustache lent him an old-fashioned style, she thought.

Her Uncle Jeff hollered out, "Marty, you made it! Just in time. We're having ourselves a little property dispute here, and you're just the guy."

Thank God. Lennon thought. She'd almost begun to believe Gabe Zemp was going to get her barred from digging on property she'd already fought for the right to dig on. She'd been calculating how much it would cost to bring her own surveyor out here. No matter how little it might be—and it wasn't chump change, not to her—it was money she didn't have even though her project had been funded. There was no spare room in the budget.

As a graduate student, she couldn't say she had the extra money of her own lying around. Hell, if it wasn't for Bailey Ann, she would be living with her parents. Bailey Ann had saved her. And now, her uncle Jeff had, too.

She knew as soon as a professional saw the property maps, they would agree that she'd stayed on the city side. Her patience restored, Lennon resigned herself to standing around waiting.

Two days wasted, she thought, by Gabriel Zemp's inept attempt to boot her off land that wasn't even his. All he wanted to do, it seemed, was disrupt her work, and it pissed her off that he'd succeeded. At least now she knew she'd prevail in the end.

It took half an hour for the surveyor to find the right spots, mark them with spray paint, and then make his final statement.

"I'm going to put some flags in along here." He said it as though this was a friendly outing and not a showdown. "These will show exactly where the city line is. This way you—" he turned, "Miss Mayfair—will know exactly what side you can dig on, and where you can't. And you—Mr. Zemp—will know that your property is protected."

Lennon fought back a gloat. She'd been well and good on her own side of the line. Now she had proof. Though she wanted to look up at Gabe and yell at him that he'd lost, she held back. Her Mama had raised a lady and—while those lessons hadn't always stuck—she let them speak for her now. This had been a shit show. It had been Zemp using his muscle with the city to bully her.

Once she'd thanked the surveyor and so had her uncle, the councilman spent a moment blustering before he said he had a meeting and bailed on the three of them. Lennon looked to Gabe and smiled. She tried to make it genuine. She did. "Now you can sleep easier knowing that none of my research has marred your precious property."

Okay, that didn't come out as ladylike as she had intended, but that man brought out the worst in her.

He didn't even respond. He just turned and walked away.

Lennon frowned after him. *No.* He didn't just get to cause all this trouble and walk away after he'd been proved wrong. She didn't even look at her uncle or say thank you to him or goodbye. She simply started down the trail after Gabe.

❧ 7 ❧

Gabe walked away from her, pissed as hell.

He could have sworn she was on his property. He wasn't just trying to make trouble. He'd read the map and he'd seen she was digging her holes well over his property line.

Okay, he thought as he paused for a moment. He had to admit to himself that even when he was certain he was right, he'd known she wasn't *well* over what he thought was the property line. But he'd been so certain she'd simply crossed the boundary and dug on his land without any regard for it.

He'd lost that one fair and square, but it still made him angry. His word might hold weight with Councilman Barrow, but not against a professional surveyor, and one who appeared very familiar with Breathless's often antiquated property maps. At least now there were flags in the ground and Lennon Mayfair knew not to come onto his space. Still, he couldn't count that as any big win. The councilman had tried his best. If Lennon had been one of those people who could be intimidated, it would have been accomplished. But she wasn't. Though he wanted to, Gabe couldn't fault her for that.

He did try to be fair. The good news was that he still had plenty to hate her for that was legitimate, like right now. He'd heard her thank her Uncle Jeff and head on down the trail behind him. Did she not understand she was legitimately trespassing now? He'd always marveled at her nerve, but today he wasn't in the mood to spar with her. However, it seemed he had no choice. She was following him and might even go all the way up to the house if he didn't end this here.

Stopping on the trail, he didn't even turn around. "You're on my land now and since you just stepped over the flags that your surveyor put into place, I know that you know it."

"I didn't call the surveyor," she said, her voice soft, almost as though she were sorry she'd won. That was not like her.

When he didn't answer—because he simply didn't care to—she tried again. "I didn't call him, my uncle did. Although it's good to have the flags in the ground, don't you think?"

Why was she even asking him? This time he turned around and faced her. This time he let his anger roll off him in waves. He was done trying to play polite games with her. This time he wished he had the bottle of Jack in his hand again; it certainly wouldn't make this day go any worse.

He wasn't a drinker by nature, but she'd caught him on the anniversary of both his brother's and his father's death. He gave himself a pass for that one and he'd spent most of the day tipsy if not downright drunk. The first few years had been the hardest, then had come the year that he'd been older than Brodie ever would be. Each year he thought about how Brodie would never be twenty-three, then twenty-four. This year it was twenty-seven.

The worst part was that on the day he was most missing his big brother, he'd run into *her*. Not today though. Fully sober, he faced her down. She looked professional. Sweet shoes, nice slacks, button down shirt. Somehow, she always managed to look gorgeous, too. If he'd run into her in a bar or out on the street, he would have desperately wanted to ask her out, but right now his chest was tight.

"What do you want, Lennon? *What do you want, Lennon?*" He

didn't know why he repeated it, only that it managed to come out even angrier the second time.

She paused, looking first toward the ground and then back up. "Here's the thing: when I was digging, I knew I was on city property."

He snorted in disbelief.

She frowned at him. "Gabe, I'm doing my thesis for my masters and after that a doctorate. I'm going to be an anthropologist and archeologist. So you can rest assured, I know how to read site maps. I know I was not on your property."

He just stared at her. She was right; he really shouldn't have gone up against someone in their chosen field.

"I didn't know whose property it was though on the other side of that line and, as you can see, I'm digging very close. There's every possibility I'll need to dig to the other side of those flags."

"Would you now?" he asked, the words coming out on a smear of disbelief. "I thought you were digging test holes or something so why would you need to dig them on my property?"

She rolled her eyes at him.

She actually rolled her eyes, he thought, and for a moment he flashed back to high school, to her standing in the hallway talking to him. Then, his older brother coming up and putting his arm around her, claiming her as his own. Back then, if she'd rolled her eyes at him, he would have read it differently.

"I'm looking for a tribe that came through here, long before we place the first Native Americans in the area. We're talking about pieces well over twenty thousand years old. It's valuable and it's important, and I'm terribly sorry if the people who immigrated on foot from other continents and into Georgia didn't respect your future property line." The tone in her voice went from excited to scientific and finally to anger about his stopping her. He could tell she was fighting hard for whatever calm she managed.

"No," he said, no inflection at all in his own voice.

"No?" she asked. "No, they should have respected your property lines?"

"No. You can't dig on my side of the flags." He didn't care if it was juvenile. She wanted something and he had the power to stop her. She wanted to dig holes on his land and the last thing he wanted was for Lennon Mayfair to be any closer to him than she already was. He didn't care if it was for science, he didn't care if it would crack open the mysteries of the world.

"It's for a good cause," she said.

He was at least glad that it must have hurt her to learn the property line she was facing was his. That, if she needed to extend her work, the permission she would need to seek was his. At least that much had come from this silly little survey.

"I'll fill the holes back in if I don't find anything," she offered.

"No," he replied again, standing his ground.

"What is your problem? You don't come out here except to harass me. You don't care about the science, and if you hadn't stumbled onto me you would have never known I was out here digging."

"So, you're saying you would have dug your holes on my property if I hadn't come out and caught you?"

"Don't be a dick, Gabe." She crossed her arms, the calm settling over her as if she'd had enough of him and all of this. *Good. Maybe she'd go away.*

But she didn't. "I told you I can read a site map. Clearly, I can do it better than you can. I knew I was close to the property line and that, if I had to cross it, I would have to find the owner and ask."

"Well, you asked, and the answer is no." He didn't let himself cross his arms. He couldn't stand to give her even that little satisfaction.

"What is it to you? You just hate science? You want to steal the city's history away from it? Stand in the way of finding out where the first Americans came from?"

"Nope." He almost smiled. "I just want to make sure that I stand in your way as much as possible. I just want to be sure that anything you want, you don't get."

"Why? We used to be friends, Gabe. What on earth did I ever do to you to make you into such a raging asshole?"

He couldn't help it. All his calm vanished. How dare she stand there and act as though she didn't know? He yelled it, wishing the sheer anger of it would knock her over. "You killed my brother!"

❧ 8 ❧

Lennon jolted at his harsh words.

"What?" she asked, her heart seeming to stop. *Of all the ridiculous things.* "Are you drunk again?"

She regretted the words as soon as they came out. Though she'd certainly smelled liquor on him the other day, he hadn't even acted poorly then. She hadn't noticed until he'd come close, and in fact, he didn't smell like a *distillery*. That was what she'd told herself, but it hadn't been that strong. She'd only smelled it when he'd come in close enough that she caught it on his breath. He didn't smell like it now, either. Not that she'd gotten that close to him. Not today.

Gabe's eyes narrowed at her as he repeated his earlier words. Only this time they weren't yelled at her for all to hear. This time they were low, mean, and accusatory. "You killed my brother."

"Your brother was drinking, and he drove his car into a tree, and he wasn't wearing his seatbelt," she responded with as much clarity as she could muster. She was almost shaking from his ridiculousness. Everyone in town knew that about Brodie. Brodie was many things, sometimes one of those things was "idiot." She had no idea why Gabe seemed to think she had anything to do with it.

"It was because of you," he said.

That, too, made her blood stop. Where it had previously just gone cold, now it seemed as though her heart had actually stopped beating. The last thing she wanted was to dredge up memories of Brodie Zemp. Honestly, when his car had gone into the tree, she had already been out of town. She did not show up for his funeral, even though she was known around town as the ex-girlfriend.

Their breakup had not been amicable, and she figured it wouldn't be wise to fly home from the semester she'd just started, to go to a funeral of a man she hated. His father would have been at the funeral. So would his mother and Gabe. Lennon had not wanted to see any of them. But mostly she hadn't wanted to be anywhere near Mr. Zemp.

Being in the same room with Robert Zemp used to make her shake. First with fear, then with rage. She'd not needed to be there.

Gabe had lost all of his immediate family in the last eight years. For that, Lennon felt bad, but when it came to Brodie Zemp, and their father, she wasn't sure which one of the two men she hated more.

She had no idea where Gabe had gotten this idea that she was in any way involved in Brodie's death. Maybe it was better she hadn't gone if Robert Zemp had also harbored such implausible ideas.

"It was an accident, Gabe," she said, enunciating each word as clearly as she could.

He was staring at her, standing still as though daring her to deny what he believed was fact. This was as bad as the crap with the property line! If only there was a surveyor she could bring in to explain to him just how ridiculous it was to believe she'd had anything to do with her ex-boyfriend dying several months after they broke up. She hadn't even been in town. And Brodie had been doing the same foolish crap he always did.

Maybe there was a possibility the police didn't rule it an accident? She said instead, "It was a DUI, and let's be honest, he wasn't known for driving sober."

Lennon watched as the muscle in Gabe's jaw started to tic, his harsh gaze bright upon her. She did not like this feeling. He still hadn't spoken, and she had no idea if she'd managed to sway him at all from the ludicrous idea that she was somehow responsible for Brodie's death.

"He did it because of you," he said.

"No way," Lennon responded. The force of trying not to laugh at something so very outlandish had her shoving her hands in the air and waving them as though to ward off that craziness. Her blood had started pumping again, anger starting to course through her at the sheer fact that she'd somehow been pushed to remember things she didn't want to. "There was nothing about me that would have made Brodie kill himse—. . . have an accident."

"It wasn't an accident," Gabe ground out the words through clenched teeth, and then his eyes darted quickly to the side.

There was nothing there, she thought. They were on the trail in the woods that he'd walked through the first day and again today. There was nothing to see. His eyes darting to the side could only mean that he hadn't intended to tell her that.

To be fair, she was shocked. "What do you mean?"

"Come on, Lennon. You think he drank that much accidentally? Did you see the reports on how fast he was going around the turn? He wasn't wearing his seatbelt."

She thought about it for a moment. Brodie was not the most cautious of guys. He often drank at parties. He often didn't wear his seatbelt. He often was a rude drunk. She knew all those facts from up close and personal experience, and so the idea of Brodie Zemp getting drunk to excess and driving his car at top speed into a tree one night still simply seemed like just another Saturday.

Gabe apparently disagreed.

"Gabe, there's nothing in that to indicate it was anything out of the ordinary for Brodie."

"He wore his seatbelt all the time," Gabe said.

"No, he didn't!" Lennon countered, almost violently. Whatever Gabe was thinking was wrong. She'd been in a car with Brodie too many times. She'd been petrified going around some of the turns. He liked the wild ride. She even thought he liked the idea that he might die doing it. He'd scared her shitless more than once.

She didn't say any of this to Gabe. The man was still clearly grieving the loss of his brother. There was nothing she could do about that, and there was nothing she could do about the fact that she'd sat in her dorm at college, taking the call from her mother and hearing that Brodie had died. Nothing she could do about the fact that she couldn't have cared less.

"He wouldn't have done that," Gabe said.

What on earth could she say? Brodie Zemp would have done *exactly* that. Brodie had done that enough times with her in the car that she'd been certain she was going to die with him.

She only shook her head. "I'm going to have to disagree with you, Gabe. I spent plenty of time in that car with that boy." She watched Gabe flinch at her reference to Brodie as merely a boy. Though she'd been eighteen and Gabe only nineteen, Brodie had been several years older than the two of them, and he had thought of himself as a man.

At the time, she'd often thought of him as "not quite being mature enough." Now, looking back, she realized, "boy" was all he'd ever achieved. "I rode around with him plenty. He sped. He sped on wet, rainy roads. He turned the music up so high he couldn't hear the sirens as the cops tried to run us down. He shouted—*gleefully*—when we fishtailed going around the curves, and oftentimes he didn't wear his seatbelt, Gabe, and sometimes he drank way too much, and sometimes he drove when he drank too much."

She'd been raised to not speak ill of the dead. Honestly, she didn't want to say this, but Jesus, Gabe believed she'd somehow had something to do with his brother's death. Hell, he thought she'd actually *killed* his brother. "Sometimes I thought he was going to kill me."

This time it was Gabe who shook his head. "He wasn't like that. You didn't know him, and I won't stand for your lies."

She felt like she had been slapped.

It was all true, every last bit of it. She had no idea who Gabe was talking about, but it wasn't the Brodie Zemp that she or everyone else in high school had known. Bookish Gabe had not been at those parties, and to be fair, she wouldn't have either if not for Brodie.

"No." Gabe interrupted her thoughts. "You can't dig on my land, and you need to get off my property right now or I'll bring you up on charges of trespassing."

❧ 9 ❧

Lennon had intended to take the weekend off from digging but, given the lost days from the dispute with Gabe, she decided to get back to work on Saturday morning. She'd figured early on that Saturdays and Sundays would be more likely to see Breathless citizens out on the city property. Not that people really came out this direction on city land, but she always figured she was more likely to run into people on the weekend than not.

Though her space was clearly marked off for research, visitors liked to ask what she was doing. Lennon always felt the need to answer their questions. However, her thesis was hard to explain in lay terms, and she was one of those people that once she got into digging, she liked to work without interruption.

Still, it wasn't as though she had anything else to do on a Saturday. She knew plenty of people in town, but she hadn't really made plans with anyone. She'd been too busy running into them in the grocery store and such. She would say hello, often offer a hug, and spend a few minutes catching up until one or the other of them realized the ice cream was melting. But she hadn't really cultivated any friendships here.

Hoping the digging would help relax her, Lennon worked on

making up her lost time. She was not yet where she'd hoped to be by Friday. Though she'd built plenty of contingency time into her plans, she didn't like feeling behind.

Getting her thesis back on track should have been making her feel better. Unfortunately, even as she dug and carefully looked for bones, pieces of clay, and other artifacts, her brain bounced around in her skull thinking about what Gabe had said about Brodie. Had Robert Zemp believed the same thing?

Lennon found it hard to believe that their father thought anything different than Gabe did. Chances were, Gabe believed it *because* his father did. Lord knew when they were little kids, Gabe had followed his brother everywhere. The family had been too traditional for Lennon and the Mayfairs' tastes, though things tended to run traditionally in Breathless, she understood.

Robert Zemp had intended to hand over all of the business to Brodie and had groomed him perfectly for the job. Gabe, knowing he wasn't required, loved and worshiped both his brother and his father, but had been encouraged to make other plans. When Brodie had died...well, Lennon could only guess everything had been passed to Gabe in his stead.

She'd always wondered how she would come back to town once Robert Zemp had died and Brodie was running everything. But now, with Gabe at the helm, it seemed things weren't any better. Though back then, if you had asked, she would have voted for Gabe over either of them any day.

Gabe at least seemed to understand that his brother had been drunk and run his car off the road. What he didn't understand was that Lennon didn't have any idea how that might be her fault. She and Brodie been broken up for several months at the time. Was anyone crazy enough to believe that Brodie had pined for her?

He'd dumped her, not the other way around. Granted, by the time it happened, everything had blown up, and she'd been glad to see the relationship be over. If *relationship* could have been the word for what had gone on between them.

Adding to the tension that she should have been instead reducing, Lennon wasn't finding anything in any of the holes she'd dug all day. After Wednesday's lucky find, she'd hoped for more, and she'd hoped it would show up quickly. No such chance though. On the bright side, no one had showed up today at her dig and asked questions, and Gabe had not come walking through the woods to accuse her of yet another ridiculous thing. She wondered what it might be this time, but she couldn't come up with anything crazier than the things he'd already said.

When she arrived home, she found another car parked under the carport at the back of the house. Bailey was here, and Lennon found herself excited and smiling for the first time that day as she threw open the back door and entered into the small area that headed to the kitchen.

They could have used a bit of a mudroom back here, she thought. But perhaps the family hadn't seen that much mud with three daughters—at least not before Lennon had become their tenant. Still, she hadn't climbed into the car with her dirty boots on. So, when she came through, she was at least clean enough to pass through the back door of the home she was staying in.

"Lennon!" Bailey Ann cried, throwing her arms around her cousin and not caring about the dirt.

"Bailey Ann," Lennon said, hugging her back. She'd missed her cousin.

"I thought I might drop by and take you out to dinner. I really thought we'd be roommates for longer than we were, and I miss you."

Lennon smiled. "I would love that. But, as you can see, I'm clearly in need of a shower." She pointed at her face where the sweat was drying at her hairline and down the front of her shirt, where she had smears of dirt collected from the day's work.

"Well, no worries," Bailey said. "I'm not planning anything fancy for tonight. Finn and I are trying to conserve our money and all."

"Yeah," Lennon said, "Buying houses and throwing a wedding and all that."

"Can you go?"

"Of course, just let me get ready? I'll be a few minutes." And so, Lennon had skipped happily up the stairs, having a good time for the first time in several days.

In the car, as they headed down the street, Bailey Ann asked if she wanted to get pizza at Bobby's. Lennon tried to hide her flinch. Bobby's was the pizza chain owned by the Zemp family and named after Gabe's dad. She'd never been able to stomach the place, not after everything had gone down.

She'd eaten there a ton when she was dating Brodie, because of course, Brodie got free pizza—even for his dates. At the time she'd thought it was cool, like he was some kind of prince-about-town. But now, she looked at it and saw he was just cheap.

"Maybe we try the new brick oven place," she offered an alternative to her cousin, who frowned a little bit at her as though *who didn't like Bobby's pizza?* But at last Bailey relented. Lennon was just glad not to be in the place since it always gave her a sense of Robert Zemp watching. He'd framed himself as the friendly "Bobby," but in his home, he was anything but.

After they were seated at the new hipster pizza joint, they ordered and waited. The good smells turned Lennon's stomach inside out with hunger. Though she was glad not to be eating something from the microwave, she would have already been eating had she stayed at home and nuked something. But being out with her cousin was a definite improvement. She could hold on a few more minutes, she told herself.

The two women chatted lightly, mostly just catching up over little things. But Lennon shouldn't have thought she could hide things from Bailey Ann. Just like she could never hide them from her mother or Aunt Della. Aunt Wes was the only one who seemed to have been passed over for the magic "Mayfair Mom" gene. Bailey Ann had it in spades.

Then again, Aunt Wes had sent Christian to volunteer in

Riley Zayat's classroom last year and they were getting married soon, too. So maybe Aunt Wes just hid it better. Bailey Ann did not.

Sure enough, her cousin asked, "What's been bothering you, Lennon? You seem off and it seems like something big."

10

She didn't know why, but Lennon unloaded the whole property line/accusation debacle onto her cousin, hoping that two sets of shoulders were better than one. She was grateful when Bailey Ann reacted harshly.

"He said *what*? How in hell could anyone even think that?" she asked.

Lennon breathed a sigh of relief. "Thank God. Honestly, I was beginning to think I'd come back into a town where I was a pariah. I wondered if everyone maybe thought I'd killed the golden boy, even though I have no clue how I could've possibly done that."

"Please," Bailey Ann said, "You weren't even here."

"That's what I said, but Gabe still insisted it was true." She paused a moment. "Were you here?"

Bailey Ann nodded. "I wasn't here when it happened, but I came back for his funeral. I mean, it was the Zemps. Our families were friends and all. You had even dated Brodie."

Lennon flinched at that and watched as Bailey Ann's shrewd gaze caught the movement.

"What is it, honey?"

Lennon just shook her head, "I don't want to talk about it.

But I will say this: by the time we broke up, there was a whole lot of bad blood between me and Brodie Zemp."

"I thought so," Bailey Ann said, "And Robert Zemp?"

Leave it to Bailey to deduce that it wasn't just Brodie who'd been the problem but also his father.

"Same," Lennon said, and that made Bailey Ann frown even harder. She should've known her cousin wouldn't miss anything. There should never have been any blood, good or bad, between a seventeen-year-old girl and the father of the boy she was dating. The fact that Lennon even had something to say about that was concerning. She hadn't seen it clearly at the time. Robert Zemp was just who he was, but looking back, she could see all shades of wrong in him long before she'd figured out the rest of it for herself.

Lennon bit her tongue and didn't tell her cousin more. It had been hard enough living through it; she didn't want to hash it out again now. It was over and done, and seemingly everybody involved but her was dead.

"Maybe one day I'll talk about it," Lennon conceded. "But honestly, I didn't kill Brodie." She leaned in closer, "I wasn't upset that he died, though. I hate to admit it. I don't think it makes me a very big person, but I'm still not sad about it."

Bailey Ann's hand closed over Lennon's on the table. "Honey, you can tell me, and it won't go any further, and I won't think any less of you no matter what it was. The look on your face alone tells me some serious shit went down, and I am sorry. I'm sorry you went through it and I'm sorry the rest of us didn't know you needed us. I didn't see that anything was wrong with Bob Zemp, or even Brodie."

"No one knew," Lennon said. "No one would've believed me anyway."

"Damn," Bailey Ann muttered.

Luckily, right then she was interrupted by the pizza arriving and she turned the conversation to happier things. "Hey, you think you could wave that left hand around a little more, Bailey

Ann? I think you're trying to catch the glint off that rock from every light in this place."

Bailey had the good grace to blush, "I'm sorry, I think it just kind of happens." She waved her hand as a gesture while she spoke, then realized what she was doing and blushed harder.

"Yeah, when you get a rock like that it does." Lennon knew it wasn't the rock that had her cousin glowing. It was the man and the two of them finally figuring things out for good. "Where's Finn tonight?"

"He's out looking at new properties. He's considering converting some homes into rentals instead of selling them outright. He wanted to look at land and rent values and crunch the numbers. He also wanted to see if it was a good idea to maybe railroad a couple of the houses, work on more than just one at once. So he's going to find the properties, bring me the numbers, and I'll do the math."

"Jeez, Bailey Ann. I mean, it sounds like a great idea business-wise," Lennon said, "But do you really want to do all that work—as a start-up—on top of planning a wedding?"

Her cousin shrugged. "I have these moments where I think we'll just do something little at the courthouse and it won't cost anything money or timewise."

"Oh, my God, *no*," Lennon said, "The new Queen of Mayfair cannot have a little wedding." She used air quotes before she picked up her first slice of pizza and took a hot bite. The cheese almost seared the roof of her mouth, but the flavor was worth the moments of pain.

Bailey responded in kind, "I'm not Queen of Mayfair. That would be your mother now, if not always."

Her comment made sense to Lennon. No one really knew how well Della or Gigi ranked in the royal hierarchy against each other. But as the surviving Mayfair wife, the title definitely belonged to Lennon's mother now.

"Still," Lennon said, "You and Finn are about the same royalty level here as Meghan Markle and Prince Harry to the rest of the world. I think you two owe it to the town to do up something big."

Bailey Ann laughed hard, throwing her head back, "Well, I have to admit, I always did have my little girl fantasies about having a huge wedding."

"I know," Lennon said. The Mayfair girls had all heard enough of them back in the day. Bailey Ann shook her head as her expression turned more somber. "I've let go of a lot of my little girl fantasies recently though. Seems I was wrong in a lot of cases, and naïve in a lot of others. Maybe it's time to let this one go, too."

"Absolutely not," Lennon told her, "This is one you should hold onto. If you and Finn are as happy as you look, then you should celebrate it. And everyone else should get a chance to see it. I mean, you don't need to go all out, and you don't actually owe the town a wedding, but if that's what you want, no one's going to begrudge you a moment of it."

Bailey Ann offered a small smile, "You know," she said, "That sounds like a plan. Finn and I wanted to get married on the date we first met. It's even a Saturday this year." She picked up her phone and pulled up the calendar to show Lennon. "I wonder if I can call someone this late at night to see if the club is available, and the church, and—"

Grinning now, Lennon spoke the words over Bailey Ann's voice for the last part, ". . . and whether or not it's a home game day for the Dawgs."

❧ 11 ❧

G abe sat at the large desk in the office in the back of the house. It had been his father's desk, his father's office, his father's chair. He poured himself a glass of Gentleman Jack into a cut crystal tumbler that had also belonged to his father.

His father had drunk regular Jack Daniels, Old Number Seven, but the taste had always been too sharp for Gabe. Rob, when he'd been alive, had teased him for it. Young Gabe had always shot back the whiskey as fast as he could to get it gone and fought his sputters at the bite. Himself, he preferred a smoother flavor. Maybe he wasn't the man his father was. Hell, he was certain of it, but at least he drank a more expensive whiskey.

He just closed a contract for one of the old school buildings on the other side of town. Thinking about what he'd accomplished, Gabe turned and looked out the window. He wouldn't have anticipated doing this. The building had been an elementary. The school had still been active even just ten years ago. In fact, some of his friends in high school had come from that elementary.

The whole town still fed into the same two middle schools and one high school as when he'd attended, but the elementary schools were getting redone. The newer suburbs were springing up on the edges of town where the space existed for bigger houses and lots. The schools were moving closer to where the kids were. They were getting upgraded, the design newer, the buildings nicer.

This old one had stood empty for some time. The city sold off the back lot long ago and businesses had come up close. The chain link fence surrounding it had grown rusted and saggy while the building sat. Gabe snagged it for a song and because of his low cost investment, he was going to try something new. He was going to try something a little more "big city" than what Breathless was used to.

Though there were many businesses in the area, he was going to convert the school into apartment buildings. He was aiming for the live-work-play model. In some—albeit much larger—cities, this was happening in a single building. In Breathless, he would bring it to one block and see how it panned out.

The building was perfect. It already had a handful of rooms cut to the right size. Because each school room had had a sink and water and drain piping already existed throughout the structure. He'd had his guy inspect it thoroughly.

In his vision, they would keep the old hallways mostly intact, leaving the wood plank flooring where they could. There were large windows that ran the length of an entire room. The charm of it would be that it was, in fact, an old elementary school building.

However, it had its problems too. While the main portion of the building was brick, the roof leaked like a sieve and he was going to have to get his guys on that first, then some specialists to help him make decisions of what parts of the old school building to keep.

He'd seen this done before. In one place, they'd pulled up the gymnasium floor, rearranged the wood planks, and created unique hardwood flooring for some of the higher end units. He thought he would probably do that. The basketball goal he might mount outside in a common area beyond the parking lot.

He had plans, he had designs, and he had a fucking headache. Its name was Lennon Mayfair.

This was a fantastic deal and he ought to be enjoying it more than he was. Instead, he was drinking more than he ought to be and thinking about the fact that she looked at him like he was nuts when he'd said she was the reason Brodie had died.

On the one hand, she was right. Brodie had drunk too much and driven his car into a tree, but he'd only done it because of Lennon. Gabe knew this and Lennon's not being able to put two and two together was making him crazy.

He wondered for a moment what his life would be like if Brodie had lived. He figured his father would still be alive now. Lennon had caused Brodie's death and that in turn had caused his father's death and then his mother's. It was easy to lay the blame for all of it right at her feet.

Almost five years after Brodie's death, his father had been diagnosed with colon cancer. That, apparently, had been the final straw. It was a shame. It was such a lightweight straw. Had Brodie still been alive, that probably wouldn't have been the end of his dad, but it had been too much to deal with.

The cancer, the doctors all said, would be curable.

It would take time, it would take drastic medication, and it would take devastating chemo, but Robert Zemp had a ninety percent expectancy of survival given the treatment and the very early stage at which they'd caught it.

But it wasn't enough. Brodie had clearly been his father's favorite son and Brodie was long gone by then. Gabe was doing his best to fill in; he'd picked up the mantle and finished his degree. Instead of continuing in the arts, he'd done it in business. He had taken economics and math, just like Brodie had planned, and he'd begun shadowing his father and helping close business deals once he'd graduated. That had only lasted about six months when the diagnosis came in.

The problem was Gabe had missed it. He'd missed whatever important flag or point he should have caught. He'd missed his father's decision. He thought that the cancer diagnosis and the ninety percent survival rate was a bump in the road.

In fact, that's the way the doctor had described it: Do the treatment. It'll suck. It'll be painful and when it's over, you'll be fine. In a year, you'll almost have forgotten about it, but it hadn't been enough. His mother had already been sick. Apparently, she had been further along in her illness than she'd told Gabe she was.

Asthma and several chronic diseases had been a part of her life since she was young. But somewhere along the way, she had gotten something else and she simply hadn't let them know she was going downhill. Well, maybe she'd let his dad know.

Even if they'd lost her and it wound up as just being Dad and him, Gabe thought that would have been enough, but it wasn't. He and his mother had heard the blast from the other side of the house.

They'd run, hard.

To this day he remembered the feeling of moving as fast as he could and yet not covering any ground. He remembered *knowing* that he'd heard a gunshot and yet reciting a litany of possible alternatives as he'd slammed down the hallway and thrown open the door. Though it had just been moments, he'd arrived a lifetime too late.

His father was on the other side of the room, his body across the couch, dead. Perhaps he'd been preserving the desk and the chair. Perhaps it had simply been his favorite spot and he couldn't stand marring it. Perhaps it had been a way of not giving them a reason to haul his precious things away.

Whatever it was, Rob Zemp had decided it wasn't worth hanging around to find out. Gabe had inherited the family business. And now, Gabe sat in the chair.

❧ 12 ❧

Lennon had woken up on Monday morning with a renewed
sense of happiness. She was grateful to be here, her day
was good, the property lines had been defined by a row of flags.
Contrary to what Gabe Zemp might think, she liked those flags.
It meant he couldn't bitch at her any more when she'd been
reading the maps correctly all along.

To make things even better, Bailey Ann had invited her to be
a bridesmaid and had asked her what color would she like to
wear. That was a gracious move for a Southern Princess. It was
the bride's choice and if she decided puke-green, then all the
bridesmaids were to happily wear puke-green. Bailey Ann was
acting like real royalty. Obviously, Harper Rose would be maid of
honor because Harper Rose was Bailey's nearest sister and that
was how it was done, but Emma Kate would be back for a big
wedding.

No courthouse quickie for Bailey Ann and Finn. Lennon
could see in Bailey Ann's eyes that she wanted the whole deal.
There would be a white dress, an aisle, and everyone in attendance. Even if it had to happen quickly to make the date the two
of them had planned.

She's had a brief moment of thought, what if Finn asked

Gabe Zemp to be one of groomsmen? Surely that wouldn't happen, the two were not close enough. But Finn had been dealing in properties and values lately. That meant he would almost have to run into Gabe somewhere along the line.

With Finn, he might have decided to make a friend. Lennon didn't know him enough to know if that would be the case, but it made her heart twist. She wouldn't want to tell Bailey Ann something that would hurt her wedding. Lennon kept her fingers crossed on that one. The town was plenty big, and Finn had other friends, and she told herself it wouldn't happen.

She'd spent her day digging holes, getting a couple of feet deep on each of them. Lennon had been excited to be back doing her research unhindered again, even though she hadn't been finding anything.

So when she hit a rock, it put the first bend of frustration into her day. She dug into it, finding it bigger than she expected. No small pebble or stray gravel, this was a chunk of rock and that was disheartening.

Lennon was afraid she'd maybe found what was a very shallow bit of bedrock, which would make it less likely someone had settled here, even for a short while. She couldn't just hit rock and walk away. It wouldn't be enough information. She'd have to dig it up even if it proved her whole theory wrong and she had to find another thesis. Somehow that sherd had wound up on Breathless property, but her thesis was that the nomadic group—whoever they were—had stayed *here*. Her heart squeezed in her chest, but she kept digging, slowly and carefully.

Twenty thousand years was a long time for something to happen, so before she quit this area and moved on to one of her other grid squares, she had to dig wide enough to prove that this either was high level bedrock or some rocky ground cover too dense for a settlement or it wasn't. Anything less and her thesis committee would give her hell about it when she defended her paper. If she got this work published, other anthropologists or archeologists would write letters to her asking her why she'd failed to do such an important step.

So she traced the top of the rock, digging and brushing back the dirt, still trying to be careful in case it wasn't just a rock. Very quickly, she discovered it wasn't as disappointing as it had originally looked. In fact, she found the edges of it and it turned out to be part of a clay brick, and an old one.

In no time at all, she'd excavated it and was holding a piece of history in her hands. Much heavier than the sherds she had originally dug up, this one might even have more to tell her. She grabbed for her camera and began documenting it.

As it was simply a brick, this one wasn't necessarily identifiable to any culture or era—not until she could get more than a visual inspection. Possibly some kind of carbon dating of any organic material in it would help figure out just how old it was, but it was clearly human made and nothing recent.

Her blood now thrumming with the excitement of her find, Lennon kept digging in ever widening circles around the spot where her brick had been found.

Before she knew it, she was deeper than she'd planned to go but had discovered a line of rock, possibly an old foundation from something long before Breathless had existed here, long before the Mayfair family had come and settled the area. She knew where the town had originally set its buildings—that had been part of the original research she'd done before starting the physical portion of this project. She'd known what those original buildings were made of, so she could avoid digging up more recent artifacts.

Lennon had also become well versed on what areas had been used by the local First Nations tribes. She'd also known, from her studies, what kinds of tools, pots, and baskets they might have carried. The tribes in this area had been more mobile societies than others. They had not built permanent dwellings, so if she'd hit something unexpected...

She let the thought trail off. She didn't want to think it.

What if she got excited and she was wrong? So Lennon kept digging and digging and digging. By mid-afternoon, she noticed something she didn't like at all, and she sat back on her heels, mortified. Surely, she had to be wrong.

As the sun went down and the light around her faded, she realized the line of bricks was headed straight for the flags. She should have quit, but she didn't. Instead, she got out her dorky headlamp and put it on, shining her own way as she went. And she kept digging.

She'd missed working on the site on Thursday and Friday, because of Gabe Zemp. She'd done a good amount of work to make up for that on Saturday, but Bailey Ann had convinced her to take Sunday off. So Lennon decided now that working late was just making up for missed time. It wasn't any kind of neurosis. She told herself she needed to follow what she found.

The line of rock, now pressed tightly together from time and embedded sediment, was far below the surface. Her work digging it out wasn't easy. The good news was the soil itself wasn't too difficult to work with, and the brick she had originally found was the only thing that seemed to be in her way.

Except for those damn flags.

She prayed hard that the outline she had found—the possible stone foundation of what might have been an outbuilding of some kind—would take a sharp turn left and take her away from those now horrid flags.

Lennon prayed as hard as she could but she couldn't change the past. The more she dug, the more she saw the line went straight up to the flags. And right under it.

She was going to have to ask permission to dig on his property, and he was going to do everything he could to deny it. Lennon sat on her butt with her hand in her hair as she looked out over the Zemp property. Now she knew it contained at least some, if not a treasure trove, of ancient artifacts.

She muttered, "Son of a bitch."

✿ 13 ✿

Lennon stood on the doorstep of the large house, surprised at just how bad it felt to be standing here again after all this time. It felt bad for any number of reasons. One of which was that it was Tuesday, and instead of getting dressed in her tank top and cargo pants and going back and digging, she was here. She was missing yet another day of work because of Gabriel Zemp.

The foundation line she'd found had been exciting. Maybe only to her, but exciting nonetheless. Small, handmade bricks had been pressed together and laid straight, indicating humans and purpose. Had it not been so late at night when she finally butted up against the Zemp property, she would have turned around and dug the other way.

But she'd kept digging toward the flags because she'd needed to know if it was going to be a battle to get Gabriel Zemp to let her dig on his land. She needed to start that battle now. She only had so much time to complete this thesis and there was already a wedding in the way. At least that was a happy thing.

There was also the possibility that if he said no and he stuck to it, she would have to go through the city and force him to give her the right to do her research there. Lennon hoped the city would be on her side. She would have to push the idea that the archeological find was far more important than land Gabriel Zemp could not prove he was using.

It was important that she not give away that little snippet of information. If Gabe knew that using the land would get in her way, he would start building something on it tomorrow. Lennon was certain of it.

She was also dealing with the harsh feelings—maybe even PTSD—of being at this house again. The last time she'd been here, she'd been thrown out. Robert Zemp had yelled at her, called her all kinds of terrible things and made harsh demands.

The things he'd called her had been untrue. In fact, he'd been completely unaware of his own son's part in the whole problem. Though, as Lennon looked back on it now as an adult, Robert Zemp must have been willfully unaware. It was clear their problem was one that, at the very least, they'd both gotten themselves into.

Lifting her hand to knock a second time, Lennon pulled back and slowly let her fist fall to her side again. She didn't want Gabe coming to the door before she was ready. Though it only then occurred to her there might be a camera and he might be watching her right now. If that was the case, she was well and screwed. He would have seen her standing here for several minutes already. So, she ought to get herself together before she knocked and set everything in motion.

She hated the way Gabe Zemp looked at her now. They'd been friends when they were younger. She'd even harbored a good-sized crush on him once.

Who wouldn't? He was a good looking guy. A prince around town. Richest kid in the city, aside from his brother, who already had finer clothes and a fancier car than everyone else. Gabe, too, had been gifted with an expensive foreign model on his sixteenth birthday. A nice set of wheels to take into the high school parking lot every day.

Lennon had not even gotten a car. Though her family had

enough money to get her a car on her sixteenth birthday, hers would never have been an Alpha Romeo. It also would not have been new. And her parents hadn't wanted their sixteen-year-old daughter out driving around on her own. Looking back, Lennon thought, a car might have saved her. It might have given her more options than Brodie Zemp.

The door loomed in front of her, a large piece of carved maple. The glass panels on either side were shaded by curtains. It was imposing, not welcoming. She felt imposed upon, certainly.

Good job, Rob, she thought, but told herself to buck up, she would have to get through this. If she didn't, she wouldn't convince Gabe to let her dig on his land. That was unacceptable. There were archeological finds there that might be important to the history of the nation. Not that anyone in the general population really cared, but scientifically, they might mean a lot.

They also might mean nothing. What Lennon really loved about her science, was that a negative result was just as important as a positive one. If other earlier peoples or tribes had not come through here, and everything she found was of native first nations people, that would simply help prove another theory.

So she tried to think of how she might get Gabe to agree. She might get him to let her dig if she could figure out what it was that he wanted. That was a hard question. He was angry. Angry at her, specifically, for something she couldn't have done.

He might want her apology, but that would mean nothing. And she couldn't give it anyway since she had no clue what she would be apologizing for. Not that she would. Brodie's death had been his own damn fault. Gabe would have come to grips with that. So how to stop him from lashing out at her?

The problem was Gabe was hurt. She could see that when she looked at him. As angry as he was, and as much as he used his energy to stop her, it was because he believed she had something to do with Brodie's death.

She could admit that would be a hard one to let go. She

couldn't imagine her brother Jackson gone, let alone think that someone she knew was responsible for it. She'd had to let go of Jackson's wife Shelle, and that had been hard enough. She'd died suddenly, just like Brodie. And purposelessly, just like Brodie. Lennon and Jackson had both struggled with the idea that someone was to blame for Shelle's death. So while she disagreed with Gabe, she thought she at least understood where he was coming from. The problem was how would she convince him where he was coming from was dead wrong? As much as Lennon had trouble with Brodie and Robert Zemp in the past, she'd never had trouble with Gabe. At least not until now.

She raised her hand and finally knocked on the door. It was only a few short moments before the large panel opened wide and it was answered, not by a butler or a maid, but by Gabriel Zemp himself.

He stared at her and sighed as if it hurt him to look at her face. "You again? Why can't you just leave me alone?"

G abe's heart quit beating when he opened the door. He hadn't looked out the peephole, and he hadn't upgraded the front door security any better than it had been when the house had originally been built. Though his heart stopped, his mouth kept moving, and he said insulting, horrible things to her.

Sometimes he didn't know why those things came out of his mouth, why he couldn't just say, "Yes," and let her dig. It wouldn't have meant anything really. What were a few holes at the edge of his property?

On the other hand, she'd had far too much to do with his family falling apart. He couldn't forgive that. The problem was, he had loved her once. He'd had a huge crush on her in middle school, before he truly understood what it meant. Then, as a couple years had gone by and he hit high school, she'd come in the year behind him, and he'd understood a little bit more.

Suddenly, he hadn't wanted to date anyone else. He'd had a girlfriend, a steady date—as one does in high school. But he'd broken things off with her because of Lennon. Though he'd known Lennon Mayfair since they were small, this time, when she showed up as a high school freshman, he'd fallen hard and fast. He'd simply wanted her to be his girlfriend.

It was his junior year before he worked up any level of nerve. They'd been friends and he either told himself he wasn't willing to risk that, or he'd chickened out at every turn. When he finally got his crap together and managed to actually ask her out, he'd messed it up. Then he'd messed it up a second time, and then he'd managed to dick it up a third time.

Each time he'd asked her, she'd said yes. But within minutes either she or he would wind up inviting their other friends along and making it into a party rather than a date. To this day, he wondered if she knew that his intent had been just the two of them. He'd not gotten a fourth chance.

He'd showed up at home one day with Lennon in tow. Tucking her hand in his, he'd tugged her through the house. It was the first time he could remember her being there. They'd had a chemistry project assigned that morning and he'd grabbed her, saying "be my partner," before anyone else could. She was sharp as a tack, and he could claim that he'd done it for the grade, but mostly he'd done it for the company and another chance to ask her out. But it hadn't happened.

They'd shown up at his home, ate snacks, made their plans, and discussed their poster. They'd been halfway through when Gabe opened his mouth to ask her again. He was going to do it. Here in his own home, where there were no friends passing in the hallway to add to the date. He started his question, and Brodie walked in.

Brodie had taken one look at Lennon Mayfair and decided that she would be his. Though Gabe had known her for years, he wasn't sure if she and Brodie had ever really met before that moment. Brodie, unlike Gabe, had no compunctions and no marbles in his mouth. It took Brodie all of ten minutes to work around to asking her out. Lennon had smiled brightly and immediately said yes, and Gabe's heart had broken in two.

He'd spent the next year and half wishing that things had turned out differently, and he'd spent the eight years after that hating her.

And now she'd come back. When she'd been gone, she'd been easier to deal with. For the first time, he wished he had a wife or maybe some beautiful girlfriend to walk up behind him, wearing nothing but a silk bathrobe. Her mussed hair would indicate they'd been doing something sexy in the middle of the afternoon.

He had no such thing. He wasn't even close, having turned into a raging workaholic, just like his father. Of course, his father had a wife and two sons, so Gabe was still falling short on that front.

Besides his work, he had nothing else in his life, except apparently stopping Lennon Mayfair.

He looked her up and down, hoping to intimidate her, though it didn't seem to work. As she asked again for permission, he simply said, "No." There was something satisfying in blocking her.

"But Gabe," she said, "the work itself is important. This has nothing to do with me. It might show that there were other tribes in the U.S., or migrants from other areas. It might show another tribe was here prior to the people that we often think of as the first settlers in this area. There's evidence now that supports that possibility."

When he didn't answer, she kept talking. "It's controversial, and no one is sure which way it goes or who was really here first. What's going to solve that mystery will be evidence. Your name and your land could be part of that."

Oh, hell no, he thought. Gabe stayed calm and simply shook his head. "I'm sorry. You're not going to sell me on some kind of archeological fame. I really don't give a shit, Lennon."

He was turning to close the door. She put her foot in it, old school salesman style, and as much as he hated her, he wasn't going to break her bones. He sighed, and she said the words that he did not want to hear. "I'll get the City Council to make you allow it."

"Really?" he asked. "You think your little research project is that important?"

"I'm confident of it," she said. "If I petition them, they do have the power to make it happen."

"I'll appeal."

"So will I." She stood her ground and while he hated her, he'd always admired that.

"I have deeper pockets," he countered, still working to stay calm.

"No," she said, in as straight forward a manner as he had denied her the first time. "You don't. The American Archeological Society does, and all I have to do is dig up enough evidence to get them behind me. Honestly, Gabe, I'm very sorry about your brother. I know that you loved him."

"But you didn't," he inserted, surprised by her sudden shift in topic, but hanging onto the conversation as it were.

"No. Not by the end, not at all."

At least she was honest, he thought. But she kept talking. "I have no idea why it is that you think I'm responsible for his death."

Gabe felt his mouth draw open. How could she possibly be that dumb? "You think that aborting his child and leaving him in a deep depression had nothing to do with it?"

❧ 15 ❧

Lennon reeled back as though she had been slapped. She almost stumbled backward down the steps and off the small porch.

He thought she was responsible for all that? How? He thought Brodie had gone into some deep depression over it? She was beyond confused now.

She needed to stop counting the number of things Gabe said that felt like a slap across the face. She suspected he had more waiting for her, and she needed to be prepared rather than surprised.

Her mouth opened and closed a few times as she tried to form words. She didn't think he could have been more wrong. She started to say so, but then, she thought of something else. As little as she wanted to be inside that house, she even less wanted to be having this conversation on the front stoop.

Though he lived high on the hill, and no one was likely to overhear them from here, except maybe the gardener, she still didn't like it. She didn't know that inside was any better. There might even be a maid in the house. But she didn't want anybody to drive by on the street front and see them arguing. That, she thought, had been the whole point of this house. That people driving by on the street could see just how wealthy the Zemps were.

"Can I come inside so we can talk about this?" she asked.

"Really?" Gabe seemed stunned by her request. "You have something to add to that?"

"I have *everything* to add to that," she said, confidence behind her voice again. She didn't have confidence about what had happened, about what Gabe might believe, or about how she'd been manipulated when she was younger, but she had confidence that she didn't want to be on this porch. And she could now add confidence that Gabe was wrong. *So wrong.*

She didn't wait for him to say yes, but she shoved past him and into the hallway that she remembered from so long ago. She almost commented that he hadn't changed anything. Not in here. And she wondered if he'd changed anything anywhere else. Had he moved into the big master bedroom? Or had he left everything as his mother had decorated it? The way Rob Zemp wanted it. She didn't know. The design had never bowed to trends, so there was no way to place it now.

"Well, come on in," he said sarcastically and closed the door behind her.

At least now people wouldn't see them arguing. Not any more than they already had. She headed into the living room. It felt like the most neutral ground in the building. She'd been in Robert Zemp's office. That was where she'd felt the worst. She'd been in Brodie Zemp's bedroom and during her time in that room, she'd felt both good and horrid in turns.

But the living room felt as friendly as this house could feel. His mother had held court there, and Lennon had enjoyed tea and small talk conversations with the woman. So hopefully this room wouldn't bring back too many bad memories. Though given what Gabe had said, she was going to have to dredge up a handful herself to make him understand.

She sat in one of the big chairs, knowing her legs would not hold her up for much longer. This conversation was going to be far too hard. He didn't know what was coming, but she held a bunch of cards that he clearly didn't know belonged in the deck. The problem was, she was fairly certain he hadn't played all his cards either.

Gabe stood on the other side of the coffee table, arms crossed and brown eyes glaring at her, blond hair looking far too perfect for as angry as he was. "I don't care what you say. There's nothing that you can say that will make me let you dig on my land."

"This isn't about your land, Gabe! *Shit*, that conversation flew out the window when you started talking about Brodie dying and me being responsible. This is about correcting an error. One that I don't know if you've been spreading all around town."

"I haven't," he said. "Why would I? His involvement with you reflects so poorly on Brodie."

Another slap. Lennon blinked. *Don't count them*, she reminded herself.

"Brodie was not depressed over me." She leaned back in the chair as if its support might get her through this. Whiskey might, but not much else.

"Oh, really? He wanted that child, Lennon. He wanted it, and you took it away from him."

She couldn't help herself. The laugh burbled up from her stomach and out her mouth. She laughed until she was almost hysterical, tears squeezing at the edge of her eyes. Gabe had no idea how wrong he was. But he towered over her, watching her, his arms still crossed. His shoulders still broad enough to look menacing as he blocked her light. But no matter how angry he was, Gabe wouldn't hurt her. She knew him. He was the best of the Zemps.

"Oh, so you're saying you wanted that baby and you just aborted it accidentally?" he pressed.

"No," Lennon said. "I did not want that baby."

He cocked his head, as though to say, *See? We're done here.* But they were far from done. Crap, this was going to be painful. She looked up at him and tried to gesture gracefully for him to sit in the chair beside her. They would both look out over the yard, and maybe not have to stare at each other while she told him. "You're wrong about your father and you're wrong about your brother. And you're wrong about that baby. You're going to need to sit down for this."

❧ 16 ❧

Belles don't swear. And if one should ever find herself in a situation when she has to, she will enunciate every single word so no one is in doubt.

LENNON LOOKED OUT OVER THE LAWN. IT WAS BEAUTIFUL. SHE imagined deer came through here during the right seasons. That might even be now. She could imagine having a cup of coffee here as the sun came up and watching the deer pass through.

She shook off the fantastical idea. It was all a distraction, she thought, from the horrible things she was going to have to tell Gabe. She'd never wanted to have to confess these secrets to anyone—let alone Gabriel Zemp. So she looked out over the lawn and took a deep breath.

"No. I did not want that baby. My intent was to give it up for adoption."

He didn't look any calmer now though he was sitting. At least he wasn't towering over her anymore. His voice still held the scorn that he'd had when he was standing. "So what, you tripped and fell into an abortion clinic?"

"Nope," Lennon said. "Your father made that happen."

This time, his head snapped toward her. "No way. He would never have done that to his own family line. You were carrying a future Zemp."

"Oh, please." Lennon was looking at him now, and she hated it. She hated staring at the face of a man she had never wanted to think poorly of her. But he thought so poorly of her right now, there was probably nothing she could do to make it worse. "Please, Gabe. I might have been carrying a future Zemp, but there was no way your father was allowing a little black baby into his family."

"Please. You're acting as if he's racist. He wasn't. You and Brodie dated for over a year and Dad didn't care at all. In fact, Brodie had talked about marrying you and Dad never said anything."

That almost made her laugh again. "Oh, Gabe. I was so young and way too naïve. But I didn't realize you were, too."

This time he just stared at her. Finally, he wasn't angry, but he was now confused. Lennon hated to do this to him. He loved his father and his brother, but he clearly had the wrong ideas.

For a moment, she thought about letting dead men have their way. But that was the problem all along, wasn't it? Robert and Brodie Zemp always got their way when they were alive, and it didn't matter who they hurt, intentional or not. So she was not going to live with Gabe's scorn to save his beliefs about his father.

"Rob demanded that abortion. No matter what he said or didn't say in front of you, he did not approve of Brodie dating me. And I think Brodie maybe did it just because he wanted to get back at your dad for something. Your father couldn't have stopped him if he tried. Not without creating some kind of massive rift in the family. But when I got pregnant, well, that was too much."

She needed a breath as bad memories bubbled to the surface, finally ready to be told. "I never told anyone this." Lennon was still looking out the window. "Only your father and Brodie knew because they were there."

"And now they're dead and you're the only one left. So how do I know I can believe you?"

Lennon let his words fall to the ground between them and continued with her horrible story. "I was standing in the hall when Brodie told him," she said, immediately countering the look of disbelief on his face. "I wasn't in the room, but I heard them yelling. I heard your father smash something, something a bit big. So here's a question: What disappeared from your father's office right around that time that was breakable? It shattered, like glass or crystal. I don't know what it was, I only ever saw the shards on the floor."

She waited. And she waited. Waited until Gabe had time to think back, until he muttered, "His decanter."

"Yeah. He didn't drop it. I don't know what he told you, but he threw it at the wall. Or maybe at Brodie. That's how mad he was. I always got the feeling that he loved that decanter."

She could see from his expression that he remembered that, too. He turned away and stared out over the lawn trying to absorb everything she'd said. And though she'd hated the sound of smashing crystal at the time, now she was glad. She was glad she had something she could call back to that Gabe remembered.

She waited another moment, because her story was only going to get worse. "He called me in there. He called me a slut and a whore. He called me the N-word, Gabe, to my face. So I'm not really sure where you get off telling me your father isn't a racist."

"I've never seen him act like that," Gabe said. "I've never seen him do anything racist. You're asking me to believe something totally different from what I know of him."

"Oh, Jesus, Gabe." Her fingers dug into the soft arms of the chair, and Lennon hated that outward show of weakness. But she kept talking. "I'm going to ask you to believe a damn lot different from what you saw. But you cannot sit there and tell me that because you didn't see it, it doesn't exist. I used to like you, you know. I didn't know you would turn into such a goddamned rich white boy who can't see beyond the end of your nose."

He at least had the grace to blink at that—and to not deny it. She sat in silence, thinking she needed to let him absorb. Instead, apparently, she'd let him form a question.

"So you're saying my father made you get an abortion? How would he make you do that?"

"Are you serious?" she asked. "You had no clue who your father was, did you? While we were in his office, he just 'took care of it.'" She used rude air quotes to make her point. "Within minutes of finding out about that baby, your father was on the phone to a local doctor. I don't know what he said, but he mentioned a few dates from years earlier, so I'm guessing he had dirt on that doctor. They had me in his office early the next week."

Lennon fought the tears that wanted to roll down her cheeks. She regretted the loss of that pregnancy. It wasn't how she'd wanted it to go. She hated the way Robert Zemp had treated her—like she was trash. Like his son had nothing to do with her getting pregnant. As though she had seduced Brodie on purpose.

It was hard to keep her jaw from clenching. Everything Rob Zemp accused her of had happened the other way around. But she'd bowed to him, caved to his threats, and she regretted it to this day. If she could change things from her life, she would have told Robert Zemp where to stick it and then run home and told her parents. But that's not how it had happened.

"I tried to avoid the appointment he made. I still thought I was going to carry that child and give it up. I didn't want anything to do with Brodie by that time. But I was walking on the sidewalk and Rob pulled up beside me. He drove slowly, his window down, blocking me from getting away. And he told me that he was going to yell to everyone exactly what I had been doing. The thing is, Gabe, what I had been doing was not what he was going to say. He had no clue what went on between your brother and me. But he was going to sit there on the street, in his fancy car, and call me all kinds of names and accuse me of trying to weasel my way into the Zemp family by getting pregnant. And worse."

Another pause hit them. As she looked over, she saw the expression on Gabe's face. Her mouth fell open.

"Holy shit. That's what *you* thought, too."

He only shrugged.

"Jesus. I fucking hate you, Gabe Zemp! I thought you were a decent person. But it's so nice to know that you would throw me to the wolves just that fast. One wrong word, and you believed him." It stunned her how much Gabe's betrayal sliced through her. She'd thought telling the story would be the worst part. She could not have been more wrong.

She took a deep breath, but it came out as a sniff to fight the tears. She spoke again, pushing through the hardest story of her life. "Anyway, he pretty much forced me to get in the car and he had me at the doctor's that afternoon. If you don't believe me, check his accounts. He paid it. The doctor's name was Marshall. You can look it up."

17

Gabe sat in the chair, stiff as a board. He did not like what Lennon was saying, and though he didn't really believe her, he couldn't quite disbelieve her either. Maybe she knew his father had dropped the decanter, and she was using it to weave her own story. He'd always known she was smart.

What he wasn't sure of was whether he believed she could be that manipulative. Maybe she'd become that way over the years. It had been a long time since they were what he would call friends. But Gabe wouldn't call himself stupid either. If she was manipulative now, in telling the story, she would have been manipulative then, too. Getting pregnant on purpose to marry into his family wouldn't have been that hard.

She let him sit in the silence for a few moments. He wondered, if she was lying, wouldn't she have said that she loved Brodie and she wanted to keep the baby? When he mentioned Brodie's name, she scoffed, said she'd hated him. That wasn't really what he'd seen, so he said that. "I saw you two together. You didn't look like you hated him."

"Jesus, Gabe. You have no idea what goes on between a teenage girl and a much older boy. And that's all he was, only a boy. I don't think he ever really made it to manhood, but he was going on twenty, Gabe. And he was your father's son. He was much more worldly than me."

She paused, and Gabe waited. This time, he looked at her. She looked sad. She didn't look mean. She didn't look like she was trying to connive him out of a chance to dig on his land. In fact, she'd said that wasn't what this was about. It was entirely possible she was trying to gain his sympathy, so he'd let her do her research. He still had no intention of that. He was not going to be manipulated. Years ago, she might have played him like a fiddle, but not now, not after what he knew.

He was going to ask her about it, but she looked at him and beat him to the punch. "Your father demanded that abortion. Your father precipitated our breakup, and I have to say that's the only thing I have ever been grateful to your father for. If Brodie was running around depressed, it wasn't about me. It was about something between him and your dad. Brodie didn't love me."

"How do you know?" he asked. "He talked about you all the time. He seemed to think you were the greatest thing since sliced bread."

This time it was Lennon who looked at him and raised her eyebrows. "Maybe at the beginning," she said.

He frowned. "What do you mean?"

"When we first started dating, everything was fun. I liked him—"

"You loved him," Gabe interrupted, still looking out the window. He didn't really know why it hurt so much to say that out loud.

"No." She waited then, until he turned to look at her. She seemed to want to be sure he understood. "I *liked* him. He was good to me—at least on all the surface ways."

"What do you mean, 'surface'?"

"You saw it. He was good to me in all the ways people saw. He took me out. He brought me flowers. Made sure I had a date every Friday or Saturday night. Took me for rides in his nice car, picked me up after dance classes."

He'd seen all that and more, Gabe thought. But she'd called it "surface ways." So he asked, "What about the non-surface ways?" Lennon looked away, those bright eyes dimming as he watched.

He wanted so badly to believe her. He wanted the Lennon he remembered back. But if she was a fairy tale then believing her would only get him hurt. Maybe it was all an act, but if it was, she was a damn fine actress.

"At first he was just controlling...and I didn't even recognize it."

Gabe wanted to tell her to go on, that he wanted to hear it. He also wanted to yell at her to shut up. He didn't want to hear things about Brodie. He didn't want her to say these things that he already recognized had a ring of truth. He'd known that side of Brodie.

Lennon looked up at the ceiling as though something more interesting than dentil molding was up there. "He told me to try his favorite pizza. When I didn't like it, he told me that I didn't eat enough to be worth getting my own half."

Gabe laughed. Brodie had taken her to Bobby's. "That's the dumbest thing I ever heard, Lennon. That pizza was free."

"Exactly. It was free and he still wouldn't let me get what I wanted. He picked the movies. He chose where we went and when we went out. He made it clear what clothing of mine he liked and didn't, and eventually he started just telling me what to wear." The anger began as a slow crescendo in her voice. "The only thing I fought him on was my homework. I should have fought harder. It was Brodie who decided when and how I—"

She cut off abruptly, but when Gabe was about to push, she said, "But after a while, he changed. He went from pushy to mean."

"Mean? That's not like Brodie. Brodie was happy-go-lucky. Everything came to him easily and he wouldn't have had to push, Lennon. You're not going to sell that story here."

But as Gabe thought about it, he wondered. Everything had

come easily to Brodie, and for the first time, he felt his own deep resentment about that. Though he hadn't had things hard, he'd not had Brodie's golden halo, either. Brodie got himself into shit, and he always managed to get himself right out of it unscathed. Whatever Brodie did, Rob forgave. Not so much for Gabe. Even though Gabe wasn't going into the family business, Rob had definite ideas about what his younger son could and couldn't do.

Could it be that Lennon was right? That Brodie had finally done something Rob didn't approve of and it hadn't, for once, rolled off his back so easily? Had Brodie just been mad at Rob? Had Brodie wanted that baby? There were so many questions that Gabe wouldn't get answered now. It had been easier when he just hated her.

"Are you sticking with that?" he asked, "that you didn't want that child but that you were going to carry it and give it up?"

"Why not?" She looked at him as though he was just pushing her, and she no longer really cared. She looked exhausted, as though it was tiring to tell him this. "Why would I change my story? It's the truth, Gabe. You weren't there, and you don't know. But I was. You weren't pregnant at eighteen, and you weren't held down in that doctor's office and forced to have an abortion you didn't want. I was heading off to college. I could've easily taken a gap year and had a baby and found a great family for it. But I didn't want anything to do with Brodie after that. I didn't want to raise his child, and I didn't want to deal with your father and his idea of money and who needed to be paid for what. I saw the way he manipulated Dr. Marshall. Dr. Marshall didn't want to do it either, but he was as stuck as I was."

Gabe's head snapped back. She was making his father sound like some kind of Mafia kingpin. But apparently, she wasn't done.

"Do you remember I graduated and couldn't get out of town fast enough?" she asked. "That whole thing went down about two weeks after graduation. I moved the next month, well before school started."

Gabe was still looking out the window. He did remember that.

He remembered Brodie was mad at the world. He'd heard his brother in his room sometimes throwing things. He'd heard fights—big blowouts with yelling and swearing—between his brother and his father. But he'd not listened to what they were about. They didn't involve him and he hadn't wanted to know.

By August, Brodie was dead.

✤ 18 ✤

Lennon had let herself out of Gabe's home. She knew her way around the house from back when she'd been a fixture there. Since he'd been sitting in the chair staring out the window as though he had nothing to add to the conversation, she'd simply gotten up and left.

She could understand why he just sat there. It was better than him calling her a liar. Still, she hadn't told him the worst parts. Not that she thought she ever would.

She'd walked down the wide front steps and climbed back into her car thinking that meeting had not gone the way she'd intended. Lennon had braced herself for a fight. She was ready to tell him things he didn't want to hear about how his land could be claimed by the city, and she'd expected the conversation to stay firmly on the topic of digging. She'd never intended to tell anyone the things she'd just told him.

Even Emma Kate only knew half of it. She'd been there for the whole thing and she'd watched it all. But still, Lennon had not told. Emma Kate knew because she'd guessed and when she shoved Lennon hard on some questions, Lennon had not been able to say no. That's why Emma Kate knew. But it had been eight long years and Lennon had told no one.

Emma Kate had never told anyone, Lennon was sure. Lennon had not even told her parents. As far as she knew, neither her Mama nor her Daddy had any idea she'd ever been pregnant. They only knew she'd been involved with Brodie and that the breakup had made her angry and upset.

She'd never once thought that Gabe Zemp would be the first person she'd tell. She hadn't wanted to break his heart about his brother. If she remembered everything right, he and Brodie had been close. They'd always been golden boys, riding about town in their high-end chariots.

Brodie had always been an asshole. At one point or another he'd managed to piss off everyone. Or so she thought. Maybe he'd made an exception for his little brother. Lennon tried to think back. She tried to see it from Gabe's point of view, but it was hard. Her own experiences with Brodie had left their scars.

Turning her car around, she aimed down the hill and back toward her end of town. As she took a right hand turn out of the driveway heading toward Bailey Ann's house, she glanced up into the rearview mirror. She thought she saw Gabe standing in his doorway, watching her go.

It was another small shock to her system, that he would watch her. She was too far down the hill to see his expression, but she imagined he was trying to figure her out. They'd once been better than this, after all. But for herself, all the small shocks were starting to add up. If she was honest, this morning had contained some that weren't that small. So she took a wrong turn and decided to drive around town a little while, see if she could shake this off.

She arrived home later after finally getting her head at least a little clearer. The day was getting away from her. She had to accept that what she'd expected hadn't happened. She'd thought she'd have a plan by now, know whether she could cajole Gabe into going along with her, or whether she would file paperwork to get rolling on a claim with the city. But instead, she'd gutted herself for him and gotten nothing in return.

Eventually, she grew tired of pacing the house. After changing clothes, she headed back out to the dig site. The day was warmer than she wanted it to be. Or maybe that was just her own internal combustion engine running in a way she had not expected.

This time, she physically turned around and dug away from the property line flags. She followed the line of the ancient foundation in the other direction, trying as hard as she could not to even think about the line behind her. She thought she'd be angry about Gabe refusing to let her dig on his land. Instead, she was sad.

It wasn't just that she'd not expected to tell Gabe those things, it was more so she'd not expected to be quite so hurt by the fact that he didn't believe her. That was startling. She and Gabe had been friends in high school, but when she'd left town after graduation, she had left for good.

Lennon hadn't stayed in touch with much of anyone besides her immediate family—which, of course, she considered Emma Kate to be. Anyone else had been dropped. She came back to Breathless only for major holidays and family gatherings. She'd been back when her Uncle Con had died. And the year before when Aunt Della had. She'd even stayed a while then. Emma Kate had needed her. Otherwise it was usually for Christmas or Thanksgiving and rarely both. She didn't want to run into Gabe. She hadn't wanted to run into Robert Zemp when he was alive. That thought had terrified her.

He terrified her and she hated him. She hated how weak she'd been when she'd been up against him. She had let him bully her and, though she told herself she wouldn't let him get away with it again, she had not looked forward to the conflict. She'd also been afraid he would come at her with something new. Or that—even if she did stand up to him—it would mean the whole town knowing what she'd done. Would she sling back the story of what Brodie had done in retaliation? She was grateful she would never have to know.

Gabe, on the other hand, she hadn't wanted to see because she hadn't wanted him to see her. It was an interesting revelation, she thought as she stuck the trowel into the ground and pulled up tiny pieces of dirt, once again looking for her ancient finds.

Her brain raced off on five different tracks. She needed to call Emma Kate and tell her what had happened. Despite being in colleges on opposite sides of the country they'd managed to stay close. Maybe because they were family, maybe because they were good friends, maybe because they were so different really that they were great for each other.

Lennon didn't know why it worked. All she knew was she needed her best friend and this time she would tell Emma Kate everything. Let it all out. See what advice she got.

She thought next of Emma Kate's older sister, Harper Rose and how she needed to get in touch with the woman so she could figure out the logistics of when the four Bass ladies were coming. It would mean rearranging things. Lennon would have work to get the house ready. Though Bailey Ann would probably insist on helping, Lennon was still looking forward to having roommates again even if they were barely school-aged.

After the debacle with Brodie she'd always considered herself an academic. The experience had changed her views on whether or not she wanted to get married, settle down, have a family of her own. All the romantic dreams she'd had in school had been thrown out the window. Maybe Harper Rose would be willing to share her girls. That would be a good chance to be a part of a family, even if it wasn't the part she'd originally dreamed of.

It sounded like she needed to hit up all three of her cousins while she was at it. But she didn't have any logistical reason to contact Bailey Ann. Lennon just wanted someone to go out to dinner with. Someone to hang out with. It wasn't going to happen magically, but all she had to do was pick up the phone and call.

Adding yet another reminder to her list, she decided she

should also reach out to Jackson while she was here. Time to reconnect with her family for real. She'd talked to Mama and Daddy. She'd seen Jax and the girls. She needed to spend more time with Salem and Scarlett. They were just bigger than toddlers, finally real kids, and she hadn't seen them or her brother other than at her mother's Sunday dinners.

She had to do better, Lennon thought. She'd been hiding from the Zemps every time she'd come into town, and it left her practically hiding from her own family, too. It had become ingrained. Gabe was the only Zemp left and she'd just told him everything. It was time to stop hiding.

Just then when she wasn't paying attention her trowel made a chinking noise. Oh, wow, she'd hit something else!

✣ 19 ✣

Gabe went to the glass cabinet in the corner of the office and opened the doors. He stared for a moment at the various tumblers, shot glasses, decanters, and of course, bottles of Jack that he had stored there. He sometimes met with clients in his home. He often had parties and would invite individuals he needed to do business with back to the office for a moment or two. They'd close the door, sign a deal, and go back out. It was the way his father had done it. It was the way much of business was done.

It made sense to have a full case of liquor and all the fixings in here. But, as he was working the top off another bottle of Gentleman Jack, it occurred to him that he'd gone through far too many of these in far too short of a time period. He'd never been an alcoholic, just the occasional drinker. Lately, since he'd hit the anniversary of Brodie's and his father's deaths and then run into Lennon Mayfair again, it seemed he was trying to become one.

With numb thoughts, he put the bottle back, even though he didn't want to quite go through the rest of the day completely sober. Lennon's words had been jarring, and he wanted the whiskey to help dismiss them. He wanted it badly. That was probably the first sign that he shouldn't drink any. Gabe was afraid if he opened the bottle and made a bad call now, he might just keep going down that road. He closed the doors to the cabinet and forced himself to turn away.

Unfortunately, she had a few key pieces of information that he wasn't able to just let go. She was right—his father had loved that decanter. He and Brodie had had that fight she mentioned. Gabe hadn't been there, but he knew that they'd had a blow up of epic proportions that day. He also knew the decanter had ended up smashed. He didn't know if it occurred the way Lennon said, but it had occurred, and there was no denying that.

There had also never been any regret from his father about some klutzy fumble that had cost him his prized possession. Never any anger at Brodie for it. And his father wouldn't have let either boy ever forget it if they had been the one to break it.

So, though Gabe had not thought it through before, he did now. His father must have broken it and it hadn't been an accident. Lennon had at least that much correct. The fact that even part of her story couldn't be dismissed out of hand bothered him.

It bothered him even more that she said she hadn't wanted the baby. She'd gotten pregnant by her boyfriend at the time, and still wanted to give the baby away. If they'd known Brodie would be gone so soon, Gabe would have almost insisted. Although he would have sworn before today that his father would have done the same, but perhaps his father had gone the other way. Perhaps he didn't know his father as well as he thought he had. He would never have guessed that Robert would have used the N-word. Or called her a slut or any of the things she claimed.

Jesus, he wanted a drink. Gabe wanted every last piece of this to be easier than it was. It was hard with Lennon coming back. It was hard seeing her again and having it rush back just how crazy he'd been about her. To remember how hard it had been to watch his brother date her. He'd been braced for that, but it was even harder to have her come back and tell her that Brodie was not the man he'd thought.

If the real Brodie was her version, then everything Gabe believed about his brother was wrong.

Nothing she said matched the Brodie he knew. Their father, maybe. Rob could be an asshole, and he was certainly hard-edged. He was a tightwad and a greedy businessman. He was a harsh task-master and an angry beast when crossed. All of that was plausible.

But Brodie? Gabe couldn't fathom it. When he'd been just a toddler, his older brother was his hero. Brodie had liked to pick him up and swing him around. Gabe remembered when he couldn't get his parents to pay attention to him, he would go to Brodie. Brodie always had time for him.

Looking back, Brodie should have smacked him away. He was an obnoxious younger sibling, and he saw other siblings now and realized no one had what he and his brother had. When Brodie was in high school and Gabe in middle school, Brodie got that car. So Brodie woke up earlier every morning so he could drive his little brother to a different school. It was a huge imposition, making sure he got both of them to school on time. But Brodie never skipped out on him, never ditched him for friends, or made him feel like a third or fifth wheel. None of this sounded like the Brodie Lennon was talking about. It was as though they were two entirely different people.

Gabe stood staring out the back window of the office, looking at trees, the smooth lawn of green, green grass, the manicured gardens. Nothing moved. Though the day rolled on in front of him, nothing changed. He didn't get the drink, he didn't feel better, and he didn't know how long he stood there before he made his decision.

Lennon had said the doctor's name was Marshall, and that he could look it up. Though given the way she spoke, it sounded like his father had forced the man. Gabe was relatively certain, if he came back and said he couldn't find a payment, she would simply say that he hadn't paid money for it, that Robert must have fully blackmailed the doctor. But Gabe went looking. If he could find it, it would be another piece—like the smashed decanter. He felt a drive to *know*.

Her story had taken place a long time ago, at least in terms of banking records. It took him a while to dig out the old statements, the bank notes, the checkbook ledgers. He went through three different systems and didn't find any reference nor payment that could have been given to a Dr. Marshall. Gabe had almost sat back, satisfied he'd found a lack of evidence that pointed to a lie on her part. Then he remembered he had access to his father's personal account.

Logging in, he pulled up old records until they didn't go back any further. The dates in question weren't accessible and he finally had to send in a request to the bank. He thought it would take days. It turned out, the entire system had been computerized all along, and it only took a number of hours for the records to come back.

It still took Gabe a while to fish through everything, but God damn, he found it. There was a payment to a Dr. Marshall, on the right date, for far more money than a checkup would be worth.

Gabe's heart sank.

How could Lennon have known that otherwise?

Fuck. The swear reverberated through his brain. That the payment was made from his father's personal account was even more damning. Hopping online, Gabe tried to look for any kind of holes or gaps in her story. He found, in Breathless, a Dr. Brad Marshall, gynecologist, obstetrician. His chest tightened more.

He told himself it wasn't true, and he picked up the phone and called into the office, asking, "Does your office perform abortions?"

It took a while sitting on hold to get an answer, but what came back was, "Not as a regular course of action," which didn't mean *no*.

He tried to think. Could it have been for his mother? But it couldn't. Drugs to treat her various chronic illnesses had rendered her infertile via full hysterectomy long before then. Gabe had known that he was the last of their line. It had never been a family secret. So there wouldn't be payments to gynecologists for his family. Not unless something else was up.

His blood boiling, even though he didn't know who it was directed at anymore, he smacked his hand down on the desk. The motion jarred the keyboard and the screen scrolled. When he looked at what popped up he saw something else that was odd.

In the last few days of July that same year—just before Brodie died—Robert made a large payment to Cambridge University. Not a donation—no one in their family had attended that university—and it wasn't an even number.

Gabe flipped through a few more screens of notes before he finally found it. January of the next year there was another similar payment. And another the following August. And so on.

He didn't know what it meant, but he knew what it was for.

❧ 20 ❧

Wednesday was a better day than Tuesday had been, Lennon decided. She'd dug up something pretty remarkable yesterday. As tiny as it was, she was lucky she'd run into it. Her methods right now were about sampling, so whether she found anything was hit-or-miss luck. She was grateful to be lucky.

This was another piece of clay—some kind of pot or vessel. This time, the piece she'd found was only an inch by two inches in size with jagged edges. But there was enough surface with enough preserved marking on it that she was able to form a good theory about where it had come from. She would have to research it, of course, but she was so excited.

She would have been online looking up the specific markings and testing for ink composition today, if not for the fact that she'd called Bailey Ann to see if she was available for lunch and had gotten invited along on an outing Bailey Ann already had planned.

Jane Copeland and Bailey Ann sat across the table from Lennon. Jane's hands pumped into the air in fists. "Oh my God. The children are all at school or with a babysitter. I have three glorious hours. Can we spend that long at lunch?" She looked to the other two women hopefully.

Lennon had not intended to take that much time out of her day, but still she laughed. Jane had four children and a recent divorce under her belt.

"We can go shopping afterward if you want," Bailey Ann offered. "Apparently I need to start looking at dresses." She made eyes at Lennon as though this were Lennon's fault. But Lennon only smiled.

"Oh, that sounds dih-vine." Jane was sighing in near ecstasy. Although it seemed perhaps Jane would be happy with anything that got her out of the house.

"Are you not working right now?" Lennon asked. Jane was a registered nurse and she thought Jane worked in the ER.

"Oh yes. Four shifts on, three days off, then three on and four days off," she said. "But I will tell you, those four days off get very long with small children. As do my days on. Kids want a lot when they haven't seen you for twelve hours."

Bailey Ann nodded. "Probably more when you're the only parent. Is Joe doing much to help?"

"Oh please," Jane rolled her eyes. "I mean yes, I give them to him, but I don't know if you could actually call what he does *help*."

Lennon felt her own eyes go wide and her mouth drop open. Bailey Ann laughed and explained what she could. "Oh, their divorce would have been epically ugly—and probably still in progress—except Jane shut it down. She got dirt on her ex." Bailey Ann turned then to look at Jane, "Is *blackmail* too strong a word?"

"Yes. Yes, it is. But *leverage* is not," Jane replied.

"Oh, my word. Are you okay?" Lennon asked. Even though Jane had a smile on her face, just the idea of an "epically ugly divorce" was concerning.

"I am, now. I still can't fully deal with him and I have to, but I'm finally better. So that's good."

"Well, I'm glad," Lennon said. "And I will say this, I am booked up to my ears with this dig but when I'm off, if you need a babysitter, I'd love to volunteer."

That made Jane's eyes go wide in turn though not quite the same way Lennon's had earlier. It was wonderful, Lennon thought to be out with these two. They were a good decade older than she was, but she guessed she was finally considered an adult and she got to eat with the big girls.

She'd been too tired last night to call Emma Kate but she'd managed to get this set up. For that, she was grateful. She was opening her mouth to ask Jane about the ages of her kids when she felt a bump that had her sliding almost a foot to the left, further into the booth.

Her breath caught in her chest and she smelled him before she saw him. Lennon wondered why she knew what he smelled like and why she'd recognized it at an instinctual level.

Gabriel Zemp was sitting next to her, his side pressed fully against hers as though they were far better friends than they were.

"Hello ladies," he said, interrupting their lunch with a smile. At that moment, she felt her blood go from a melting sensation she'd had no control over when he made contact to ice cold.

Was he going to sit here with a smile on his face and tell them? Was he going to finally accomplish what Rob had only managed to threaten all those years ago? She felt her breath suck in and her spine straighten and turn to steel.

Let him do his worst, she thought as she braced herself.

But he turned to her and said, "Lennon," in a voice that had her melting all over again. Jesus, what was he doing to her? Was he trying to disarm her so he could get the upper hand and shatter her? She had no idea.

He looked to Bailey Ann and Jane with another charming smile. The Zemp men were never above using their looks to get their way, but she didn't know why it was working with Gabe right now. Her relationship with Brodie should have made her completely immune. But clearly, it didn't.

"A minute, if you will?" He produced a small stack of papers. She had no idea where he'd gotten it from. Apparently, she hadn't been looking when he'd slid in next to her, she'd only been reacting and missed the obvious. He slid the legal-looking file, held together with a binder clip, across the table toward her.

Lennon looked down at it, probably frowning. On closer inspection, it looked like a contract, she thought. She didn't know and as she peered up at him, he didn't smile in response. There was no way to read his expression, but he said, "It's a contract so you can dig on my land."

Her heart stopped and she thought for a moment just how badly she wanted that ability. The contract might allow it, but she had a second thought. Was it more important for him to know that she had not told him what she had in order to gain use of his land? In a split second, she decided she would regret it if she let go of her principles for access to property. She would never forgive herself if she let another Zemp manipulate her. So she pushed it back at him.

"It's okay," he said, once again scooting the contract toward her side of the table.

She looked up to find her two friends across the booth looking at her with bright, questioning eyes. *Oh, Jesus.* Now was not the time to start any rumors around town. Lennon glanced around the restaurant, suddenly noticing it wasn't as empty as she would have liked.

She wasn't ready for "Didn't you used to date his brother?" and all the other questions that would come up. Working hard at it, Lennon tried to keep her expression neutral and her skin from heating up. She offered a half smile at Gabe. "I wasn't trying to get access to your land."

His smile wasn't halfway nor was it neutral. "Nevertheless, you have it if you want it." He tapped at the papers. "Read it. You'll find it's only enough to keep someone from suing me over anything regarding your digs, and that I want to see what comes up from my property. It's all up to you at this point." He smiled once more and began to slide smoothly out of the booth. "Ladies, I'll let you get back to your lunch. My apologies for interrupting."

Both Bailey Ann and Jane offered him kind passes against his sitting down uninvited. They both expressed how happy they were to see him. And they managed to keep their faces in a relatively neutral zone until he was gone.

Jane craned her neck until she announced, "He's gone." Then she turned to Lennon. "Holy shit, what was that? Y'all about set the table on fire."

Even Bailey Ann was sitting on the other side, fanning her face with her hand.

Oh no, Lennon thought. This was not what she had wanted. But the heat under her own skin called her a liar.

21

Gabe waited almost a week, though he told himself he wasn't waiting and that he wasn't doing anything...not really.

He told himself he was just checking on her progress. After all, he had a signed contract from her and anything she dug up on his land had to go through him first. Though he promised not to restrict her showing it to any archeological societies or giving it back to any native tribes to whom it belonged, he'd had his lawyer add in that she had to show him each piece. If anyone asked him, he would say he had a legal need to know what was being removed from his own land.

But he knew it was more than that.

Something had changed while he'd looked through his father's accounts. Lennon had become credible, and he felt like shit that he hadn't thought she was before. In his defense, she was challenging everything he thought he knew about people he probably knew better than she did. The payments to Cambridge University had been the nail in his father's coffin on that one. Rob Zemp would not have allowed himself to get blackmailed, so Gabe's only conclusion was that his father felt guilty.

Gabe had the contract written up within twenty-four hours

of finding the damning numbers. He'd signed it and admitted to himself that he wanted to believe her. His father wasn't here anymore, but she was. The question was, had he fucked up their relationship beyond repair? He was going to find out.

He grabbed an apple and was out the door before he thought about it. Heading down the trail in his work clothes, he realized he should have changed into more reasonable shoes. It wasn't an easy trail, so he wouldn't be able to say he was just out for a walk. Gabe took a bite of the apple, telling himself it was just a casual checkup. As he came through the other side of the trail, he saw her, but she was on the other side of the flags.

Dammit. This would've been easier if she'd already been on his land.

He slowed down carefully and called out to her, "Lennon."

Her eyes were wide as she looked up, an almost smile on her mouth at seeing him, though he couldn't quite believe it because if she was happy, if she trusted him, wouldn't she have dug beyond the property line? Maybe she had and he just didn't see it.

"Is there anything over here I need to worry about stepping in? I'd really rather not turn my ankle."

"No." She shook her head and waved her hand around. "Take a look at everything I've dug. Everything is flagged and marked. You shouldn't be able to accidentally fall into any holes. Besides, I wouldn't want you accidentally stepping on something that's twenty thousand years old."

He nodded. She'd stuck yellow flags at various points around her dig. When he looked closer, he saw that she had written dates and times and labels on them in black sharpie. They were clearly hers, clearly different from the ones that the surveyor had put in to mark the property line. None of the yellow flags showed up on his side yet. "You're not digging over here?"

She shook her head and headed back to the hole she was working on, slowly putting in the trowel just like she had the first day, though this time she wasn't quite as studiously ignoring him. Taking a chance, Gabe stepped carefully over the flags and navigated the places she'd already dug. He saw a deep trench with something at the bottom, though he couldn't identify it. Other holes had gaps. Some went straight down like a cone, and some had been dug out to one side or another. He could only guess that was where she'd found something. Judging by the number of cases where that had happened, it looked like she'd found a small handful of items. He wanted to ask, but for once, he held his tongue.

He stood over her, waiting while she ignored him a little while longer. He amused himself by taking another bite of the apple. Eventually he gave up. She wasn't going to speak first.

"It's okay," he offered. "You can dig on my side. The contract lays everything out. All I want is to see what you pull up. I'm not going to take anything from you or your research. I'm not going to fight you for any of it."

She signed the contract and returned it through his office in town. Had she not wanted to see him? But if she'd signed it, she must have thought it was all kosher. So why wasn't she digging on his side?

Lennon sat back but didn't stand up to face him, her trowel finally coming to a rest, and she looked up at him. "I don't know, Gabe. That was not my intent in what I said. I told you that so you might stop hating me, not so you'd let me dig."

"I know," he said.

It took her a moment and she swallowed hard, looking like she wanted to ask *how did he know?* Instead she asked him something much more direct. "Did you find the records from the doctor?"

He nodded. He didn't tell her the rest of it, though. He let a moment of silence fall between them and, as they so often had these past weeks, they let whatever painful topic they were discussing fall into the space. He waited a handful of heartbeats and asked, "Did you find any more artifacts?"

She pointed with her trowel. He didn't see anything, and she eventually crawled a few feet over and put the trowel, point down, in the dirt next to a very tiny piece of...he didn't know what it was. He leaned over and looked closely.

"It's broken," he said.

"Of course it's broken. It's possibly been in the ground for twenty thousand years, Gabe."

He hated that he loved her sarcasm and he laughed at himself. She looked up then, her stomach growling.

"Are you hungry?" he asked.

She shrugged. That was a yes. He remembered that. She didn't like to tell people when she needed something. It was surprising to him how quickly their high school friendship came flooding back and he held the apple out. A Granny Smith, her favorite. He remembered that, too.

She shook her head. "I'm okay," but her stomach growled again, proving her a liar.

Gabe simply stood there holding out the apple.

"My hands are filthy."

"Do you want me to hold it for you?" he asked, almost laughing again. This was the Lennon he remembered, all the bad blood and years in between them almost seeming to disappear, but not quite.

She peeled her glove and took the apple, taking three large bites, the look on her face almost orgasmic. His muscles tightened and he almost regretted coming out here. She handed it back and then pulled her hand away at the last minute.

"I probably got it dirty."

Without a word, he took the apple back from her and took his own bite. He didn't care. He asked her about lunch and she only shrugged. "Are you just not going to eat?"

When she gave a monosyllabic non-answer, he pushed. "Do you not bring a lunch with you? Or do you go out?"

"One or the other," she finally relented with another not-quite-an-answer, but she didn't look up. "I forgot today. When I forget, I try to do drive-thru."

"But not today?"

She almost laughed at him. "Look at me. I'm too filthy to get into my car and it would take me so long to clean up enough to go anywhere. I shouldn't—" her stomach growled again, cutting her off.

He was looking at her, and that was half the problem. There were no other Zemps to get in his way this time, if he could admit that's what he was doing. Gabe was almost to the point of throwing all his lies and sidesteps out the window. "So walk through the woods with me and let me feed you. Come on. Your stomach is growling. You'll get light-headed and fall into one of these holes. Then what good will you be?"

Gabe waited, holding his breath, to see if Lennon Mayfair would say yes.

❄ 22 ❄

You can tell a good man by how he treats his mama.

LENNON FOLLOWED GABE THROUGH THE MANICURED BACK yard with hedges all around and up to the back door.

"I'm too dirty," she said. She didn't belong in the big, pretty house with its shiny floors and big, clear, glossy windows. Her mother's home had window toppers and curtains. Gabe's home had valances and silk drapes. Lennon would probably never fit in here. At her best she'd stood up to the occasional party in this fine house. But now? She certainly didn't belong, not with her hiking boots, cargo pants, and tank top—with mud splotches in random places and her bra strap showing.

Before he opened the door, Gabe turned and looked at her. "So we'll take off our shoes. I mean I've been walking in the woods, too, and I'm assuming you wash your hands before you eat?"

She tilted her head at him, thanking him for being sarcastic. Luckily, that seemed to be enough. He must not think of the big house as a mausoleum quite the way she did.

In stocking feet, she followed him into the kitchen, trying not to watch his ass. She tried to remind herself that this man was much cleaner than she was. More powerful. Richer. So many "er"s. But as he led the way through his home, he didn't treat it or her that way. They headed into the kitchen and Lennon looked around. She remembered this room. There had been a few times she'd interacted with Mrs. Zemp in here.

"You haven't changed anything, have you?" she asked.

"Of course not. This was my Mom's kitchen. I don't cook like she did, but I like—" he paused as though he'd decided not to say whatever it was, but after a moment he picked up, surprising Lennon. "I like to think that I could walk in here and find her again. Maybe just for a moment."

Damn him for melting her heart like that. It was not fair. "Have you changed anything else in the house?"

"Only my bedroom."

That seemed to fit with what she had seen. It was like stepping into a scene from her own past. Then she paused. "You're still in your same old room?"

He nodded, letting it lie at that.

When she really thought about it, she was amazed that he lived here at all. She didn't fault him for not staying in the master bedroom. His mother had died there and though it had been a relatively peaceful death, it had been a long battle. And his mother had been the last one. Her death had not been sudden nor violent like his brother and father, but for Gabe it must have been the end of an era. The way Lennon heard it told, he'd been by her side for every moment. Though that would have made sense as something anchoring him to the house, the rest did not.

His father had died in the office, his gun under his chin. He'd made a mess for his still-grieving son and sick wife to clean up, in more ways than one. That Gabe continued to work in that office was a tribute to the man or the cleaning crew or both. Lennon didn't want to have to make that distinction.

She didn't like this place and the deaths here. She would have thought he wouldn't either, but he'd stayed. And he seemed to fit. The fine weave of his clothing and the high-end stitching made him look like he belonged in this kitchen and it made her feel just a little more out of place while he opened cabinets, stepped into the pantries and pulled down a pan.

"Grilled cheese?" he asked.

Lennon couldn't fight the laugh that burbled up. "You do know how to seduce a woman."

As soon as the words were out of her mouth, she clamped her jaw shut but Gabe only offered a half smile and turned back to the stove.

"Okay, I have...cheddar, garlic havarti, ..." He looked into the fridge again and kept rattling off cheeses. Of course, his list included Brie and Camembert.

"Garlic Havarti," she said.

Then he told her he had Black Forest ham, a thin sliced roast beef and more.

"Roast beef," she said and then was allowed to pick several kinds of bread. "Jesus, Gabe," she said. "Who is stocking your kitchen? Are you some kind of gourmand that I wasn't aware of?"

He laughed again. "No, I have a maid. I make her do the shopping. She knows what I like and sometimes gets a little overzealous."

"Do you have a family?" Lennon asked and watched as his head snapped back to her suddenly as though the question was odd. "Oh no, no, no. I mean like some secret family. Or a stowaway that you're feeding? I'm curious who's eating all of this food."

"Oh. Well," He walked over and opened the fridge again, this time so she could see in. He showed her that—aside from cheese and sliced meat and a couple of loaves of bread that he apparently thought it was necessary to keep in the fridge—there wasn't much else. He then turned and opened the pantry to show her several rows of various size and color boxes. Cereal, mac and cheese, rice dishes. No basics, just box dinners.

She frowned. "Please tell me everything is in the freezer."

"Well," he reached down and opened the bottom drawer showing her piles of single serving, man-size dinners. Pastas, beefs, things like that.

"So you've been living off frozen dinners and grilled sandwiches?" she asked.

"Mostly. I mean, sometimes I don't grill them."

Lennon nodded feeling a reluctant kinship with this man. Despite his fine clothing and fancy cheeses, he wasn't doing any better than she was. "Me too."

He tipped his head, raising one eyebrow at her. "Do you want me to make something different? We can get pizza."

She shook her head quickly. He would mean Bobby's. He owned the whole chain now. She certainly couldn't ask him to take her to a competitor and she'd blown her weekly budget for eating out at lunch with Bailey Ann and Jane the week before.

"Grilled cheese is good," she said to him and watched as he deftly made sandwiches to a perfect crispness, demonstrating just how much practice he'd been getting at this.

He served them up on plates, cutting them in half on the diagonal with the spatula, as though he were serving them to children. He opened the fridge, pulled out a bag of precut carrot sticks and served up a handful of those on each plate as well.

"You know how to live in style," she said. At least this time she hadn't mentioned seduction. Though to be fair, given the grilled cheese and carrot sticks, seduction was clearly not his goal here.

"Gotta be healthy," he told her.

"True, eat enough boxed dinners and you start going for the carrot sticks."

He poured her a soda but of course it was some artisanal variety made with cane sugar. She smiled though he didn't quite seem to get the joke. Sitting at the table inside the dining room, she was suddenly flooded with a barrage of memories. She'd come here once to make queso for a Spanish class project.

A whole group of them—four students—had been charged with bringing the food to the class party. Other groups were making pinatas and showing off traditional clothing. Gabe had snagged them the food gig. When she'd arrived to do her part, Gabe had been the only one here. Had it been Brodie, she would have been uncomfortable, but she'd always felt safe with Gabe.

It seemed, in that respect, nothing had changed. So she ate her sandwich as they talked casually about nothing. He asked about what she'd found and triggered a barrage of information pouring out of her. Eventually, Lennon had reached up and put her hands across her mouth. "Oh, I'm sorry! Shut me up."

"No, I asked. I wanted to hear about it." So he asked about the painting technique used on the broken sherd she'd shown him. Had he been reading up? She didn't know but told herself not to think things like that.

Later, after hand washing the plates as a way to thank him, she said good-bye and that she'd walk herself back to the site. But she didn't understand the knot in her chest. She worked out here all day, alone. So why did leaving him back at the house—his house—to head to her site, suddenly make her feel lonely?

🎏 23 🎏

Four days later, he did it again. This time, he didn't bring an apple but a sandwich and a banana. Gabe put it in a cloth bag. Not one much for picnic baskets, and not one for making a complete fool out of himself, the basket seemed like overkill for a woman who wasn't expecting him and was maybe only starting to feel something more for him than anger or irritation.

He'd made only one sandwich—albeit a large one—and brought it along as though it was his own lunch. As though he was just walking through the woods with his meal in a bag when he had a full kitchen right behind him.

It was stupid. He knew it. For some reason it sounded fully believable when he was cooking up his little scheme to see her again. But now that he was walking through the woods with his lunch, he felt as though there were a thousand holes in his plan, or that he was simply too transparent for words. He was a grown man, but he was taking his lunch out into the woods to find the woman who was digging.

When he arrived, he discovered Lennon still wasn't digging on his side of the property line. In fact, he'd arrived just in time, catching her as she sat down on the sidelines to eat her own sandwich.

Without asking, he headed over and sat next to her. He didn't say anything at first but smiled as she took out her food.

She didn't seem upset. In fact, she smiled.

"Watcha got?" he asked, trying to be casual.

Luckily, she didn't fault him for being stupid. "Chicken salad."

He frowned. That looked good. Maybe better than the sandwich he brought, and he had to admit to himself that he had tried to do it up.

She held the thick cut sandwich up toward him. "Do you want a bite? It's wheat bread, and the chicken salad has diced grapes and dried cranberries."

"Cheese?" He asked, thinking he might see a slice lurking in there.

"Muenster."

He took a bite of it and moaned, "Oh, my God, that's good." Gabe chewed and regretted his own sandwich choice. "That's a serious sandwich. That's almost like cooking."

Her laughed changed the way his heart beat and the way his lungs took in air. He was a goner. He realized it sitting here on the side of her thesis dig. She wouldn't be here for long, and he was both thrilled at the feeling and sad at the knowledge simultaneously.

Lennon didn't seem to notice. "It's the diced grapes that make it. Most people don't bother. They put them in whole or maybe halved, but you have to dice them so they are all throughout the sandwich."

"Well, I'm calling bullshit. That's hardly the lunch of a woman who's living on boxed meals."

She laughed at him. "Oh, I didn't make this. My Mama did."

He nodded. Yes, it made sense that Gigi Mayfair would make the best chicken salad in town. "What kind of bribe should I offer her to make some for me?"

"Oh, there's no bribe that will get you her famous chicken

salad sandwich," Lennon said, the look on her face clearly one of pity. "She has to love you."

He nodded. "I guess I've got my work cut out for me."

"What's in the bag?" she asked him then between bites.

"Oh, my own lunch." The part where he had to own up to what he'd done. Was it painfully obvious that he'd just come out to see her? He didn't know if he hoped that it was or that it wasn't.

"Whatcha got?" She mimicked his earlier statement.

"Turkey, cranberry jelly, and cream cheese on a croissant."

"Oh," she said. "So you're stuck with grilled sandwiches and boxed foods? I don't think so. You're just a pretender, rich boy."

"Rich boy?"

"Please. It's almost months before Thanksgiving. Those are not leftovers. You can't even pass that off. And a croissant? Nope. I'm not buying your sad tale."

Gabe threw his head back and laughed. It had been a while since he found something so funny. It was even funnier because all of it was true. He had Garlic Havarti, and four kinds of sliced meat in his fridge that would only not go bad because he would send it home with the maid. It was high school before he'd learned his friends didn't have houses as big as his. That even their parents didn't have cars as nice as the one he'd gotten for his birthday. That they didn't have specialty deli cheeses in their fridge all the time. And yet, here he was, with a poorly stocked fridge and no one to eat with. His cheeses might be fancier, but he was still surviving on sandwiches and boxed meals.

Pulling his sandwich out of the bag, he unwrapped the plastic wrap from it and held half of it out to her teasingly. "You want a bite?"

Lennon nodded, and she took the bite right out of his hands. Something about it triggered a flood of heat in him. For a moment, he stopped and wondered what he was doing. This was Brodie's ex. A few weeks ago, he'd hated her. Where had all his anger gone?

He'd been so convinced that she was the reason Brodie had died. He'd understood that Brodie had a hand in it. He'd known all along that while the family used the term "accident" that it was really a suicide. He'd known that, even though no one inside or outside his family had ever had the balls to say it.

For eight years, Gabe had blamed Lennon. But something about the way she told that story had made it all fall away. Brodie had been angry. Gabe remembered. Brodie had probably either driven into that tree on purpose in a drunken, poor-decision-making fit, or he'd just gotten too drunk to know that he needed to stay alive, but he'd been angry for months.

The way Lennon told it, Brodie had been angry at Rob, not her. If he had wanted the baby and Rob had driven her away, forcing her to abort it, well, Gabe could understand that too. He still didn't know exactly how it had happened, but both cases fit the evidence, both fit what he remembered had happened with his brother.

For the first time, he found he couldn't lay that blame at Lennon's feet. It had been easy when she wasn't here, when she wasn't sitting in front of him, when she wasn't smiling at him with that lush mouth, and the wide eyes, and the memory-triggering glances reminding him that he'd once loved her himself.

He opened his container of honey-roasted mixed nuts and simply placed it on the ground between them. Occasionally he held his sandwich out toward her, silently offering her a bite, and secretly he rejoiced when she accepted. It was better when she traded him for the chicken salad. "Tell me what you found since I was out here last."

As they ate, she talked, telling him about the brick and how she'd found another one, how she'd followed the foundation line away from his property and out to where she'd finally come across a corner.

When he looked at it, he said, "It really looks like it only goes about fifteen or so feet. It's not that far."

"It's really far when you're on your hands and knees digging it up and making sure that you don't damage any of it," she replied with a slight sarcastic bent.

He nodded. That made sense. "You really should dig on my side of the property line. Then you'll know just how long that foundation wall is."

He could see where the trench went right up to the flags and stopped. Clearly, she should keep following it. "Do you need help?" he asked before he thought better of it.

Lennon threw her head back and laughed. "Are you going to send me a team to help with my dig?"

He hadn't thought of it that way, but he frowned at her, wondering if maybe that was the right thing to do. He'd been a royal ass.

"You can't send me a team." Just like Lennon, she'd refused his offered before he'd even confirmed it. "They won't dig correctly. It's painstaking work and has to be done carefully."

He nodded. "I could help."

But she didn't say yes. Instead she looked at him and said, "Why did you do it? Why did you set up that contract letting me dig on your land?"

He took a deep breath. *Confession time.* He should lie to her, tell her he had some hidden stake in it, but he didn't. "Because I blamed you for something that I don't think was actually your fault. Because I feel bad about that. Because I didn't want to be an asshole."

🌿 24 🌿

Lennon sat on her bed, propped against the pillows she'd leaned on the headboard, her knees drawn up under her chin and her phone tucked between her ear and her shoulder.

She'd frozen there, as she listened to Emma Kate's final analysis.

"Lennon, you've got it bad."

"No, I don't." It had been the obvious first words out of her mouth. It was simply instinctual to protest what Emma Kate was suggesting. "Em, there's no way."

"There's *so much* way," Emma Kate replied. The tone in her best friend's voice was much happier than Lennon would have expected, given that she'd unloaded the whole sordid deal from her senior year of high school into this one conversation.

Emma had been, in turn, sympathetic, outraged, livid, and threatening to come back and kill every last Zemp. Though, as Lennon quickly pointed out, the only one left to kill was Gabe, and he was the only Zemp who'd probably had zero part in it. It was possible even their mother had known and at the very least stayed quiet.

"You don't think Gabe knew?" Emma asked.

"No." That "no" had come just as fast as her denial of Em's

idea, Lennon thought. But then Emma Kate suggested that Lennon was falling for him. "There's no way," she said again. Even as she did it, she heard that she protested too much. Still, she wasn't able to stop herself.

Lennon wasn't able to process what her friend was saying, and she decided shutting up might be the better part of valor. Unfortunately, that didn't work either, because Emma Kate knew her, and she let the silence hang for just a moment.

Then she spoke again. "Here's the thing, Lennon. You called me, and you told me about what happened, and I'm grateful that you did. Honestly, what you told me isn't very far off from what I figured out for myself. I mean, given the way that you reacted at the time, when you showed up on my door, the night you spent at my place crying and us hiding you from my parents and yours, so that no one would have to know... I had pretty much put all the pieces together without you saying the words." Emma Kate paused again, and Lennon found herself hanging on, waiting. "But this time, when you told me the story, you told me about Brodie, and you told me about Mr. Zemp, but you also told me about Gabe. Lennon, Gabe wasn't really involved back then, but you told me about him anyway."

Shit, Lennon thought. She had done exactly what Emma Kate was suggesting. She'd woven Gabe tightly into the story. When she told of being in the office with Mr. Zemp, how he'd broken the decanter, she mentioned that Gabe had not been there, as though that were somehow important to that day. It hadn't been at the time, but. . .

Emma Kate interrupted her thoughts. "You told me the story that way, because it's important to you *now*. It's important to you that Gabe wasn't there and didn't have any part of it. The reason it's important to you—" her cousin offered yet another dramatic pause. Lennon knew what was coming. "Is because you have feelings for Gabe."

"No. I don't," Lennon denied again, though even as she said it, she felt it for the lie that it was.

She did have feelings for him. Fuzzy ones. Dramatic ones. Concerning ones. And it figured she needed her cousin pointing it out to her—repeatedly—for her to get it. Em heard what Lennon was really saying and how she was saying it, and she held it up for Lennon to finally put two and two together.

Shit, she thought again. She did not need to deal with a crush on Gabe Zemp. Their dealings were already tangled enough as it was.

"Okay," Emma Kate said, "So, I get that you didn't realize you had feelings for Gabe until just now when I told you, but you're going to want to sleep on that for a few days, because you've got a decision to make."

"What decision is that?" Lennon asked. What did it matter if she had feelings for Gabe or not? It didn't change anything. Sure. She could dig on his land, but he'd written her a damned legal contract. It was hardly the move of a man trying to flirt, and why would he?

The two of them were a mess before they even began. She was his brother's ex. His brother was dead. Possibly in a way related to her. Her past with the Zemps was so messy, there was no way she'd be able to have anything with Gabe. Even if she did have a crush on him and even if he did have feelings for her in return, how would they sort it all out?

They wouldn't. That's how. She would dig on his land. She would enthusiastically tell him about tiny broken pieces of clay pots or brick foundations that she found and what they meant, and that would be the end of it.

Except it wouldn't.

Emma Kate pointed out, "Do you think he'll bring you lunch again? You should take advantage of that. Start bringing something extra that you can share with him."

"Oh, lord, Emma Kate! I am not trying to seduce the man. I'm trying to dig up artifacts."

"Uh-huh. Whatever."

The conversation quickly turned, Lennon steering it this

time away from the man her cousin didn't believe her about. While Lennon was working on her masters, Emma Kate was still working on her bachelors degree. Though they graduated high school just a year apart, Emma Kate was not keeping up, achievement wise. She'd taken a gap year and then would have only stayed two years behind Lennon, but she quit after her sophomore year. Luckily, she got the school to allow it and she picked up again a year later.

School had never been Emma Kate's thing, not like it was Lennon's. She'd not been bad at it. She'd been a solid student, landing herself at UCLA, but she'd never quite figured out what she wanted to do. She was supposed to have already graduated but was putting it off. And still hadn't started her thesis in time. Lennon knew Em hated being asked about it, but she wanted to know. "How's your thesis coming along? Do you think you'll graduate in December?"

"Geez, Len, you're as bad as everyone else!"

"No, I'm a college student like you and I'm poorer than everyone else." Though probably she was as bad as everyone was, wanting to be sure Em was doing okay when she always seemed to be barely at "okay" and more at "just getting by" academically. "I have to plan my plane tickets super far in advance to get the cheap fares. So I need to know now if I'm going to LA in December for graduation."

She almost prayed she wasn't. December travel would be more expensive. But when Em responded with, "Better plan for June..." Lennon felt her heart drop.

Was her cousin ever going to finish? She was so close. "Do you need help thinking of something? Or getting started on the research? I'm happy to help edit and all."

She shouldn't have said it. Lennon knew as soon as the words were out, that Em wouldn't appreciate it. *Crap.*

"Nope. I'm good. I have several ideas, and we're just trying to narrow it down. But I don't see it getting done and defended in the next month!"

Lennon understood. December graduation meant everything had to be wrapped up several months before. "Okay, then I'll start looking at flights in June then."

She was thinking she could pull the school calendar and find out when graduation would be when Emma Kate said, "Well, don't buy your ticket just yet."

"Em!"

"No, I just mean, what if I screw it up? And you paid all that money?"

"I can push it back." Lennon was arguing now. She didn't like where this was going. Did Em just not want to graduate?

"I'll tell you when to get it. Right now, you need to decide what you're going to do about Gabe." A short pause and then, "I always thought he was hot."

"Sure, I mean he does have a great ass. But more importantly he's really smart and he's a decent person. Maybe even a really good one."

"Yeah, that's exactly what people say when they don't have a crush on someone." There was a smirk in her cousin's voice as she hung up on Lennon.

Lennon was left curled in a ball on her own bed thinking about Em maybe not graduating this year, her fifth year of school! And of Gabe and the way her heart rolled over every time she was close to him. She was in all kinds of trouble.

❦ 25 ❦

Lennon had packed her lunch this time with Emma Kate's words ringing in her ears. Her worry about Em and her concern about her cousin's senior thesis not getting finished *again* also followed her, but she'd packed a lunch to share.

Now she found herself wondering if Gabe would show up. She'd done the same thing the past two days, but he hadn't come. It figured. She'd been left eating her over-planned lunch on her own.

Emma Kate was probably wrong, she told herself. Plus, the man had a business to run. It wasn't as if he could just show up every day. Also, they had such a tangled past that it basically didn't allow for anything to happen between them. She shouldn't have even tried this. It was ridiculous, waiting on a man who wouldn't appear and didn't even want her—not that way. So, she thought at least she would enjoy her turkey sandwich, her Granny Smith apple, and the little pot of peanut butter she'd brought to dip it in.

She'd managed to keep digging—and not get sidetracked by a phone call or a need to research something—through almost half the morning before she got a surprise.

"Hey, Lennon." The voice came from behind her, almost startling her.

She knew better. She'd learned long ago when she was on a dig for one of her professors, that if you were near something or digging in an unknown hole, you couldn't get startled. You might jam your trowel into something, break a piece of clay or bone, fall back and step on something already excavated. The likelihood of damaging an artifact was too great, so no matter what happened, you stayed calm.

She recognized his voice, but the timing surprised her. If her hands hadn't been covered in gloves and the gloves in turn covered in dirt, she would have pulled her phone from her pocket and checked the time. Instead, she just asked, "You're here early, aren't you? I mean, I thought you might come for lunch."

Well, she shouldn't have said that. She shouldn't have let on that she might be expecting him, but then again, he'd probably already figured her out. Emma Kate surely had, and she wasn't even on this side of the Mississippi.

"Yes. It's only ten. I finished up early for the day, so I thought I'd come out, see if I could help."

"Watch where you're stepping!" She pointed with the trowel, an automatic gesture, as it was almost always in her hand. She'd set everything out, not expecting company. At least not other than Gabe maybe showing up for lunch, and he usually walked around things. Today, he was already standing in the middle of several of her flags.

"I see you've been digging on my side of the property line."

She nodded and though she liked his smile, she had to tell him. "I had to pull up a few of the flags."

He frowned. "Of course, you did. The trench goes right through them."

At least it didn't seem to bother him. "Well, I was just thinking how hard you fought to get them put there."

She shouldn't have said that, shouldn't have reminded him

of the day they had stood glaring at each other, while a surveyor, a councilman, and the mayor had to come out and break up their fight. It seemed like something that probably hadn't even really happened. Not now, when they had become almost friendly. When she was harboring thoughts of more. But the flags were there, constantly reminding her of just how angry he had been.

Her heart turned over in her chest. No matter what Emma Kate thought was a good idea, her cousin wasn't here. She didn't have to live with it. Besides, Lennon was leaving in a few months anyway. As soon as the dig was over, she'd head back out of town. She couldn't let anything happen between her and Gabe.

Gabe still didn't know the worst of it, but she wasn't going to tell him here, today, so when he said, "Put me to work," she had a hard time telling him *no*.

"I can't have just anyone pick up a trowel and dig, Gabe. You have to be careful. It takes patience, certain techniques."

"You'll teach me," he said it with a calm certainty.

As she looked at him, getting ready to tell him he was too well dressed for a dig, she realized he wasn't. He'd planned ahead. She almost said, "I don't have tools," but to be fair, she could give him the rake and let him scrape the holes, checking to see if she'd missed anything. It wasn't a bad idea actually, but even as she thought it, he pulled a bag off of his shoulder, and it clanked.

"What do you have there?" Her frown gave away her doubt about his planning ahead.

"I brought a trowel, a hand rake, and some old, but clean, firm-bristled paintbrushes." He said the last part as though they were silly.

It was, but she smiled. "Congratulations. You get a one-hundred percent on your first pop quiz."

When Gabe smiled, it went all the way to his eyes and lit up his face. Lennon felt her own mouth smiling in response as though she had no control over it. She was in big, big trouble.

For herself and her own sanity, she tried again to talk him out of staying.

Gabe refused. "Come on, Lennon. I want to do this."

"You want to kneel in the dirt doing backbreaking manual labor to dig up your own property?" she asked, incredulous.

"I do. But I didn't think of it that way. I thought of it as *being part of a cool project.*" He paused a moment, then proved he'd been listening all along. "You said you're pulling up artifacts that may be as much as twenty-thousand years old. When else am I going to get a chance to hold something that was created that long ago? Something that survived right here in the dirt on my land longer than, well, what? Fifteen thousand times longer than it's been my land?"

She laughed at how bad his math was. "Yeah. You need to divide that better. I don't think you should have gotten your MBA with that kind of math."

At least he laughed in response. "When else am I going to get a chance to say that I was on an early dig with the world famous anthropologist/archeologist Lennon Mayfair?"

The problem was it wasn't his argument that swayed her, but his smile. She leaned over and pulled up a small hand-rake and held it out to him, her heart beating harder than it should have. "Fine. Use this rake, and I'll show you."

❦ 2 6 ❦

The bridesmaids dresses must match the table linens.

LENNON STOOD IN FRONT OF THE FULL-LENGTH MIRROR, feeling a little bit shell-shocked. She'd been running around in dirty cargo pants and tank tops earlier in the day, sweating in them actually. She'd been wearing that almost-uniform for long enough now that it felt bizarre to be standing in a bridesmaid's dress in a clean reception area in front of a three-way mirror. It felt odd to see herself dressed all the way up.

The dress was a dusty coral that somehow managed to be bright enough to look good on her darker skin tone, as well as on Jane Copeland's fairer one. Jane was Bailey Ann's only other bridesmaid who managed to be in attendance today. They were missing both of Bailey Ann's sisters and her cousin's best friend from college. And Sioban—Finn's sister, whom Bailey Ann wasn't overly fond of. But that was a wedding for you.

Lennon was standing on an eight-inch-high pedestal, the dress swishing around her ankles and revealing satin heels with a sexy band around the ankle. The shoes were white enough to blind, but the shop attendants had been assuring Bailey Ann they'd be dyed to match perfectly. Lennon wasn't sure when she'd ever be able to wear them again, but she wanted to. They did look like satin bridal shoes though...

An attendant had accompanied the small group into the changing room and now pinned the bodice of the dress on both sides to make the needed measurements. This dress was a floor sample, and the store would have to rush order the exact ones needed for Bailey Ann's fast approaching wedding. The couple had picked a date in the middle of October. And while it bought them some time, it was still fast by wedding standards.

As Lennon looked over at the glowing bride, she thought it was worth it.

Bailey Ann was ooh-ing and ah-ing over the dress. Never mind that she stood behind the two women, looking short next to their pedestal heights. She touched the dresses and looked a little dreamy, as though she were imagining the look all together.

Jane stood on a pedestal just to Lennon's right, while she, too, smiled as the attendant moved to her dress and began to pin it up and measure various points.

"Okay," Bailey Ann looked at Lennon, "You call Emma Kate, and I'm calling Harper Rose, and we're going to get all this worked out."

Bailey Ann was tapping at her phone and had Harper Rose on the line before Lennon even managed to get to her purse and pull up her friend. It had taken a call, a voicemail, and a text, and just as Bailey Ann was getting Harper Rose's measurements, Lennon's phone rang with Emma Kate's picture on the screen.

Em didn't even bother with a greeting. Bailey Ann, possibly the most organized woman on the planet, had already alerted all the bridesmaids that they would be on call this afternoon. Emma Kate knew exactly what was going on. "Please send me a picture."

"I'll go one better and put you on video right now."

"When you didn't call earlier, I headed out to class." Emma Kate said a bit of concern in her voice.

"We took a little longer than we thought meeting up and then finding a dress that will look good on everyone...No, that's not true, we found one right away, but it was for a summer wedding." Lennon explained.

"I'm standing in the hall and class is about to start."

"No. No. Go to class," Lennon protested. After all, she herself thought class was perhaps the most important thing ever.

Emma Kate apparently disagreed. "Oh, no you don't. Show me that dress right now."

Obligingly, Lennon turned the phone toward Jane, who turned and modeled the dress.

"Oh, my God. That's gorgeous."

"I know, you'll look beautiful in it." Lennon told her even as Emma Kate asked after her sister.

Lennon held the phone up facing the oldest of Em's sisters. Bailey Ann managed to talk to both her youngest sister and still be on the phone with Harper Rose.

"Bailey Ann, you did great," Emma Kate said, and Bailey Ann put Harper Rose aside for a moment.

"Are you sure this is okay, Emma Kate? I hate to see you missing classes."

Lennon watched the exchange. She was glad to see the worry on Bailey's face, if only because it meant she wasn't the only one worried about Emma Kate graduating on time. Which was already late.

Em replied, "I know you scheduled it for my long weekend. I'm only missing a Monday of classes and I would not miss *your wedding* for the world."

"Maybe we should postpone until you have a real break," her sister frowned, letting her concern cross the distance.

"Shut up, Bailey Ann. I'll be there," Em said. "Lennon, if you need to, you hang up on me before she can protest again."

"Well, why don't you go to class?" Lennon suggested. She was torn. She knew what it was to be the younger sister. Though she had an overly alpha older brother and Em had two sisters, they'd been the babies together—coddled, worried over, over-protected, and maybe not protected enough.

Lennon wanted her friend to find success, but she understood the need to have everyone stop hovering and get out of her way, too. She aimed for handling the logistics of the dresses. Em could handle school, and if she couldn't then she could learn to ask for help. "I'll text you what measurements we need."

Bailey Ann interrupted then, "But we need them by tonight! So we can do the rush order."

"It's not a problem. I've got you covered." Emma Kate said as though no one would really believe her. Lennon wondered. "Let me get to class. Then I'll get home, and I'll get them to you in about two, two and a half hours?"

"Perfect."

Lennon hung up the line and waited while measurements were recorded from another state and cataloged for Harper Rose. The middle sister had answered each question Bailey Ann asked, producing each measurement on the spot from memory. *Of course*. And they were waiting for Emma Kate's. *Of course*.

"The whole order will go in this evening," the sales lady told them. "That takes care of the bridesmaids dresses. Now, how about your wedding dress?"

Lennon watched as Bailey Ann's entire stance changed. She knew she was seeing a pivotal moment for her cousin. Her whole life was changing. Even though it had already changed, it was a *statement*—getting in that white wedding dress was saying that she wasn't just letting her life change, but she was making it so and making a commitment to it.

It was an interesting thought to Lennon, and she wondered if she'd ever have that moment herself.

As the seamstress unpinned the bridesmaid dress, a fleeting thought of Gabe passed through her mind, but she brushed it away. She was ushered into an attached changing room, through a curtain where she removed the dress and handed it back. It was taken from her hand as soon as she held it out, the staff consistently on their toes. But she still had a corset that she had to get out of. A loaner she been given to wear to show off the dress, so she didn't have bra straps hanging out.

Jane was in a curtained cubby like Lennon's on the other side, but the staff ushered Bailey Ann into the big middle changing space. They had already pulled out three wedding dresses early for Bailey Ann to try on with different necklines and overall styles. The attendants were hanging out, ready to pull more stock like the one she liked best.

Lennon was just putting her own skirt and blouse back on when she heard a yowl from Bailey Ann in the other room. "Oh, dear God, No."

Lennon laughed and stepped out, her shirt not quite buttoned. But she stopped dead as Gabe's face peeked through the curtains to the dressing room.

"You can't be in here," she waved him away.

It didn't stop him, and his head stayed there, pushed through the curtains as though protecting her from the world—but not from him. He smiled as he apologized. "Sorry. I thought I heard your voice."

"Well, you did, but this is a women's dressing room, and Bailey Ann's trying on her wedding dress."

"Ah," he said. Then he motioned to her shirt. "Might wanna button up."

She gasped as she tugged her shirt together. "You know what? Maybe you shouldn't stick your head in the ladies' room."

"I'm sorry, I didn't realize," but the curtains were already falling shut behind him, his non-apology trailing him. It was Lennon who ran over to the curtains this time, buttoning her shirt as she went. "What are you even doing here?"

Was he following them?

Gabe turned and smiled, one hand in his pocket. "I'm trying on a tux. I've got a wedding to go to. Want to be my date?"

❦ 27 ❦

G abe sat in the old principal's office of the elementary school building he'd bought. He couldn't tell if it felt good to sit in the most revered seat from his childhood days or not. He hadn't attended this school per se, but the city had built six elementary schools at once in the mid-fifties. Like many towns, they'd used one set of blueprints for the job. Sitting here was like being in elementary school again. Everything felt the same, from the shape of the front office desk, to the tiles in the cafeteria, to the overly shellacked gymnasium floor.

At least he'd gotten himself out of the house. Gabe had needed to talk himself into it, telling himself that if he didn't leave his home, he would likely wind up putting his jeans back on or his cargo pants and heading out into the woods. Obviously, he would say he didn't have anything better to do and see if Lennon would let him dig with her.

It was a lie. He told himself he'd finished his work that first day. But truly, he'd only finished the things that absolutely required attention. He'd not been doing his job and things were piling up. It wasn't the first time he'd let his work slide over a woman. Probably not surprising, the last time he'd let his work slide it was also over Lennon Mayfair.

He'd done basically the same thing as he was doing now when he was in high school. When he'd decided it was time and he was going to ask her out, it had taken him several months to get around to it. During that time, he and his father had watched his grades dip. Out loud, Rob had wondered if it would keep Gabe out of the college of his choice, but it hadn't. Then his grades dipped further when Brodie and Lennon had started dating, but Gabe didn't like to admit that that was why. It was just a rough patch, his mother said, as teenage boys often went through. It was a rough patch named *Lennon Mayfair*, and so was this one.

Right now, his "rough patch" involved getting behind on renovating this building. While he hadn't been paying attention, the work had come almost to a stop. He hadn't called in enough contractors, and of the few he'd thought were qualified, several turned out not to be.

The building was old. Beyond that, he was completely repurposing it. That meant the remodeling required special care to take care of the kind of features that one found in an older building. Beyond that, it took even more specialized care to handle the features that one found in a school, specifically.

Gabe hadn't really thought far enough ahead, and that was unlike him. It had seemed like a neat project, but now he sat in the office, wanting to go dig. Instead he was dealing with forty child-sized toilets—the industrial kind, with black seats, and lever flush bars mounted on pipes in the back. He had to offload them somewhere. Surely, they'd be useful for someone. Right? But as of right now, he couldn't find a single buyer. It was looking like he was going to scrap them.

The toilets were just one of several similar problems. Like other pieces he'd come across—things he'd thought he'd recoup some of his money on—they were actually going to cost him. The place was turning into a money pit and he'd barely even started.

He had to deal with twenty-five large, old, wooden teacher

desks. They were part and parcel of the building, and they were in great shape. Gabe had expected they would fetch a pretty penny at auction. Sadly, he'd now been informed that too many old schools like this had been overturned lately, and the market was more than saturated with desks.

The original school windows that he thought he would leave intact, and had been industrial at the time they had been installed, had aged well but not well enough. Too many of them were leaky, and he couldn't pass inspection with the kind of heat and air conditioning loss that they were allowing. There was almost no way to insulate the building well enough when half the windows leaked like sieves.

He smacked his pencil down on the desk. He'd had a much better day yesterday when he was digging up rocks with Lennon. In fact, that's what he'd been doing—just digging up rocks. He dug up a little mound of pebbles, setting them all to one side, as she'd instructed. She'd been smart enough to sort through them and point out that he'd missed a mud encrusted piece of clay. He'd thought it was another rock. And that's why she was in charge.

Lennon had now found a handful of artifacts and was relatively convinced that she was on to something. He'd watched her face light up, but he couldn't think about that now. He had to save this building. He'd put far too much money into it, and he'd sat on it for a little too long now. It needed a new business plan, and he needed to figure it out, but he couldn't concentrate.

He and Lennon had talked the whole time they'd been digging the day before, and she was right. His knees did hurt, and it made him feel old. His lower back ached a little from the use of normally untouched muscle groups. He didn't think they had a machine at the gym that had prepped him for this.

Gabe couldn't remember the last time he'd felt both so keyed up and so relaxed around someone. They'd talked about her school and she'd asked about his degree. But she'd topped off that short conversation by asking what he'd wanted to be, because she knew it had all been thrown off when Brodie died, and Gabe had suddenly become the heir apparent to the Zemp family fortune.

Not that it was a real fortune. It wasn't. He knew. He wasn't so much a billionaire or anything like that, as he was a big fish in the small pond of Breathless. Put him in any slightly larger pond, and he'd be nobody.

He'd seen the differences between him and the other kids when he'd been in high school. Then he'd gone off to college and seen that, well, he wasn't that different from those guys. Just more big fish from little ponds. But Lennon was the one who had asked what he'd intended to do.

It wasn't where he'd ended up, that was for certain. He'd gone into the liberal arts, studying English, history, and even visual art. He dabbled a little in theater, but quickly abandoned it, as he had little talent for acting. But while there, he'd been prop master for more than one play and in charge of scenery for several more.

He'd taken two years of his college life that way, before his father had convinced him that math and economics were what he needed to get his degree. Rob insisted Gabe was done dicking around, and it was time to buckle down.

Unable to tell why, Gabe sensed there was something in her question, something about the way she asked it that almost disapproved of what he'd eventually chosen. She hadn't asked him point blank, but he could hear it, almost as though it was waiting on the tip of her tongue, "Did you choose that, or did your father?"

He hadn't really thought of it that way before. If everything she said was true, Rob had made choices for her without her consent, and Gabe was now wondering not only *if* Rob had made some for him, but how many choices and which ones?

✤ 28 ✤

Two days later Gabe was sitting in the office at the elementary school for the third day in a row. He had managed to find somebody to tear out and haul away the forty child-sized toilets. While it frustrated him to pay extra to have the crew remove the adult-sized ones too, no one wanted industrial type school toilets. At best, he could keep one or two for staff or for a public restroom maybe by the lobby, but no more. They had to be dismantled and hauled away. They were old, and they were so far from "water efficient" that there was no saving them.

Luckily, he had found a team to come and reclaim the basketball floor from the gymnasium. The owner—who had first come and given him an estimate—was now suggesting Gabe also tear up the wooden flooring from the small stage at the far end. Gabe hadn't even looked at the stage to see that it had hard wood. Of course, it was different from the basketball flooring and could only be repurposed in a separate smaller space.

No, Gabe had missed all of that. In fact, he'd sat in this office reading reports and looking at blueprints. Measuring square footage and trying to figure out who to call to check for load-bearing walls and get advice on whether it was worth keeping or tearing out the ramp that ran alongside the stairs in each hallway. While he'd been crunching the numbers—and thinking about Lennon—he'd been missing the realities of the job.

He'd found a company to replace the windows, but their estimate was an arm and a leg and it would leave the whole building looking different. On the one hand, he liked the proposed style. It was far more modern and would satisfy the requirements of not being drafty, thus dramatically reducing the power bills for the people who would live here. That would be a big selling point and help with the rent, but it was going to cost him up front and he was going to pay it, because that seemed to be his only option.

Though he'd been pleased when he initially looked to see that each of the classrooms had plumbing installed, he now also had forty old metal sinks that he had to get rid of. Again, it wasn't something that was needed or even that he could repurpose in the apartments. He had to find a place to put a laundry room or create washer and dryer attachments in each unit. Or he could do it at the end of the hall, but he preferred the in-unit variety, given the clientele he wished to sell to. But it wasn't looking like there was a good way to do it.

He'd had two different designers bidding on the basic classroom-to-apartment remodel and he was wondering if he even liked any of the ideas they'd come up with. Neither had yet found a way to incorporate the washer and dryer without building an obvious closet into the space.

Gabe was frustrated and rubbing at his now aching neck when his phone rang. Reaching into his back pocket, he pulled it out and was surprised to see that it produced a smile. He'd taken Lennon's picture while she was digging the other afternoon. He'd called to her, letting her turn her head and catching her by surprise. She hadn't fully appreciated it, but he loved the picture enough to set it to his phone. He smiled again at her hair scraped back from her pretty face, but poofed out in the pony-tail behind her head. She looked both strict and adorable and he was in trouble.

"Hey Lennon," he answered the phone wondering if his grin translated into his words.

But her return tone was not the same level of chipper as his. "Gabe, I've got a problem."

"Uh oh, what's that?"

"I've run into a cave on your property."

"A cave? We don't have caves in Breathless." He'd never heard of such a thing, and wouldn't he and his brother have found them?

"Actually, we do," she said. "Though not very many." With that she launched into a short explanation, making him smile again.

"How is this a problem?"

"There are sturdy trees that have grown in front of it for years. I need to excavate and that will take some equipment. I obviously need your permission as this isn't part of our contract—"

He was resenting that bloody contract. He should have just given her free reign, but he couldn't take it back now. Pushing his attention away from regret and back to the phone, Gabe listened as she was still talking.

"I need to show you where it is, probably need to get another contract signed."

As frustrated as she sounded, he really liked hearing her voice. "I'll tell you what. I'm at the school. So why don't you mark the cave on the map and bring it down here, and we'll sign off on it."

"Come on Gabe, you know I'm a mess. I have mud embedded in my knee pads and. . ."

"And you're going to bring me a map because that's what you do. In fact, you probably already have it marked. So just show me what you have so I can sign off on it."

He'd seen her marking each of her finds on her own blueprint. She would record what she found there and probably even an estimate of the age of the contents. "So go home, shower, come meet me at the school. Help me out here. I need advice about this building. Tell me whether I need to continue with this project or not, and we'll solve the problem of your cave."

Okay, he thought, *that sounded like a bit of an innuendo.* But she didn't seem to pick up on it, thank God. Instead, she huffed a small sigh as though irritated that he was asking her to come down.

He tried again, "You'll want to come see this. I'm at Greer, the old elementary that closed down?"

"Oh, I know that one." At least her tone perked up. "Some of my friends went there."

"Mine too. It's one of the last of the original school buildings and they sold it to me, and I want to convert it into apartments." He suddenly found himself babbling to her the way that she did to him about pot sherds—not shards, he'd been corrected.

It bothered him how much he'd hoped she'd say yes, and how much his heart had flipped over when she finally did. After hanging up, he struggled to wait patiently and didn't really achieve it. He did less work in that hour than he usually did in fifteen minutes.

Of course, he was watching as her car pulled up, because he'd calculated about how long he thought it would take her to get there. He'd also headed out toward the lobby to check and see if she'd arrived no fewer than three times. At least this time he was right.

She was parked in a parental drop-off lane that would've gotten her ticketed had the school been active. Lennon had pulled her old car up right behind his new one. Her car sported a handful of dings in the silver doors, a marked contrast to his shiny, clean, new model sports car, but he found he liked that about the two of them.

She wore a skirt that was a little too short for the cooler weather, and a heavier sweater. It was definitely a different look from her usual dig clothing. He liked that, too. Was there a side to Lennon he didn't like? He hadn't found it yet.

Holding the door open, he ushered her inside, reaching out for the big leather bag she'd slung over her shoulder. He knew from past experience that it held all her paperwork for the dig.

She was looking up at him expectantly, but he tried to quell her worry. "Look, I'm going to sign off on excavating the cave."

"It will possibly require heavy equipment coming on to your land," she offered as a warning.

"Are you going to tear down my house? Break my windows? Cost me all new landscaping?" He raised his eyebrows as they talked while he led her back to the principal's office.

She only shook her head at him, frowning. "Why would it even get near your house? It's so far away."

"Exactly. So, I'll sign off on it." He watched as she nodded just a little and seemed to understand. Setting her bag down on his desk, he took her hand in his as though it were the most natural gesture in the world. "Now, while there's still good light, come help me figure out what to do with this building."

He was tugging her down the hallway behind him, pointing out the problems he was facing, when she tugged back a little. "Gabe, I have no idea how I could possibly help with this. This is not my area of expertise. . . I don't know anything about modern building remodels."

Stopping, he turned and smiled at her, though he noticed he didn't drop her hand. "I know. That's why I need you. You're smart, you're a fresh pair of eyes, and you aren't looking at it the way the rest of us are. I trust you."

He watched as his last phrase startled her though she tried to hide it.

Gabe wondered if he'd hidden it well enough that it surprised him, too.

29

Lennon felt the nostalgia hit as she trailed Gabe down the hallway of the old elementary school. The pale wood planks of the floor lined up longways to the hall, almost as though they were leading her back down to the classrooms, the same way she had followed an identical hallway through her elementary school career. It was bringing back surprising memories of being a small kid.

The old-style classroom doors had a solid bottom half and a nine-pane window in the top. The school had been built in a time before craftsmanship went out the door and before school shootings and bullet-proof everything was the norm. The doors were wood, the windows glass without even the wire webbing in them.

When Gabe pushed his way into one of the classrooms, she saw the first crack in her nostalgia. The floor was covered in ugly, gray industrial style carpeting. It was worn almost through in places. It occurred to her that the city had not been keeping the school up in its last years, once it became apparent that the council might close this school down.

Gabe tugged her into the center of the now almost empty room and finally let go of her hand, which was a shame. It was only then that he looked at her expectantly. But Lennon shook her head and shrugged.

She wanted her paperwork signed, so she could excavate the cave. Not that she had been planning on doing any excavation work tonight. Not that she didn't like spending time with Gabe —which was something to examine more closely at a later time. But she hadn't intended to be walking the old school building.

"I don't know what you want from me." She looked at him, waiting for further instructions.

"I want you to take a look at this place and tell me what you would do."

"Well, what's the point? It doesn't matter what I would do with it. I'd open a school or something. The real question is: what do *you* want to do with it?"

"Apartments," he said quickly. "I think that this area of town —with all the new business growing up around it—would be a great place for people to live. It's not a singular live-play-work building like in New York but it would be close to all those things. There's a grocery just down the block, business around the corner, a gym getting built right now across the street. The area is up and coming."

She nodded, still not sure she saw the vision. "What kind of apartments? Families, solo people, couples, a mix?"

She watched as he thought for a moment. "Probably not families. I'm thinking something younger, hipper, more modern, in an old building."

"You're going to make an old elementary school into a place for a young, urban, hip, people *without* kids?"

"Well, when you put it that way," he said.

Lennon only shrugged at him, still feeling she was missing something important in his grand design.

"Okay," he explained. "I saw this done in Chicago when I went to visit for a meeting. One of the presenters had turned an old school into a set of unique condos—high end. Now her old school was from a multi-story building. And she had turned each of the classrooms into a reasonably open space floor plan. But hers were each designed by a different artist and sold as is. So there are some differences."

"Too many to just copy that idea?"

"Well, we don't have multi levels. We don't have small enough classrooms to make one-, two- or three-classroom units. And I'm not selling, I'll be renting. Breathless really isn't the place for avant-garde, artist-designed lofts. Still, I think the basic idea will work."

"Well, what are you thinking about how to make this classroom into one apartment?" She listened as he talked her through adding a wall that would divide space for separate rooms.

"It would make the bedroom completely enclosed—I'm not a fan of open concept that's too open—and then this section will be a bathroom." He waved his hand around the area, pointing to the old formica classroom countertop in the corner, and the set of silver sinks. "So the bathroom would be on this side, and I can put the kitchen over here as well since we already have plumbing, which makes sense. It would be away from the windows because you'll want to have cabinets in the kitchen."

Gabe kept turning and pointing as he talked, getting more and more excited.

"It sounds great. I don't see a problem."

"That's just it," he told her, almost spinning now, with his hands held out wide. "The basic idea is fine. It's all the little pieces that offer up a problem. For example, the roof leaks and there's some damage up in the attic. I'm going to have to fix that. I don't see that there's any way around that."

Lennon didn't either, so she shrugged to him. "Okay. That makes plenty of sense. What else?"

"I think I can turn the offices into another apartment, but I don't know what to do about the restrooms. It's a lot of space and I pulled out a decent sized boys room and a girls room down at the end. I'm going to do something with those areas because having a community restroom at the end of the hall doesn't make any sense in an apartment building. But I don't know how to make that space into an extra apartment. Next, I'd like to get a washer and dryer in each of these units. Don't know how to do that, either. I also want," he turned and looked at her before pointing behind him into the corner. ". . .to get rid of these desks. I thought I was going to sell them off and make some profit on it. Thought I was going to sell off a lot of things in this building, but nobody wants them. It seems I'm not turning any profit here."

Lennon frowned at him. "So what are you actually trying to do?"

"I'm trying to make apartments."

"But what you just said is that you're trying to turn a profit. Which one is it?"

"Well, they're both the same thing."

"Not really. If you're just trying to turn a profit, then you slap some walls in and get some people to move in and you don't care. But if you're trying to make some really interesting and unique apartments, well, then you have other problems. Which would require other solutions."

He stared at her for a moment and Lennon tried to elaborate. "I mean you're treating this like it's some kind of dream, like it's this big plan that you *have to* make these apartments. Yet you also seem to think that you're going to easily do a thing which is unusual for this area and obviously you don't have everything hammered out on it. Somehow you think you can take this gamble, but also cut corners and still miraculously turn a significant profit on it. I get that you *might* be able to do both, but planning to do both is apparently killing you," she said.

She watched as he stopped and blinked for a few moments, trying to absorb all of that. "So. . . ?" he asked, still looking confused by what she'd said.

"Pick one. Are you trying to turn a profit or are you trying to make apartments?"

"What would you suggest?"

"I really don't know. I'm clearly not a businessman of any kind. I operate on grant money, and probably will continue to do so well into my future. But if it was me deciding? I think you should make the apartments."

"Why?"

"Because it was the only part you seemed excited about. Do you need the money? If it fails, is there something horrible that you're going to lose? Are you in some dire financial straits that no one knows about? Something like: if you don't get these apartments profitable by the end of the year, you're going to lose your home or some part of your business?" He was shaking his head at her the whole time. "So you don't need the money."

"I guess not."

Must be nice, she thought, but then she said out loud, "Then make the apartments. Screw the profit. It will come later. Make the apartments you want to make."

30

Gabe left Lennon to wander the school while he headed back to his office, supposedly to write up the documents for the work she needed to do at the cave. He had promised her he would sign off on excavating the cave and so he'd offered to create an addendum to the contract. He could write it, print it, and sign it right there in the principal's office. That wasn't the problem.

The problem was, he was a little bit boggled by her questions. She was right. He hadn't done anything like this before.

He'd spent the last several years following through on business deals his father had already put into place before he'd died. Gabe had opened a few more Bobby's Pizzas in the neighboring towns. Hell, Rob even picked the lots to build on, the buildings to renovate, and when each should open. Gabe had merely followed through.

Bobby's Pizza made money. As his father had always said, "If you were going to start a business, sell a service. But, if you must sell a product, sell pizza."

Looking back, Gabe found he'd been satisfied with the job he'd done. But he'd not been *excited* about any of it. He would happily mark things up as a win when the new store turned out well and another on the day each new store paid itself back. He enjoyed opening day and ribbon cutting at the new Bobby's Pizzas, but they weren't his baby. None of it had been.

This was, and Lennon was right. He hadn't even seen it, but he'd been trying to do too many things in one space, maybe even contradictory things. He didn't *need* a profit. It would be great if the place did become a money generator. Thinking it through, he realized he would probably be able to get it to that status several years down the road even if it didn't bring in gobs of profit right away. But even if it flopped, it wasn't going to change his lifestyle that much.

It was just going to be something else to put under his belt. And what was he doing with his lovely lifestyle? *Nothing.* That's what. He didn't have a life *style;* he just had a comfortable income. That was all.

He didn't own a boat, nor did he really want to. He had the car he wanted. He wasn't driving a Lamborghini like he'd planned in high school. But that was it: he *could* drive one if he wanted, he had simply long since learned it wasn't what he really wanted. His father had left him in very good shape. Financially, they owned the house. They owned the businesses. The businesses were profitable.

When he thought about it, Gabe realized he had more than enough money—as long as the economy didn't crash so hard that people would no longer buy pizza—to send his kids to private school, to have a wife who didn't have to work, to cover his greens fees and annual dues at the club and be a generous donor to the library. He could easily pay for staff to clean his house, wash his car regularly, and keep up with the maintenance on things he didn't want to bother to pay attention to. Unfortunately, of all of those things, all he had was the staff.

He hadn't even become a generous donor to the library. He was signing the pages he'd printed up and he almost stopped dead. He'd always thought he'd get his name on one of those little brass plaques. He'd loved the library as a kid. But here he was, town golden boy, and he'd not done it. He'd made zero moves of his own when he was shadowing his dad. And it seemed he was still shadowing the man, even though Robert Zemp was no longer alive.

Gabe had expected to ask Lennon about the school and have her answer about the school. Instead she'd held up a mirror to his face and he wasn't sure he liked what he'd been doing—or as the case was, *not doing*. And she'd managed to do most of it couched in answers almost like the ones he'd expected. Except for the part where her answers kept surprising him.

When he'd asked her about the teacher's desks, Lennon had replied, "Leave them in the rooms. Put one in each apartment. Anyone who wants to live in an old school building—the kind of person who would enjoy having a hardwood floor made out of a basketball court with the occasional red and blue stripe across one of the boards—is going to really enjoy having an original teacher's desk."

He hadn't thought of that. It hadn't been in the other apartments he was copying, and since those had been profitable, he was trying to run along the same path. In his plans, he was making only the smallest changes to that original design—only the ones that were necessary for *this* school, *this* area, the people around here who might live in his apartments. But maybe Lennon was right.

She said maybe he would attract other people to the town of Breathless. It was far enough outside Atlanta that they probably wouldn't commute, but they might start building some downtown businesses if there was an upscale apartment building where they could live in the heart of the town.

When he'd asked her about the windows, she'd asked, "How many leak?"

It was a kicker, he thought. "About every third one."

"Can you just replace the ones that leak?" she'd asked while she looked up at them with a frown as though she could see the air escaping.

At least that was something he'd already thought of. "Well, if I do that, then I'll have random windows that look different."

"Well, maybe you replace all the windows on only one side. The building has a definite front and back, so pick a side and replace all of those. Use the good ones that came out and see if you can replace the ones that leak on the other side."

He would only wind up replacing half the windows. The two sides of the building would look different, but as she said, he clearly had a front and a back. "Which ones do I replace?"

"Depends. Do you want to make the front of the building look modern, or do you want it to call back to its old school days?"

Her answer was relatively easy and one he hadn't thought of. He didn't know if it would work, but he liked the way she was thinking. And he liked that she was thinking not about profit margins, but merely about doing enough to make the building do what it needed to do, to give Gabe a project that he could be proud of.

He'd not yet had a project he was proud of.

She pushed the door to the office open then, her head ducking into the principal's old domain. Her feet stayed beyond the threshold outside, and she leaned in, almost as though she was afraid to step in maybe without an invitation.

Gabe understood. He'd felt that way himself. He held out the new pages for the contract. "Here, I have this. If you want to just come sign it, it gives you free access to clear out the cave."

She finally came in gingerly and sat in the chair he'd left there. It, too, was original to the building. She took the paper and twirled it around to where it faced her. Then commented, "You've marked out a big area around where the cave is."

"I know. You should be able to excavate without problems. I want to be sure that you can bring in any kind of machinery without worrying that you're not cleared for it."

"I won't bring in machinery. It might be heavy and damage things underground." She was now leaning far across the desk, coming close as she raised an eyebrow at him. "And if I find another cave?"

Gabe leaned toward her, catching a whiff of her perfume or shampoo. He couldn't tell. But instead of turning his head and brushing his lips across her skin, he merely tapped to a paragraph on the lower portion of the page. "You didn't read far enough down."

Her eyes widened to discover that he'd already thought of that and signed away permission for any additional caves that she found as well as the one she'd already located.

"Caves tend to exist in clusters." He was proud of knowing that. He'd looked it up. He handed her a pen, having already signed his own line across the bottom.

It was Lennon who hesitated. "I don't get you, Gabriel Zemp. First, you tell me that I can't come near your property line and demand that I'm digging in the wrong place and have to stop. You create a scenario where I lose two days of work to get a surveyor out, and now you're signing away the rights for me to dig wherever I want and drive machinery all over your land."

Gabe thought about it. But he didn't have any brain power left. She'd thrown him for loop after loop. His own feelings for her had only complicated it. So he let the only words that made sense come out of his mouth. "I don't get me, either. But it's a good deal and you should sign it." Then he startled them both. "I trust you."

❧ 31 ❧

Belles are encouraged to find creative solutions to their problems. Everyone has been stood up, but a belle will just go have a better time without the jerk.

LENNON HAD FINALLY BROKEN DOWN AND ADMITTED SHE HAD a horrendous crush on Gabe Zemp. Worse, she'd not only admitted it to herself, she'd admitted it—out loud—to Emma Kate.

"I don't know, Em. I've been working for five days straight, and I've heard nothing from him." She paused and tried not to be so irritated. "I have lunch out there each day. He knows exactly where to find me."

"So you're saying he gave you free reign on his land, then he ghosted?"

"Pretty much. What am I supposed to think?" She was looking for some support in her frustration. But Emma Kate had never been one to validate anything she didn't fully believe.

"Maybe you should think he's busy. You know, you could reach out to him," Emma Kate said, as though it were some kind of casual piece she had thrown into the conversation.

Lennon didn't let that slide. "I suppose I *could*." She used all the snark she could muster and stuffed it into her tone in that one phrase. But—and she didn't say this—she'd never had to make a move with him before. Gabe had simply shown up, and...*shit*.

Her cousin was right. He'd not made Lennon do any of the work. Until now.

"Do you think he's testing you?" Em asked, riding directly on Lennon's thoughts, even though she'd not put any of it into words. Emma Kate was like that.

"Maybe." She drew the word out, hating to admit it but it was the right thing to do.

"So," Em posed, "is this a test you want to pass? Or do you want to just let this fade away? If you want to maybe let it go, now is a good time, because you have an easy out while he's not coming around."

"I—"

"Nope!" Emma Kate cut her off and Lennon could almost see her friend's finger slicing the air as if to tell her to zip it. "Do not answer that right now. It's something you need to think about. Seriously, this guy's a Zemp. That is one messed up family history you've got with them, and I suspect it would be a lot of work to have something good happen. But, you really do like this guy, and you always have. So maybe it's worth it. But if it's not, don't reach out. Let it fade now, while it can."

Lennon sighed. "Damn, Em. I don't understand how you can't finish your thesis, because you are on top of this." She regretted the words as soon as they were out of her mouth.

"I'm finishing, Lennon. I'm just not you."

"I know. I'm sorry." Lennon cringed, and wished that Em could see her and know she really hadn't meant it. "I didn't mean it that way."

"I know," Em said. "I'm the family fuck-up."

"No, you're not," Lennon protested, almost out of rote.

"I *am*. I'm the one who's taking six years to do five years of attending class for what should have been a four-year program. I've spent a massive ton of money on a degree I still don't have. Although I guess luckily, there's enough family money in the house or something that I'm not going to have to pay for this too harshly."

"You're not going to be buried under student debt for your five years?" Lennon asked. She'd wondered if Della and Con had left the girls well-enough off. She'd hoped so. It was hard on Emma Kate losing both her parents in such a short time. That probably hadn't helped her finish school at all.

"No, in fact, though I had fully intended to be buried under mountains of debt for this," Em said. "It turns out Mama and Daddy stocked enough away that I should be okay."

"That's at least good news. What about grad school?"

"I guess I could be okay with that, if I can get myself a scholarship. I've got good enough grades, I just. . ."

"You haven't decided," Lennon filled in.

"I haven't decided on anything!" Em wailed. "I don't know what I want to be. I don't know what I want to do. I mean, this is what you always wanted, and me, I just floated along. I was the baby, and everyone took care of me, and I. . . I don't even know, Len, but I'll finish, I promise, *someday*."

She muttered the last word, making Lennon wonder a little bit, but she'd pushed too hard already, and she dialed it back now. "I have faith in you, 'Cuz. You'll make it happen. Remember, it's getting your degree that's important, not getting it in the right thing. Do you remember your Daddy told me that all the work of the degree was half of it? The other half was *finishing*. The degree is a stamp from a university that you can finish something."

Lennon had meant it to be a helpful statement. She'd meant to remind Em of her father and what a good person he'd been. But Emma Kate's response had been garbled and unenthusiastic. Lennon wondered if she'd put her foot in it again. But she told her cousin how much she loved her, and that she needed to do what was right for her, before they hung up.

She'd not slept well that night, thinking about Em's question.

Gabe said he trusted her. That had been eye-opening, apparently for him too. It was more than possible that that was why he was holding back. Maybe he'd just realized he was getting in deeper than he intended. Bringing her out to the school and getting her involved in his decisions. He'd come out and dug with her for almost two whole days. Maybe he'd realized it was just too much.

For the past several days, Lennon had continued digging in the flat open area of Gabe's land. She'd not been able to go into the cave, because she hadn't been able to get the right workers in to excavate the front of the cave.

When she hit her dig site the next day, they'd finally shown up.

So she hadn't slept well the night before, and now she was struggling to direct people to do a very, very careful job that they wanted to do quickly and with very large tools.

"No." She stood her ground, hands on hips as she guarded the tangled mass of trees and brush in front of the cave. "You can't drive your trucks in here."

"But, ma'am, you want that cleared? That's the fastest way."

"I hired you because your boss said you would hand clear the brush. No trucks. No machines. You'll have to walk the tools in from the parking lot. I'm paying for a *gentle* clearing."

"There's no such thing as a *gentle* clearing, lady."

Though it was unlikely that they would destroy something with the small backhoe or bobcat they wanted to use, driving the truck in just might. She couldn't risk it. So an hour later, three guys had shown up with chainsaws and a few other hand held tools. She watched and it all went well until they got to the stumps. They wanted to remove them with blasting caps, but again Lennon demanded they had to be dug out by hand.

The men did not understand, and they argued with her about

how much easier it was to blast it out. Lennon explained, and then explained again, and again one more time, why that couldn't happen. In the end, though they'd done as she said, they were quite angry about it, and insisted on charging her extra. Luckily, she had a fund for the research, and she'd set aside some money for things that came up, but this had about eaten all of it up.

The men had stayed well into the afternoon trying to get the job done, and Lennon had stayed to watch them work. She was afraid that they might blast the trees out as soon as she wasn't looking. It was six p.m. before they finally finished and packed up their gear and went home.

Now that the cave was clear, Lennon desperately wanted to take a look inside, but told herself she was better off waiting until the next day. God knew it was dark, and no one was around. Gabe apparently wasn't even going to come out and offer to share lunch with her. So, if something went wrong, if she twisted an ankle, or got stuck, or God forbid, found an amazing set of cave paintings and left herself in there with a headlamp for twenty-four hours, no one was going to notice.

Forcing herself not to look, she turned away and headed home. Tomorrow was another day. Besides, she had to get to her late dinner with Bailey Ann, Jane, and Riley—her cousin Christian's fiancé—that night.

Smiling for the first time that day, she headed home to change and get her salad out of the fridge. She had friends to meet. Gabe could wait.

L ennon watched as Stella ran up to her on chubby legs.

"L'nin, L'nin," she said, almost as though Lennon were an old communist Russian leader, rather than a girl named after her great, great grandfather's surname, as she were.

She tugged Lennon's hand, insisting that they go upstairs to see her room. It was Jane who said, "Stella, maybe you need to leave Lennon alone for a little bit, okay? Lennon is mommy's friend."

"I'm good." Lennon offered it up with a smile, enjoying having Stella take her own hand in her small, chubby one. For whatever reason, the little girl had decided Lennon was her new best friend, even though she knew Bailey Ann much better and had just met Lennon. Lennon was apparently the cool one and had to be shown what was in her room.

The house was a beautiful, old craftsman style and Stella led Lennon up the stairs and around to the smaller room up top. All three bedrooms were nestled up here and as she walked by, Lennon saw that there was a crib in Jane's master bedroom and the two boys were playing in what was obviously their bedroom. They were neither quiet nor gentle but seemed to be getting on fine.

"Are you getting a baby sister in your room soon?" Lennon asked.

"Yes!" Stella's face lit up and that made Lennon happy. "Her crib will go over here. And I'm going to get a big-girl bed!" she pointed to the toddler bed that was pushed into one corner. "When baby Claire cries, it will be my job to get mommy and help take care of her. Because I'm the big sister now." If she was going to get a roommate, at least she was excited about it.

A-ha, Lennon thought. *Good way to sell it, Jane.*

Stella sat them down on a fluffy rug shaped like a flower and pulled out several tiny ponies along with a couple of dolls and an airplane.

"Here. You be airplane," she said, handing the toy to Lennon with authority. Lennon readily agreed, having no idea where the game was going. The dolls were three times the size of the airplane and the multi-colored ponies were about the size of fairies, compared to the dolls. Lennon could not figure out what situation they would all possibly get involved in.

Stella unfolded a story with the dolls flying to China, a turn that Lennon had not expected. "Why China?"

"My daddy goes to China," Stella said. Though, it wasn't said with anywhere near the enthusiasm that she had previously mentioned getting a baby sister as a roommate.

The dolls and ponies arrived in China—where apparently the ponies must work as airport employees—before Jane appeared at the top of the stairs. Apparently, she was attempting to rescue Lennon, but Lennon didn't need it.

When she protested that she was having a good time, Jane let them both know it was time for the kids to go to bed. She'd invited Bailey Ann and Lennon and Riley over for dinner but promised them a real adult dinner and that she would feed the kids early and that the women could have the place to themselves.

Lennon laughed as she watched her new friend clearly attempt to override three young children who were excited about having guests. Guests they were apparently no longer allowed to interact with. Baby Claire handled it with the most grace, though all the kids were in their pajamas by the time Lennon arrived. She was grateful to be included, aside from hanging out with Gabe at the school almost a week earlier, she'd spent real time with almost no one.

Bailey Ann and Finn had been wrapped up in remodeling their next house and planning their wedding. Lennon wondered how they were handling two such big projects at the same time. She was busy enough with one. Still, she'd been fielding a flurry of texts with her cousin about colors, shoes, Emma Kate's measurements—which were late—and so much more that she'd not seen Bailey Ann at all, not until now. At some point while Lennon had been upstairs, Riley had arrived. Having been banished to the downstairs while Jane got the kids all to bed, Lennon used the time to ask both women how it was going today, as weddings could turn on a dime.

Jane eventually returned to find that Lennon, Riley, and Bailey Ann had set the table. Lennon put out her salad—partially from a bag, but who was counting?—Bailey Ann had a rice dish for a side, and Riley had showed up with a Middle Eastern dish that Lennon didn't recognize but Bailey raved about. Laughing, they'd dug through their friend's kitchen drawers finding the necessary silverware and utensils with no help at all, but eventually coming up with the right pieces.

Jane sank into her chair and raised the glass of white wine Bailey Ann had poured them all. Even before she spoke, she made Lennon feel like a real friend.

"Here's to kids in bed, weddings going off without a hitch, and somehow swinging an archeological dig that landed you a hot guy!"

Jane and Riley were sipping their drinks before Lennon managed to stop choking on air. *Did everyone know?* She was going to ask, but Bailey Ann beat her to the punch with a topic change.

"I have something to tell you and I don't want you to be mad."

Uh oh, Lennon thought, *but also, good gossip?* Maybe Bailey Ann was pregnant...But no, she was drinking the wine, so it wasn't that.

"I'm trying to tell all the bridesmaids and groomsmen, because we didn't want anybody to be upset, but Finn and I are already married."

"*What?*" Lennon cried out, listening as Jane and Riley echoed a similar sentiment.

"Remember I told you how Finn and I thought about just going down to the courthouse? Well, this date—the one that we are planning for—it was a backup date. It was homecoming weekend our first year together. But, we actually met closer to the beginning of the school year. That had been our original plan to get married exactly twenty years after the day that we first met. But this year it was a Tuesday and..." She trailed off until the three women nodded at her to go on.

Lennon took another drink of her wine as her cousin continued. "Well, we had this backup date planned, but that day we woke up and looked at each other and said, 'Let's do it.' So, we went down to the courthouse and got married then and we didn't tell anybody because, well, it wasn't what we had thought we would do. We knew we would have the big wedding later, so. . ." Bailey Ann rambled for a moment before Lennon realized what she needed was reassurance.

"That's wonderful," Lennon offered, reaching out and taking her cousin's hand, watching as she grasped it, as Bailey Ann's face changed. Lennon looked to Jane and saw that the third member of their party also looked happy. "It's great. It means no one gets cold feet, no one has to worry if the bride is already pregnant, any of that crap. We can all just have a great day with a party."

"We are doing the whole ceremony."

"As you should!" Jane chimed in. Lennon was grateful that

Jane was happy about the wedding. She had every right to be bitter about marriage given the way hers had turned out.

"You beat me to the punch!" But Riley was laughing as she raised her glass in salute. She and Christian weren't doing the bridesmaids and groomsmen thing. And having a smaller ceremony that still didn't have a date set.

Bailey Ann looked between the three of them. "We just didn't want you to find out later and be mad or think we had lied."

"Not at all," Lennon told her. "Congratulations!"

It turned out that all Bailey Ann had needed was reassurance. Maybe that's what Gabe needed, too.

❧ 33 ❧

Lennon stood at the entrance to the cave, her heart pounding as she wondered, not for the first time, just what she might find. She reminded herself it could easily be nothing, literally nothing, or worse some kind of animal droppings.

She had on her dorky headlamp, and of course she'd brought her camera, notepad, phone and more. She was also wearing her favorite pair of jeans, the ones that fit like a dream, and a cotton shirt that was made out of t-shirt material and hung on her *just so*. She wasn't digging today, and she'd known that when she left the house. It was time to explore the cave.

There were holes in the ground outside the cave, some she'd dug but most left over from the men removing the trees and brush. Other than that, once she navigated them, she should be on pretty sure footing. She wasn't in nice shoes, but she had on a cute pair of sneakers. Though she repeatedly told herself that she hadn't yet decided whether she would walk over to Gabe's at the end of the day, it would seem that her wardrobe admitted that she already had.

Trying to ignore what she fully intended to do later, she clicked the button on her headlamp, flipping the bright light on. She offered up a small prayer that she didn't leave a disturbing mark in her hair, then another that she find some really great artifacts or information in the cave. With one last deep breath, she stepped slowly into the dark.

The cave was just large enough that if she stayed in the middle, her hair would not brush the ceiling. Pulling a GPS app up on her phone, she recorded the exact location of the entrance. She would record as far inside the cave as she could get signal. Who knew? She might get all of it. Next, she swept her head around moving the bright little lamp to every corner so she could see.

At first sweep, she saw nothing obvious. But she wasn't discouraged. She re-checked the rock at the edge of the entrance more thoroughly the second time, then aimed her light down to the dirt at her feet. Next, she tilted her head to shine it a little further along the walls as far in as she could see.

The headlamp, it turned out, was a terrible idea, making her tilt and tip her head to get the light the right direction. So she pulled it off, grateful not to have hat hair, or worse, headlamp hair, by the end of the day, and began aiming it with her hand. It meant she had too many things to hold, but she was still excited about what she might find.

The work was slow and painstaking, because had anyone painted on the walls, there was a reasonable possibility—especially here at the entrance—that it would have worn away over the years. The original drawings, though once vibrant and probably large, might now have left only the tiniest traces for someone like Lennon to find. She trusted herself to find it if she was diligent.

As an undergraduate, she'd learned that diligence got you recommendation letters. Diligence found tiny chips of bones that could then be tested, carbon dated, and possibly even more learned from them. Diligence was her job here, so she'd embraced it. While she wasn't patient for most things—lord knew, she wasn't patient about Gabe not showing up for a week —this walk into the cave the first time would be done right.

Everything would be recorded. Every nook and cranny inspected.

A few moments later, after she'd done everything she could from standing at the entrance, she took another large step into the cave and repeated the process. An hour later, she was less than ten feet into the cave.

She'd found several places that had something black pushed into the crevices. It might have been paint, so Lennon spent copious amounts of time taking pictures. She'd recorded the spots and tried to see if she could connect any of the splotches she found into something meaningful. As of yet, she didn't have anything. She'd have to print them up and look them over later. When that was finished, she grabbed a tool from her back pocket along with a tiny vial and took a scraping. Once it was labeled, she turned back to cataloging the dirt on the floor, the cracks in the walls, and wondered what kinds of stalactites or stalagmites she might encounter that might not have been here when the original people were.

Though fascinating, it was a painstaking process, and she forced herself to stop for a late lunch before heading back in. The cave led back until it forked about twenty feet in, leaving Lennon wondering just how deep it went. It was possible it connected to other caves, and if she went far enough in, she would emerge in another spot. She didn't know yet.

She'd spent the entire day doing that, but at six p.m., she called off the dogs. Finally, she admitted fully that when she'd gotten dressed that morning, she'd known what she was doing.

She'd still had no texts and no calls from Gabe. It had been a week. If he was waiting for her, well, she was going to have to finally show up.

After stowing all of her gear in the trunk of her car, she locked everything up and turned around. This time when she headed back toward her site, she took a last turn past the dig and followed the trail through the woods to Gabe's house.

The whole time she walked the path, the daylight dimmed

around her. She told herself that even coming out here was ridiculous. What if he wasn't home yet? It seemed he'd been working at the school, and he might be working late. What if he was home and he'd already eaten dinner? It was a good six-thirty in the evening before she'd even entered the path to the house.

Worse, what if he was home and he had a date? He hadn't done anything to indicate that he *wasn't* dating someone. He may even have a long-time girlfriend. Lennon didn't know. And shouldn't she know that before she just showed up unannounced?

Fifty times, she almost turned around, but when she arrived she saw his car in the driveway and figured it was time to make a fool of herself. If nothing else, she could thank him for giving her permission to excavate the cave. She could easily pass off her foolishness by telling him she had just come by to say what she had found. That would work, especially if some beautiful, half-naked woman appeared behind him in the hallway. Lennon raised her hand to knock, her nerves almost getting the better of her. With a deep breath, she took her chances.

"Hey, Lennon." Gabe answered the door only moments later, his face lighting up as he saw who it was. In that moment, she realized he had been waiting for her. Now, she had to convince herself there wasn't somebody waiting down the hallway for him.

"Is this a good time?" she asked.

"It's great. It's great. Come on in." He stepped back and waved her inside. He headed into the living room, and as she followed him she began telling him about the cave, about what she'd found.

He didn't quite seem to stop and sit. Which meant she wouldn't make this into some formal meeting where they sat around the coffee table and discussed research. But as they turned the corner into the kitchen, she heard the ding of the microwave.

Gabe ignored it. "So you didn't find anything you can definitively say is an artifact, but you found a few things to test?"

Lennon ignored his question. "Do you want to get that?"

"Oh, no. I told you I eat microwaved dinners most of the time. I guess I'm just proving it now..." He reached back and scratched his neck, almost as though he was nervous.

Lennon frowned. *What was going on?* "It's okay, you can eat the dinner that I interrupted."

"No, it's fine—I—"

"Gabe? What is going on?" She was smiling, because it was funny, but what was he hiding?

Rolling his eyes, he opened the microwave and gingerly grabbed at the corners of the cardboard box. Setting it on the cooktop, he sighed and showed her what he'd been nuking. "Happy now?"

"No." She was shaking her head. "You're eating microwave mac and cheese? The box version was too hard?" That was a new low.

"I didn't want to show you. Besides, this has..." He paused and read the top of the box. "Five different cheeses in it."

"You're eating mac and cheese that was once frozen."

"Well, what do you propose I do?" He held his hands out to her.

"Cook something. Even boxed mac and cheese is better than frozen." She was laughing. She understood, but it was fun to tease him.

He tilted his head at her, his eyes lighting and his expression heating just a little. "Then stay and cook dinner with me."

❧ 34 ❧

G abe watched as Lennon searched through his kitchen for anything to make dinner out of.

"You weren't kidding when you said you didn't have anything." She only found sandwich meats and such, exactly as he'd said the last time she was here. He was wondering if she was going to come around to the idea that maybe microwavable mac and cheese had actually been his best option.

She didn't.

He was leaning back on the countertop of the island while she scrounged. Unless she was magic, there wasn't anything she was going to find to make things look better. So he waited, while she searched through the fridge and the pantry and opened all the cupboards. Gabe grew more and more embarrassed as she saw the foods he'd chosen for himself. He didn't have anything foreign, even something as simple as Chinese. Just a few meat and rice dishes, and everything repeated. He liked what he liked and he ate it—apparently all the time. That thought passed through his brain right as she discovered four more boxes of frozen gourmet mac and cheese.

She only turned and raised one eyebrow at him as she held up the box from the freezer, as though to ask what he was doing with so many of them. Gabe only shrugged.

On her second pass, Lennon began grabbing various items and putting them on the counter. He had a variety of cheeses for all the grilled sandwiches he'd been making. He also had pasta so she put that out as well. She even managed to find a tuna salad kit, and she grabbed a jar of pesto he'd stashed in the fridge, too.

At last, she turned and looked at him. "Is there a vegetable in this house?"

He wanted to say "probably not" or "doesn't pesto count?" but what he did say was, "Possibly I have frozen peas. Hold on."

He had to pushed past her to get into the freezer and dig behind all the boxes of frozen meals. He'd stacked them neatly, which was embarrassing, as it indicated he was a bit of a pro at being a slack. But he had to have a vegetable in here, *right?*

As he searched, he spoke to her over his shoulder. "Some of the frozen dinners come with vegetables, you know."

He barely saw the movement in his peripheral vision as Lennon nodded. "I know. It's where I get a large portion of my own vitamins."

Maybe she wasn't judging him as harshly as he was imagining. At last, he produced a bag of frozen peas which he did not bother to check the expiration date on. Surely, peas could not go so bad as to make something terrible happen.

Taking the peas from him and adding them to her collection on the countertop, she said, "Alright, let's boil some pasta." After a pause she grinned and asked, "Can you do that?"

"I can do that," he assured her, trying to keep an answering snark out of his tone. Her question hadn't warranted any snark in his reply given that he was surviving on frozen boxes of mac and cheese.

Once she'd gotten the water over the heat, she looked up at him. "Salt?"

At least he could hand that to her quickly, for which he was grateful.

"Next, I need a cheese grater," she said.

Obligingly, Gabe began looking through the cabinets until she laughed at him. "Why are you laughing at me?"

"Because, you don't know where your own cheese grater is."

"I'm sure it's right here." Even as he said the words, he pulled the stand grater out of the cupboard. *Good.*

"This is obviously not a kitchen that you designed." She took the grater from him with a smile though, and he decided to just confess to everything.

"Please. If this was a kitchen that I designed it would have one burner, one large pan for making sandwiches, and a huge microwave. Nothing else."

She laughed at that too, and something flooded inside him at the sound, at the bright shine to her eyes and the width of her grin. Lennon was standing with her back against the counter as she smiled up at him and asked for a spoon to stir the pasta. Gabe reached around her to the ceramic holder with all the spoons and handed that to her as he felt the heat flare between them.

She turned to stir the pasta then, and Gabe frowned at her back. "Your momma's quite the cook, did you not inherit that?"

"Oh, I can cook," Lennon replied, the grin back in her voice. "I just don't. I mean, usually it's only me eating and it feels like a lot of work. Mama taught me how to make a casserole in a nine-by-thirteen inch pan, which would feed me for. . . well, I don't think anyone wants to eat Turkey Tetrazzini for six straight days."

There was something about watching her here in his mother's kitchen that made him feel both a bit nervous, his cells fluttering as though he were doing something he shouldn't, and also as though this were the most right and natural thing in the world. For a moment, he thought that she belonged here with him. "What's next?"

He threw the words out there, knowing they could be interpreted the obvious way or in a grander sense.

Lennon turned, putting her hands on the counter behind her and leaning back again. "Well, mostly we have to wait for the pasta to cook, and then we can microwave the peas. When it's ready we'll throw them in—"

He touched her then. One hand out and around her waist. He didn't really know what inspired it. She was giving him instructions on how to make tuna pasta with peas and pesto, but...she'd *showed up*.

All week, he'd wondered if she would. He had been afraid the feelings were all on his side, but as he moved in closer, he felt and heard the hitch in her breath. He realized that it wasn't only him. She felt it, too. She moved toward him just a fraction of an inch as he leaned in, his mouth closing on hers. The heat that had already flooded him, kicking up a notch and melting down.

This time, her breath didn't hitch, but sucked in long, and slow, and steady as he slowly kissed his way across her mouth. When he reached the other side, his arms tightened against her, pulling her closer as he deepened the kiss until neither of them could breathe anymore.

Here, he thought. He could stay here forever.

35

G abe let himself in through the back door, discovering as
he turned the knob that he hadn't even thought to lock it
on the way out. He tried now to look around and see if anyone
had come in and robbed the place while he was gone, but he
didn't have enough sense to do that either.

After merely looking around the back entryway to see if it
felt weird, he admitted his brains were too scrambled to do
anything else. He'd walked Lennon through the woods, back to
her car, and kissed her again before she climbed in.

It was something short and quick, so he didn't get caught up
the way he had the first time. That time it had been so deep and
had gone on long enough that he'd been certain she'd realize
what he was doing—what *they* were doing. He'd been afraid she
would run off and leave him with a boiling pot of water and a
cold, microwaved mac and cheese.

But she hadn't run off at all. And, until he'd gotten back into
his own home, Gabe hadn't stopped to examine what it was he
was doing, either. *He'd been kissing his brother's ex.*

If Brodie had been alive, Gabe would have asked permission
—at least that's what he told himself. Right now, he questioned

his ability to make any level of reasonable decisions. That kiss had scrambled his thoughts in the best possible way.

But, had Brodie still been around, Gabe would have needed to be certain that Brodie said it was okay first, because Brodie was his brother. Family was family, and no matter what, Gabe wouldn't put someone else before that.

He sighed. He was worried about family members that had once been here but were now imaginary. Because no matter what he did, he was out of family, and Brodie wasn't here to ask, and he wasn't coming back. None of them were.

Gabe tried playing out different scenarios for what might have happened if Brodie hadn't died. Would he and Lennon have stayed together? If so, might they have eventually gotten married?

That was the thought that almost killed him. He'd had a crush on Lennon since he'd first met her. Back then it had been a crush. It had grown into something more even before Brodie asked her out. But now? Would he have had to spend Christmases watching his brother get to be with the woman he was in love with? Would they have had kids?

He told himself that wouldn't have happened. Rob had driven a wedge between them, and they had been fully broken up before Brodie died. Still, Gabe wasn't convinced that Brodie hadn't been sad about the break-up; his brother may have missed Lennon terribly. She seemed to think it had more to do with Rob controlling his son's life than anything else, but Lennon was gone before Brodie had done anything stupid. And looking back, his brother had done a lot "stupid" that summer.

Gabe consoled himself that Brodie and Lennon had run their course and Brodie would have said it was okay for his little brother to date his old ex from high school. It was a weird thing to imagine his dead brother giving him permission to kiss a woman, and it was a weirder thing still to think that he might need it.

Part of him wanted to ask what Lennon thought of the whole thing because while she was Brodie's ex, Brodie was her ex as well, and she was still here, and she was kissing Gabe.

She hadn't kissed him back politely. *No.* Her touch had contained nothing of the, "Oh, he started this, so I won't be rude and push him away," variety. *No.* She'd been fully involved. Wrapping her arms around his neck. Shifting as though she wanted to be as close to him as possible. Leaning into all of it.

Each time Gabe thought it couldn't get hotter, she would do something—use her tongue, her mouth, her hands, kiss him deeper. Anything, and he'd boil over again.

Finally remembering to turn around, he closed and locked the back door behind him, wondering if she would text him when she arrived home. He thought of it and wished she would despite the ridiculousness of the idea.

Breathless was not large. It was a simple, small town, with a main street and the houses all clustered relatively neatly around that, unless you lived in one of the new subdivisions out beyond the edges of where the town used to stop.

No, it was the Zemp house that was a little out of the way, up on the hill for everyone to see when they drove by. Lennon's house—or Bailey Ann's where she was staying—was right in the heart of everything. She'd gone to elementary school with her cousins across the street from the home they'd lived in, and she'd walked back with them in the afternoon until her Mama had picked her up. She wouldn't be texting him to let him know she'd gone barely two miles down the road.

With a deep breath, Gabe finally admitted he had no idea what he was doing. Hell, a month ago, two weeks ago even, he would have told anyone who asked that he hated her. He hated what she had done to his family. The fact of the matter was that he'd probably been dead wrong all those years. The other fact was, even if he'd only been mostly wrong, he no longer cared. Lennon was Lennon. She'd been barely eighteen at the time.

Chances were that she and his brother and his father had all messed up. She got a pass for being so young. Or she should. And that was as far as he could take his anger now.

Tonight, they'd cooked and eaten their pasta together, smiling at each other across the table occasionally and talking. That was the part he had liked best: he'd reached for her and kissed her like there was no one else in the whole universe, but the conversation afterward while they ate had not grown awkward.

He'd asked her about the testing on the smudges she'd found that might be paint, and she launched into the science of carbon dating. He'd loved every minute of it. She told him she'd made the pasta with six cheeses. Lucky that he had that many in his fridge so that he could guarantee it was superior—by one cheese —to the one he'd unfrozen earlier.

The food had been good, better than what he'd intended to eat before she'd showed up. She'd asked about his business as though she really cared. Lennon remembered details from her visit to the school and asked about them. Gabe found himself telling her what was happening with the same excitement level she used when telling him about old, clay bricks.

He stood now in the hallway that ran the middle of the house and his heart rolled over in his chest. It had been a week since he'd seen her. But every time, he'd been the one to ask her out, to show up at her work site. Not the other way around. So he'd thought, if he left things to her and she didn't show up that she was saying she wasn't going to do anything with it. He'd told himself that it had been a week and Lennon had made her decision, but then there she was, suddenly. And suddenly he had a guest and dinner, freshly made just when he'd given up on that too.

He hadn't planned on any of this. He hadn't planned on getting involved with anyone, and he certainly hadn't planned on it being Lennon Mayfair. He hadn't thought she'd ever come back to town. Instead, contrary to every plan he'd made, he stood there looking into his kitchen as though he could see the two of them. He could almost feel it all again, the wave of heat washing through him as she wrapped her arms around him. As he'd finally kissed the one woman he'd always wanted to.

❧ 36 ❧

Lennon noticed that Gabe texted her the next day. He'd done it relatively early in the morning, asking her if she wanted to go to lunch. But he hadn't been quite early enough, and she'd been far enough in the cave the next day that she'd lost some signal. Her phone hadn't chimed that she had a message until she'd walked out of the cave and it began pinging as it loaded all her missed notifications for a handful of hours. By then, it was too late to meet up with Gabe. She was elated about the cave, but pissy about the missed text.

With her heart in her throat, she called and apologized profusely, figuring he'd spent the morning thinking she couldn't even return a text to him. Which would mean he'd thought that she'd probably brushed him off.

Lennon had not brushed him off, not even close. Last night, she'd kissed him back with tongue and full body contact. The last thing she wanted was to look like she'd ghosted on him the next day. *Not cool.*

Apologizing for the fourth or fifth time, she waited while he told her it was okay. "I'm just glad you didn't disappear on me."

Her heart thumped at the sound in his voice and she almost asked if she could make it up with dinner. But her mouth didn't form the words. Her rational brain was pushing her to think about things, let everything hang for a day. She wanted to be certain this was what she wanted. She wanted him to be sure this was what he wanted, too, not just something that had happened.

This morning, when she'd woken up, she found his text waiting for her.

"I was too late yesterday, probably too early this morning. But please call me before you go in that cave," it said. It was almost a command, but it still made her smile.

And so, as she stood in the woods looking at her dig site, she realized she was possibly less than a mile away from where he was right now—if he was in the office at his house. He might be back at the school, she didn't know. Lennon decided quickly that it was better if she didn't get too involved this early on. She didn't need to know his every move.

Still, she couldn't stop herself from calling him.

"Can I take you out to lunch today? I just wanted to ask before you get too deep in the cave and you lose signal."

"That would be wonderful. I'm not quite sure when I'll have a stopping time, though."

There was a pause and she figured that was the end of it, but after a moment, he said, "So how about if I show up at noon and I'll call out to you. If you don't answer, I'll wait. When you get a good stopping point, you come out and join me for lunch? I'll bring something I can work on."

Her heart fluttered. The man was willing to wait on her. She was thinking it through and had barely said yes when he offered up, "Pizza okay?"

"No." She almost barked it out, staccato and harsh.

"*Oh?*" he asked. "I mean, obviously Bobby's, but you don't—"

"I'd rather not," she blurted, interrupting him this time.

"*You don't like Bobby's pizza?*" he asked her, an incredulous lilt to his voice.

Shit! she thought, though what came out of her mouth was an undramatic, "Not really."

She shrugged and left it at that, hoping Gabe would drop it. The last thing she wanted to do was tell him that his family's pizza joint gave her something akin to PTSD. She let him make an offer on another place, thinking if it was anything halfway passable, she'd just say yes. And so when he did, she jumped at it. "That sounds wonderful."

"Then that's where we'll go." He was agreeable and she didn't doubt that was what he would do, but there was a tone to his voice—one that said he was curious why she'd reacted as she did. One that said he was interested in finding out why. She was not interested in sharing.

Lennon wanted to go to lunch with him. She did not want to explain her history.

So she'd worked through the morning and made an effort to find a good stopping point and head out of the cave just after noon. Sure enough, she found him there, looking over notes and tapping away on a tablet.

He looked up and his face lit up at the sight of her. "Hey, you ready?"

She nodded and said she understood when he explained about taking separate cars. First she followed him in her car, then through the door, and through ordering. Everything was stilted and she didn't think she'd ever had a lunch that was such a disturbingly awkward affair.

They'd chosen a new café that served soups, grilled sand-wiches, and pastas. Lennon noticed, laughingly, that neither of them had picked a sandwich. Probably they'd both eaten enough of those to last a lifetime. But much of the rest of the meal had been rough around the edges, as though they hadn't really decided yet what they were or what they were going to be.

At one point, Gabe had reached out to hold her hand and then dropped it just as quickly.

Did he not want to be seen in public with her? Not want people to know what they were doing? Or was he thinking maybe *she* didn't want them to know? Truth be told, she didn't know.

Lennon couldn't decide if she wanted the whole town of Breathless to know what they were when she didn't even know. Back in high school, her relationship with Brodie had been plenty of fodder for the gossip mill—one of the town princesses going steady with the town golden boy. She'd almost been voted Homecoming Queen, and Lennon was pretty certain that that was because she was dating Brodie. With Gabe? She wasn't ready to deal with the gossip. At least with Brodie she'd been ready to say "Yes, I'm his girlfriend." Now? She wouldn't know how to even answer.

By the time they'd finished the meal and put their trash into the waste can and stepped outside, she remembered they were going to separate cars. He had to leave to get back to the school, since he'd waited on her a good twenty minutes for her to finish up the piece of the cave she was looking at before they could leave.

Lennon paused a moment, asking how things were going with the remodel, if the estimates were coming in any better. If he had found something to do with the space at the end of the hallways that had used to be the bathrooms? If someone had come and hauled away the awful carpeting yet in the classrooms?

Gabe answered each question and, each time, he would step toward her and then step away. Lennon was doing much the same thing, the weird little dance discomforting, even though his presence felt warm and wonderful.

Just then, she decided that, whatever she was doing with Gabe Zemp, she should *stop* doing it. This was clearly already awkward. And she'd realized that if she got any more involved she was going to have to tell him everything, and she didn't know if she could. So she would have to end it, and it might as well be now.

So, at that exact moment, when she decided she had gone as

far as she could, he held out his hand and picked up hers, suddenly not caring if anyone could see.

He traced the bones in the back of her hand with his finger and he watched their hands together as he did it. Almost as though he were sad or regretted something. "Can I take you out to dinner tomorrow night? Not like this."

He waved his free hand back toward the restaurant they had just come out of. "A real date. I don't care who sees us. I don't care about the gossip mill. I just want to do this right. I kind of fucked it up for lunch."

Well, crap. She couldn't break up with a guy like that. It wouldn't be right, and she didn't want to. She'd never wanted to. *She wanted Gabe.* With that question hanging between them, and his wishes shining brightly in his eyes, there was no way Lennon could tell him no.

"I'd like that."

✣ 37 ✣

*O*ne LBD (little black dress) is a must for every belle, three to ten
is the preferred number.

LENNON SAT ON THE EDGE OF HER BED AND WATCHED WHILE
Bailey Ann rifled through her closet muttering to herself.

It was T-minus two hours until her date with Gabe. Bailey
Ann—once she had heard about it—had rushed to the dig site
and immediately taken over. Her first step was to get Lennon out
to the local spa to get their nails done.

Lennon had looked down at her already dirty cargo pants and
laughed hysterically. "You know I work in a cave and dig in the
ground most days?"

"Of course, but you wear gloves. And you should do this."
That was so like Bailey Ann to say *you should do this* and act as
though it was all decided. "I mean, I'm working in home remodeling. I can swing a sledgehammer like nobody's business now."
Her cousin grinned at her as she pulled Lennon into her car,
enticing her to abandon her work for the rest of the day. "Come
on, you've been working hard. I've been working hard. I've been
working weekends. I bet you have too."

Lennon only nodded in response. Her cousin was right. So she let Bailey Ann pull her along and take her for a manicure and a pedicure. It felt positively sinful and it felt even better when Bailey Ann paid for it only letting Lennon cover the tip.

She was looking forward to the day when she was done with school and her income could be a net positive for once. This morning she'd thought about getting her hair done. It was a real date after all. And it was a date with Gabe Zemp; everyone was going to be watching.

But given Lennon's history with his brother, everyone was going to be gossiping about it three minutes after they watched. She talked herself down from getting her hair done. She had neither the money nor the time to invest in what it would take to do it right. Also, she told herself, though she was willing to dress up and let Bailey Ann play fashionista in her closet, she was only willing to go so far. A man either liked her or he didn't. Truly, the majority of the time Gabe had seen her in cargo pants and tank tops, in her gardening gloves sitting on the ground digging like a child. Manicured nails, her own stab at a hairdo, and Bailey Ann dressing her was going to have to do.

"This!" Bailey Ann exclaimed as she spun around, hanger in hand.

"Oh, God no." Lennon could only shake her head at the long red dress. Then she asked, "Isn't that yours?"

"It is. Come on, it's not *too* flashy. When have I ever been crazy and wild?"

"Well, I would guess whenever you wore that red dress you were." Lennon pointed. "The answer is *no*. I am not wearing a red dress—certainly not *that* red dress—on my first real date with this guy. Try again, please."

Bailey Ann raised one eyebrow at the "real" Lennon had let slip. But she poked her head back into the closet, still brushing her way through the hangers. Pulling out a skirt, she held it up at arm's length in front of herself and closed one eye. It took a moment for Lennon to realize she was trying to imagine what

Lennon might look like wearing it...if she wore it under her armpits. But her cousin just shook her head and put the skirt back into the closet.

A few moments later, she found a blouse that she liked and told Lennon to hang onto it. But apparently Bailey Ann never found the other half of that outfit and, a few moments after that, she took the blouse back and hung it up again.

Murmuring a few things to herself, she then turned and stared at her cousin as though she wasn't really looking at her. This time Bailey Ann had nothing in her hands. While Lennon wondered if Bailey Ann was going to suggest she just go naked—which Bailey Ann at least would never do—Lennon simply looked up with a question in her eyes.

At last her cousin made her pronouncement. "I don't know why I didn't think of this before but, this is *you*. This is *Gabe Zemp*. He's not taking you to Zemp's up on the hill, is he?"

"No," Lennon said, glad she'd put her foot down on that one, too. And also glad that the way her cousin said it made it clear that it wasn't kosher for him to do so. It was good to be reassured that she wasn't being snotty or unreasonable. Gabe probably didn't know it, but she'd had enough of Zemp men taking her out for free meals.

"Good." Bailey Ann's teacher-like reply said it all. "So you're probably going a little out of town but still, people will catch wind of this. I think that means you have to play it classic." She reached into the closet and shuffled down to the far end. "Hmm. . ." she murmured. She pushed one hanger, then another, and at last, she pulled out the chosen one. "You can't go wrong with the LBD."

Lennon almost laughed out loud. It would figure that Bailey Ann would come all the way over here to dress her and then choose a little black dress for her to wear. To be fair, it's not what Lennon would've chosen. "Isn't that more for parties?"

"No," Bailey Ann said. "This is why you need me. It's for first dates to nice restaurants. We won't dress it up, we'll dress it down. No high heels or anything crazy. Maybe..." she seemed to pause and think. "If you have heels with color on them and some kind of matching necklace? *Not* pearls. That would say too much."

"What would it say?" Lennon felt the urge to know just what her cousin thought pearls spoke of.

"It would say that would say you're looking for a ring." She paused. "Are you looking for a ring?"

"Oh, God no!" Lennon burst out what might now be her favorite phrase. She almost came off the end of the bed in response. No, she was not looking for a ring.

"Good. Then no pearls. Let's see, let's see. Oh. . ." She leaned down and into the corner of the closet. "You have bright blue ankle boots. I'm so jealous, these are great." Then she looked up at Lennon, "Please tell me you have a sweater that will go with this. Even a white one is okay, just not black."

Lennon smiled. She loved sunshine yellow, hot pinks, and bright, electric blues. She merely pointed into the closet, letting Bailey Ann pull out a cardigan in nearly the same color.

"Perfect. Casual, but LBD. You're all set."

"Your work here is done?" Lennon asked laughingly.

"It is." And with that, Bailey Ann hugged her, kissed her on the cheek, fairy-god-mother style. Then she was out the door to return to her new husband.

Lennon had offered her thank yous and promised to send a picture when she was ready. It was so easy, she wound up with almost half an hour to spare. She'd really overshot on getting ready to go out with Gabe. So she'd sat in the living room chair, reading a home magazine than was still coming in her Aunt Della's name. There were recipes that looked good but would be out of style before Lennon found the time to make them. There were tips on how to decorate the home she didn't have.

But when the doorbell finally rang, she stood up and slowly opened it. She felt her heart do a long tumble in her chest as it pulled strings inside her from all her feminine places up to her brain. The man had showed up in a dark charcoal suit that had clearly been tailored to fit him exactly. Her mouth watered just a little as she started at his shoes and worked her way up.

She figured when she got to his face, he'd be grinning at the way she was checking him out. But all the effort was worth it when she found that he wasn't smirking at her at all. He was standing there, almost open-mouthed.

Score one for Bailey Ann.

Lennon could get used to the stunned look on his face.

❧ 38 ❧

Lennon had closed the front door behind her and put her hand in his to walk down off the front steps. Only Gabe didn't escort her down.

He pulled her directly into his arms and up against him. With the heels on her hot, blue boots, he was now only a few inches taller than she was, and her startled glance up put her directly in range.

She heard him suck in a breath the moment before his lips touched hers. It should have been a savage kiss, hunting and stealing from her, but it was gentle. Searching. Asking its own permission as his mouth moved along hers.

A fleeting thought crossed her mind that the neighbors could see them here, making out on Aunt Della and Uncle Con's doorstep. But the idea flitted on by and disappeared under the feel of his arms around her. The undertow grabbed at her, enveloping her whole world, stealing her breath and ripping her out to sea.

She was supposed to do this for fun, she thought, as his tongue traced the seam of her lips. As her own mouth parted to let him in.

This is temporary, crossed her mind, as she cinched her arms around his neck, having no idea how they'd gotten there.

Her back arched into his touch and his tongue found hers as her mouth opened further under the onslaught. Her cells were on fire. Her insides twisted. Her foundations of reason crumbling.

She had buried her secrets long ago, yet here she stood on her porch melting for the one man who could force her to dig them up.

She could walk away from this, she told herself. But she couldn't walk at all, and she didn't want to. This was going to pull her under and mess up all her plans.

She was thinking of pushing away, of finding herself and separating "Lennon" from "Gabe," but his hands traced down her sides, thumbs trailing. She stood there, entranced as she felt the touch from ribs, to waist, to hips.

She heard him suck in air as though he, too, had been underwater, pulled out to sea by whatever this was between them. He stepped back, just a few inches, but enough to put space between them.

Then he leaned in and whispered, his breath warm on the shell of her ear. "I almost started to pull at your zipper. And we're standing on the front porch under the light."

As he pulled back to look at her, she smiled up at him. "And Bailey Ann is so efficient, you know she has the best LED bulb in that light." Lennon pointed up and over her shoulder. "It won't burn out for something like eighty years."

He laughed, but his words were, "Damn Bailey Ann for that." Then he did step off the porch, her hand still tucked into his. "We should go, we have a reservation."

Her heart was tumbling as he handed her into the passenger side of his low-slung sports car. For a moment, she wondered what the hell she was doing, as flashbacks to Brodie hit her in waves. Her family had never been poor, but the Zemps were the richest family in town. As an adult now, she knew that might not be true, but they were never quietly wealthy. The Zemps did everything with flare and dollar signs.

She'd dated Brodie at first because he was startling. What did a *man* several years her senior see in her? He was popular. She was small town royalty, but no one followed her the way they followed Brodie. Then she was part of his flare and it felt good to be shown off. But what did that make her really?

So as Gabe climbed in the other side of the car, she turned and looked at him. Because here she was on the passenger side of a flashy Zemp sports car that no one else in town could either afford or would drive. As soon as he turned and smiled at her, she sat back.

The difference was clear. Whatever Brodie had liked about her stopped at the surface. He liked that she was pretty. He liked that she was half African-American and that pissed off his dad. He liked that his dad could never say that out loud. And he hadn't, not until that last day. Brodie had liked that young Lennon was malleable. Gabe liked that mature Lennon had her own thoughts and didn't let anyone push her around. Including him.

Her heart settled in her chest and she asked, "So where are we going?"

"Well, I didn't pick Zemps because it seems wrong to take you there." He paused a second. "I don't want to be interrupted by staff who know me and have questions, and I'm torn. I'm not trying to impress you with money or anything, but taking you somewhere I get free food seems a little crass..."

He let the sentence trail off. Then he picked it back up. "So there's a new seafood place between us and Alpharetta. *Oh shit!* Please tell me you're not allergic!"

"Not allergic," she reassured him, laughing at his sudden panic. She crossed her legs and smiled at him until he muttered, "God, those boots are sexy as hell."

She was just raising her eyebrows as her heart tripped when he pushed his eyes back to the road and resumed what he'd been saying. "So, I have no idea if the food will be good or the service adequate, or what. It's an adventure, if you're up for it."

"I'm up for it." Lennon found herself smiling. God, she was having fun. Gabe tripped her buttons, that was certain. The man was hot, and the charcoal suit only made it harder to ignore her attraction to him.

Dinner was an adventure. Upon finding out how much she loved shrimp, he'd bought a sampler and placed it in the middle of the table between them. Though they'd tried to eat like a gentleman and a lady, the barbeque got the better of them. She'd tried to subtly lick her fingers once and found him staring at her with more heat than the Cajun shrimp had been able to garner. They didn't make it to dessert and the check came far too quickly.

Gabe was signing for it when his head popped up, "Come dancing with me."

Her eyes blinked and she realized she was nowhere near ready for this evening to end. "Where?"

He grinned. "The Six String. They have dancing and drinks and...it's no seafood restaurant. We'd be a little overdressed, but..."

She only nodded. She'd never been to the Six String. It had sat on the edge of town her whole life, and though she'd been to country western bars before, she'd not been to this one.

An hour later she was at a high-top table, her sweater sleeves pushed up and a margarita in her hand. Gabe was nursing a double rum and coke and had abandoned his suit jacket in the car.

She smiled at him, acknowledging if only to herself that she was falling way too hard for this man. She wouldn't be staying in town. She'd never give up her master's degree or any level of her education for a man. And Gabe wouldn't leave. The Zemps were as much a fixture in Breathless as the Mayfairs. His businesses were all here.

But she reminded herself she had another month or so. And she should enjoy it.

"Finish that up and come dance with me."

She saw that his glass now held only ice and she was close to the bottom of the margarita. She tipped it back and said, "I'm not much of a line dancer."

"That's why you bury yourself in the middle. So there's always someone to watch."

She'd done that before and figured she might as well make an idiot out of herself. If she had some fun that was great. If he thought she was too much for him, well, that would apply some much-needed brakes to this runaway affair.

Two line dances later, the band broke into a slow song and she found herself in his arms again. Only this time she stayed there. He was a good solid lead, letting her follow along without thinking about it. She could dig a site like nobody's business. She could spout the history of the world with ease, but dancing was not her thing. Gabe made her feel like it was.

Though they weren't doing anything too crazy for public, it felt like they were. The heat between them fueled the air and she was waiting for an electric arc to form. Gabe's hand was on her waist, holding her close, but it felt like he should be grabbing her ass and hauling her against him. She almost wished he would.

Then he leaned in and whispered. "I can stop at one drink, and in about thirty minutes I can drive you home....Or we can stay and party a little more and walk to my place. It's less than half a mile behind here. But I won't be able to drive you home until...later."

The sensible answer was the first one. She knew it. He knew it.

Pulling back, Lennon looked up to tell him just that, but the heat in his eyes stopped her. The open need and the vulnerability —that he'd laid it out there, what he wanted, and she could just cut him down—tugged at her. She told herself not to let that vulnerability play her. But it was more that he knew what he'd handed her, and he was willing to ride it out.

Lord, help her.

"I'll take 'Or.'"

❧ 39 ❧

L ennon stood behind Gabe as he put his key in the lock and opened the large front door to his home. They'd each had several more drinks, but the line dances and even the walk here hadn't fully sobered her up.

She couldn't tell if it had sobered him up either, but the bright sheen in his eyes when he smiled at her told her he was having an amazing time. With her. Her heart thumped in her chest as he closed and bolted the door behind him.

What had she gotten herself into?

Lennon was leaning back against the hallway wall when Gabe turned and looked at her, frowning. "Do you need that wall to hold you up?"

She shook her head but didn't say anything.

"Soooo," he drew the word out and she knew what was coming, to a certain extent. His expression turned serious then and she held her breath. "I can sober up and go back to get the car and drive you home. That will probably be a good hour or so. Or you can stay over here tonight."

"Or," she said. The world rolled out of her mouth, filling the space between them.

He started to smile, then it fell away. "You can stay in the guest room. You can eat all the...sandwiches we can make from my fridge. You can tell me to go away or stop at any time. Or we can just see where this takes us."

"Or." It came out on a breath, her chest heaving now with the thoughts of what "or" represented. She was definitely getting in over her head. Definitely moving beyond what she'd told herself her boundaries were. But she wanted him. So bad.

He was slow and cat-like as he closed the distance between them. If the hallway hadn't been so big she wouldn't have had time to say "no" or change her mind, but she didn't want to. Lennon just stayed there, leaning against the wall as though her legs might give out from under her.

She'd leaned against it the first time for something solid to brace her thoughts about what she was considering. Now, she thought her knees might actually give way. The look on that man's face was turning her to jello.

His hand hit the wall beside her, bracing himself and caging her in, but she didn't feel trapped in any way. She was melting, but not stuck. Then his expression changed.

"Jesus, I didn't even ask. Are you seeing someone? At school? Someone I don't know? I—"

She shook her head. There was no one waiting for her to get back. "You?"

She should have asked that a long time ago. A guy like Gabe? A man with the money the Zemps had, one who ran in his circles? There would likely be a quasi-fiancee waiting in the wings...

But he shook his head no. "There's no one. I don't do this. I don't fall like this, and God, Lennon, I have wanted you for so long."

So long? But she'd only been in town for—

His mouth closed over hers, his hand still on the wall, their lips the only thing touching. She kissed him back, her head lifting to meet him, her hands pushing off the wall behind her to get closer. But still he didn't touch her, other than the heat of his mouth and the soft touch of his tongue tracing the kiss.

She was simmering. Every part of her longing for his touch. She felt the clench of her muscles, the ache in her breasts, the need that perfused her entire body as he gently kissed his way along her jaw.

Too little, she thought, and reached up for him. Her arms encircled his neck as her back arched, brushing the tips of her breasts against him.

What had been a simmer flashed and boiled over. His arms were around her, his kisses changing instantly from sweet to drugging. Her hands roved over him, loving where his sleeves were rolled up and she could touch skin. Her head tipped back, and his mouth descended from her neck to her collar bone.

His hand reached down to find her knee, just under the hem of the skirt of her little black dress. *Good job, dress!* she thought, but then she didn't think anything more as that hand slid slowly upward, tugging her leg along with it. By the time his warm hand was cupping her ass, he was moaning how good she felt into her ear and her leg was practically wrapped around his waist. She was still pushing against him, still wanting more as his hands roved, up her arms, along her shoulders, under her chin until her face was turned upward to kiss him again. And again.

She felt and heard the tug of her zipper as it slid down her back. Lennon watched helplessly as her fingers reached for the buttons on the front of his shirt. He helped her tug at it and she liked watching as his muscles rippled with the movements of shedding it. He tossed it behind him, hitting the black wood, ladder-backed chair that had sat by the entry table for as long as she could remember.

His hands were on her now-bare back and her dress was peeling downward until his mouth was on the tip of her breast, his tongue making lazy circles while she squirmed.

Gabe was breathing heavily by the time he pulled back and

looked at her. Her dress was askew, her lips bee-stung from his kisses, her chest heaving in time with his.

"Not here," he whispered, but he didn't look around at the entryway hall. Instead he held his hand out to her and waited until she set hers in his, then he tugged her up the stairs. He didn't even make it to his bedroom door before he began kissing her again.

It was heady, the feeling that Gabe Zemp just couldn't get enough of her. But she couldn't get enough of him either, and her breath hitched as she realized, *yes, she was going to do this*. She reached for his belt as he opened the door and led her into his room. The room was dark, but he let the hall light shine in on them.

He was kicking his own shoes off as her fingers worked the button and zipper there, feeling him hard behind the fabric. His voice filled her ear as he groaned aloud at her touch. She did it again.

Then she found herself on the bed with this golden god kneeling before her as he took off her shoes, ran his hands up her legs, and tipped her backward onto his mattress.

He was trying to go slowly, she could tell. So was she. It just wasn't working. Her dress was gone and though he stopped for a moment to admire her lace undies, they didn't last long either.

Lennon was reaching for his pants, even as he was shoving them down and stepping out of them. Sitting on the edge of the bed, she went for him, stroking her tongue up the length of him and eliciting a shout.

"Jesus, you can't do that." His breath soughed, and his chest heaved, and she could tell he was torn between pushing her away and letting her try. But he tipped her back again, saying, "I want to be inside you."

She could only nod, all words having fled her. His smile was tempered by need, his gaze hot enough to set her on fire if she hadn't already been there. She watched as he fished a condom out of his wallet, swearing the whole time. But before she could laugh, he was there again, so close she could breathe him in. And that's what she wanted.

Her back arched, though whether that was a conscious response, she didn't know. Conscious or not, it was an invitation and Gabe took it. She felt him, hot and ready just moments before he pushed into her.

"God, baby, you're so wet." He breathed the words as he moved inside her, slowly at first. Then when she arched her back, bringing them closer together, he gasped at the sensation and began a harder rhythm.

She was gone. She was here, in his arms, joined with this man. She was nowhere. The world had fallen away, and it was just the two of them, just this moment. As everything swirled around her, she called out his name. Twice. Three times. "Yes! More!"

Her fingers clutched at his shoulders, pulling him to her, and she wasn't sure she didn't leave marks. But she moved with him and against him until she screamed out his name as she came apart.

𝕾 40 𝕾

G abe wandered downstairs with a warm weight settling in his chest. He'd rolled over in the middle of the night and found Lennon still there next to him. It had been a surprise, not that she hadn't run away during the night, but that she'd never questioned staying with him in the first place. It was as though she'd said she was in, and she was all in.

He hadn't intended to wake her, but he'd managed to do a fine job of it anyway. So when she mumbled his name, he reached for her. They were both already naked and coming together seemed as natural as breathing. It was only later, when they were both falling asleep again, that he jolted, his back straight, and cursed out the word, "Condom."

His heart was hammering. His brain suddenly very awake and thinking about babies and Lennon being pregnant and how mad she might be at him for making that kind of colossal mistake.

She, on the other hand, barely even woke. "No worries," she murmured, tucking her pillow up under her head and hardly opening her eyes. "I'm on the pill. Just tell me you didn't give me anything."

He barked a harsh laugh, his forearm thrown over his forehead. "God, no. I haven't been with enough women to have caught anything."

He shouldn't have thrown that kind of information out there. Not in the middle of the night when she wasn't even really awake. Not the first time they were together while they were still finding their way to each other. Lennon didn't need to know who he'd been with or not, and he already knew too much about where she'd been.

She hadn't taken it that way though, and had only replied, "You only need one, if it's the right one."

"Oh, really? The *right one*?" he asked, now turning his head to the side and looking at her in the dim light of night, a grin on his face. It was the dead middle of the night, he was awake, and he was smiling. He seemed to always enjoy being with her, no matter what they were doing, though this was definitely very high up on his list.

"It's a quote from *Little Women*," she told him, now seeming fully awake herself.

"Yeah, I don't think the Little Women were talking about STDs, though."

She, then, had barked her own laugh. "Yeah, I'm clean."

"And, yes, I have been tested. Recently. *Sooooo*," he drew out the syllable into the dark sometime around four a.m., "should I invest in more condoms, or no?"

He'd meant it as a question of *did they need to keep using them?* but of course he realized too late that, given his choice of words, he could mean did she ever want to sleep with him again? It would be an equally valid reason for not having more condoms on hand.

"We're good without," she said confidently, putting all his fears to rest.

Gabe curled his arm under his head then and pulled at her. Lennon came in close enough to abandon her pillow and let her head rest in the space he'd made. Her hands settled on his chest, the conversation over and everyone content, and they'd fallen back asleep like that.

This morning, when he'd woken up, she hadn't. She'd been out cold, and he wasn't surprised. He normally went to the gym for his exercise, because he spent a lot of his days behind a desk. But she got her workout on the job. Plus, he'd put a couple of margaritas in her last night, and a couple of rum and cokes in himself. So letting Lennon sleep late seemed like something decadent that he could do for her this morning.

He couldn't say that either of them had been completely sober the night before, but he could say he'd made the same decision he would have made if he was, and he was confident that she would have too. Well, they might have been more reasonable, and tried to hold out another week or so. They might have said they needed to know each other better, but they'd known each other for decades. Besides, even if they had said that, he was confident they wouldn't have made it.

Gabe headed down the stairs, thinking he would start coffee for the both of them. But as he hit the hallway, he saw her bra lying on the hardwood in the entryway. Something about the idea of that caught him.

He'd been here before. He'd had women over. He'd found pieces of clothing scattered around his house, but before, he'd always thought, "I have to pick that up. She'll want that back." This time, however, it seemed symbolic. Lennon was in his house. Lennon had let him undress her. Lennon had come at him with such wonderful passion that she'd left her bra on the floor in the entryway of his home.

That was a good feeling.

Wearing only the boxers he'd quietly pulled on as he snuck out of the room, he headed into the kitchen. He only walked past the bra on the floor as though, by not picking it up, he was making a statement about that symbol. He wanted it to talk to him again when he came back around the corner.

He sat on a stool at the counter after turning on the coffee machine, waiting and thinking while it grumbled and sputtered. The machine and even the coffee pot in it was the same one his mother had bought for his father years ago. Gabe felt about it like many things, the same way his mother had thought. If it still worked, why would he replace it?

He didn't need a newfangled, one-cup coffeepot. He tended to drink two or three cups each morning on his own. He'd also learned, like many people had before the one-cup machines had come along, how to simply put less water in the machine.

He thought about that for a moment. His father had always liked to flash what they had, but his mother had some level of contentment, that she never felt the need to show off all she had. Gabe, it seemed, had inherited a little from both sides. Lord knew, his sports car was plenty expensive, and he loved driving it around town. He loved the feel of it, and he loved being seen in it. Hell, it was still sitting in the parking lot of the bar.

For a moment, he entertained the idea of running back down the hill, getting it, and bringing it up into the driveway. But to do so would require getting back into his room, and getting dressed, maybe waking Lennon up. He realized, too, that having the car here would be an excuse for her to ask for a ride home sooner rather than later. So he ditched that idea. If she had to go, he could call her a ride or go grab the car himself. It wasn't far.

He contemplated waffles, and found he also had to contemplate whether or not he had the ingredients to make waffles, and/or the skills to make waffles. But—layered on top of the thoughts of breakfast—were thoughts of Lennon. How long would she be staying here, in Breathless? And what would he do when she went? Because, though he'd had affairs and relationships before, he'd not done *this* before.

He'd dated, he'd liked women, and he'd even, slowly, liked one or two of them more and more as time went on. He'd maybe been in love once, but when it was over, it had seemed a natural decline. Not a hideous breakup, but a natural end to what they'd had. He'd never fallen so hard like this.

He was heading downward at high speed with no parachute.

And the ground was approaching fast.

🕮 41 🕮

Lennon dug with renewed vigor at the site. She'd even held off going back into the cave. As she hadn't really found as much as she'd wanted, it had turned into an entire other avenue of research—possibly someone else's thesis.

Nothing in the cave seemed like it was going to be the obvious find she'd hoped for. Putting it off let her think it would be a good project for rainy days, days when she couldn't dig.

She'd driven to the site from Bailey Ann's house today, having slept in her own bed in the second bedroom all by herself. Though Gabe had wanted her to stay over again, she'd begged off, saying something inane about not wanting to get too involved, too fast. She'd said it to him with an air of confidence, as though she could put the brakes on something already running so wildly out of control.

He'd kissed her on the front doorstep when he'd dropped her off and said, "I think this makes you my girlfriend now."

The words had pulled a wide smile up from inside her and made her immediately regret telling him they should stay apart. But she'd only said, "As long as that goes both ways."

His answering grin and nod managed to light her up even more.

Her phone pinged and she saw the next in an ever-extending series of texts he'd been sending throughout the day.

"Please come stay tonight with me. I'll make dinner. Real dinner."

She wanted to, desperately, but ... "If I do, I'll have to get up early and go to work."

"So will I," was all he replied. It had pinged back quickly, as though getting up early and acting like they were already at the level where they spent the night on work nights was of no consequence. Her protest didn't change his invitation at all.

"Fine. I'll be there."

He sent back a goofy picture of him smiling. Then a second one of him spinning like Julie Andrews in The Sound of Music. So Lennon sat there in the dirt and laughed at her phone until she finally got it together enough to write back.

"I see you did that in your school office. Be careful or someone will catch you."

"Don't care. See you."

She was still grinning as she wondered if they would actually get up and get off to their respective jobs the next morning or if they would hang out in bed for a few hours like the first time. It had been nice—lazy, decadent and perfect—with Gabe there. So she sighed and thought *yes, they'd try it out, see if it worked.* Neither of them had a job with a boss who made them clock in. They could all too easily just skip out on their work. Even though she couldn't afford that in the long run and neither could he. She'd have to wait and see how she handled it.

Before she'd left the other morning, he mentioned that he was more than willing to make to trip and stay at her house if she wanted to be more comfortable in her own bed.

"Oh, dear lord, no," she'd replied quickly. "I'm already a guest at my cousin's house. Screwing in her extra bedroom just doesn't seem like quite the thing."

He'd laughed at her and said, "Trust me, I think Bailey Ann

and Finn have done enough in that house that you don't have to worry about offending her. It's yours right now."

"I know," she said. "But Harper Rose and her girls are moving in sometime soon too. I still don't know quite when. But it could be any week now."

"Alright," Gabe had replied, his chin resting in his hand as they sat at the counter. "Just remember that when they get here, that's when it will be too late. And if there's any rooms in there you feel the need to christen, well then, we'll need to get on it right away."

She'd laughed and called him dirty-minded. And he'd only replied, "When it comes to you, yes."

She ignored that they'd only spent one night together and yet they were already making plans for many, many more. She ignored the number of weeks on her calendar before she was slated to go back to school. She ignored that she'd gotten involved with her dead ex-boyfriend's brother.

She ignored all of it and tried to simply enjoy being with Gabe. That part, at least, was easy to do. Though her brain was wandering off and Gabe was interrupting her work with silly texts and calls, she still felt as if she was better able to focus on her work now. He had decided they were officially boyfriend and girlfriend. He'd told her he wasn't seeing anyone else. They'd agreed to this arrangement, whatever it was, and there was a level of settling that came with that. Something that allowed her to let go of her worry that he might only want her to show up at his back door unannounced. It was the confidence that she didn't have to ask if he was flirting with her or if she was reading it wrong.

Sure, she still thought it was possible some society belle would show up, someone who's mama had decided her daughter was engaged to Gabriel Zemp. He might even have an ex-wife somewhere. She didn't know and she hadn't asked. Even so, on her one evening alone, she'd immediately picked up the phone and called Emma Kate. Lennon had told her what she'd done, giddy in her retelling. No details of course.

A lady might kiss and tell, but only to her best friend. Besides, Lennon held most of it to her heart for only herself to take out and relive, but she'd certainly told Emma Kate that she'd been kissed well and good.

Em had squealed, overly excited for her, and said, "I told you so! You know, I never really thought you should have dated Brodie. You always should have gone out with Gabe."

Those words almost caused Lennon to choke on air.

"Really?" *Is that what people had thought?* She didn't know.

"Of course. He had this huge crush on you all through high school."

"He did?" Lennon was beginning to wonder if she'd gone through high school blind and deaf to everything around her. According to Em, Lennon had suffered a long-term crush on Gabe she'd been barely aware of, and now she was saying Gabe had liked her, too, back then. *Had she picked the wrong brother?*

Maybe. Though, if she'd gotten pregnant, she had no doubt it would have gone down much the same way. Robert Zemp would no more be willing for Gabe to father a black child than he had been for Brodie to do it. He still would have insisted on the abortion and he still would have broken them up. So maybe it was better that she got her relationship with Gabe now, when they could be adults. When she could do it without Robert Zemp interfering.

She only mentioned a little of that to her cousin, though. And when the conversation turned, and she asked Emma Kate how school was going, her cousin immediately became vague and dismissive.

That was unusual and the way Em brushed it off bothered Lennon. Though Emma Kate was never one to really embrace school, she did well, always showed up for her classes, and wasn't the kind of slacker that everyone hated. She simply couldn't make decisions or finish the degree. Now, the un-clarified brushing off regarding her honors thesis was really starting to concern Lennon. But every time she asked or pushed, Em built the wall up a little more. She ended up wishing Em well and hanging up despite the fact that she felt something was going on. She wasn't going to get any answers now and she didn't have any decent theories about what was going on with her cousin.

Shifting her thoughts, Lennon decided what she would need to take to Gabe's that night. She thought about swinging by the grocery store and getting them something other than the few limited items in his fridge. She was planning a menu when her trowel made the noise she both loved and hated—the *chink* that said she'd hit something.

She loved the discovery of something new. But hated that she might have damaged it before she even saw it. She should have been gentler in her search. But carefully scraping acres of dirt, just in case, was more work than even she could muster a passion for.

Telling herself it might be a rock—though rocks tended to make a different sound—she carefully excavated what she'd hit. By the time she had it out of the ground, she was looking at the biggest piece of clay pot she'd seen yet.

❧ 42 ❧

"I don't understand," Gabe said to Lennon, leaning forward onto the small eat-in breakfast table where they sat in his kitchen. "If this is the biggest piece you've found, with the most markings on it, why aren't you more excited?"

"Because it's ambiguous," she uttered, her voice clearly showing her frustration, which Gabe still didn't quite understand.

He thought her goal was to dig up pieces—as many pieces as she could possibly find. The more evidence she had, the better, or so she'd said. He thought she didn't care which way it turned out, and he said so.

"No," she sighed in near disgust. "I *don't* care which way it turns out. But this piece is going to require much more research than I'm capable of during the time for my master's thesis. The master's thesis was intended to be a small project. I wasn't supposed to dig up a foundation line or find a cave. And now I've got a big enough piece with markings I can't readily identify and a composition I can't easily date."

He smiled at her despite her frustration. "You have to admit, that's a good problem to have, right? To have found something so big and now have far more to do than you expected. Isn't that better than digging and finding nothing?"

She nodded, but only reluctantly. "Had I dug and found nothing, I would have had a short and sweet master's thesis. It would have been pretty easy to defend."

"Yeah, but it would have been nothing. You would have been so disappointed." He said, wondering why that didn't console her.

"True." She sighed the word out again, not coming around to his enthusiasm about her find. Lennon at least tried to explain. "But I'm actually kind of disappointed now, too. I want to do the work on this piece. And I won't be able to do it, because if I finish my master's and I stop there, then the piece will get handed off to someone else. If I don't want to hand the work off, then I have to go on and get a PhD."

"Aren't you already in line for that?"

"I am. I just hadn't quite decided. I thought I would take a solid look at the job market before I graduated. See what's out there, calculate my options." She hadn't cheered up, and he was at least beginning to understand. She'd found something huge and wanted to keep it for herself. But she might be forced to give it up.

He nodded. "What is the job market like?"

"That's just it. It's real hit-and-miss. Sometimes, something will come up and jobs will open up all over, and the next year the graduating students can't find anything in the field. I could always do something adjacent to my field. I mean, I might get into some kind of forensic anthropology job, even though that's not really where I've studied. I can go out and be an assistant on a dig, but that's not going to earn me much money. With a master's, I can teach at a community college, but I'll probably be teaching very basic things."

"Not what you want to do?"

"No. PhD's cost a shit-ton more money, though," she said, her word choice making him smile. "And, well, I had a scholarship for undergraduate that covered everything, so that was nice. But even with tuition covered, my master's hasn't been cheap. A PhD will cost even more. It will possibly double the debt I have now. So, I have to balance that out with what I can earn afterwards."

Gabe had gone very still at her words, but Lennon didn't seem to notice. The notion of her undergraduate "scholarship" bothered him. How could she just list it off so easily? Call it a "scholarship" to his face? Had she used that term specifically thinking that he didn't know?

But she didn't see his distress and kept talking. "If I get a PhD, I can become a professor. But these days, the academic market is crap. Honestly, it used to be that you would wait until somebody died to get a position. But back then—all of a decade ago—you could at least get tenure. You could get your research funded. Now, with everyone pulling out of science funding, getting grants has gotten three or four times as hard. A lot of the positions that are available now are not guaranteed jobs, not unless you bring in grant money to cover your own salary. And grant writing is a whole other art. I have no idea if I'm good enough at it to sustain a career or if I even want to spend a good portion of my time writing grants. It's definitely not what I love."

She paused, but only for a moment. "So, doing further research on this piece might not be in my budget. I could totally see taking out loans and funding all of my future education if I knew it was going to pay off, but I don't know that it will."

Gabe tried to rein his disturbing thoughts back in. "How much longer would it take to get a PhD?"

"Probably just a couple more years. I've really been on track to do it, and my classwork will all be done. It'll just be research."

"Could this be your PhD dig?" he asked. He hoped his tone was even because his brain was rattling, trying to figure out what she thought he knew about her so-called "scholarship." He tried to stay on track, "A continuation of your current thesis?"

"Probably, given the way it's going. I mean, I found a lot more than I thought."

He was torn. He didn't like the way she'd rattled off all the money his father had paid into her education as though it meant nothing. But he had to admit that his heart sat up like a happy dog at the idea of her staying around here and doing digs for a few more years.

That was an easy thing to hold on to. Besides, she'd brought him dinner. She brought chicken breasts and salad. She brought potatoes to put into the oven, though she threw them in the microwave first, telling him, "We don't have all the hours to let them bake."

When he'd questioned her methods and use of the microwave, she'd brushed him off with "This will work," and he'd smiled.

There was something in her motions that told him that she cared, and something in the way she'd rattled off her "scholarship" money that told him it didn't bother her. Maybe it didn't. Maybe it was something they'd set up—her and his father. She just didn't seem like the type to have done it any other way. He wondered if it was considered payment for an abortion she hadn't intended to have. The problem was he didn't know. And if he'd learned anything this last month, it was that he really didn't know even many of the things he'd believed he did.

So Gabe had helped her cook, letting her direct, but both of them taking equal time in the kitchen. He'd tried to pull his weight on the work, chopping chicken and fetching her the things from his pantry like salt and garlic.

While she cooked, she asked about the school remodel. It was only then that he realized she never asked about his other businesses, never about the pizza chain, nor Zemp's restaurant. Maybe he hadn't talked about them and she thought they just ran themselves. They certainly didn't, but then again, he hadn't given her any reason to believe otherwise. Maybe now was the time, so he told her.

"The windows are coming out next week, and we're going to keep the old windows on the front, bring some of the ones around from the back, and replace the entire back row."

"Well, good. I'm glad it worked."

"And, I didn't get to work at the school yesterday. I had to resolve some issues at Bobby's." He watched as she stiffened at the mention of the name and realized there was more going on there than he knew. "What is it?"

"Nothing." She asked him to open the oven and check how done the chicken was. But he was confident the still-raw-looking chicken didn't need a check and she knew it. Lennon was merely trying to distract him.

It wasn't nothing. But Gabe didn't know what it was.

❦ 43 ❦

When one makes tea, it must be sweetened with real sugar. Anything less isn't Southern. It's best if one can stand a spoon up in it.

LENNON STOOD AT THE BACK DOOR OF HER CHILDHOOD HOME, where her parents still lived. She had a plate of deviled eggs in her hands and Gabe at her side.

When she'd spoken to her Mama earlier in the week about what to bring, her mother had insisted she bring her young man along for Sunday dinner. GiGi had tried to get Lennon to bring him the week before, but she'd managed to decline. This week, her mother pushed harder, as though she somehow magically knew her daughter had slept with this man and the relationship had moved to another level—one that required he come for Sunday dinner. Lennon had not been able to say *no* this time. She'd hoped Gabe would have a good excuse, but instead, he'd thanked her and said he was free.

So here she was on the porch with deviled eggs in one hand and Gabe's hand tucked in the other. It wasn't that she didn't

want Gabe here, it was that she didn't want the others interfering in her relationship. Sunday dinner was a longstanding
family tradition.

Her parents attended the same church they had when she
was little. Her brother Jackson and his two girls now did the
same. He'd gone with his wife Shelle when she'd been alive. And
they'd all come back to make Sunday dinner afterward. Lennon,
too, usually went with them when she was home, though this
time her attendance had been sporadic at best. Still, she'd never
missed the dinner—she wasn't really allowed to. So when Gabe
had asked her out and she told him that she'd been getting pres-
sured from her Mama to bring him anyway, it seemed the natural
progression of things to actually bring him along. It would make
her mother happy even if it made Lennon a little nervous.

Though everything had gone well so far, she wondered if this
would wind up being the thing she'd regret. After all, she'd
brought Brodie here years ago. Her mother would remember
that she'd dated Brodie, but would she understand what it really
meant that she had Gabe here?

It seemed, as Lennon opened the door and came in, that her
mother looked between her and the man at her side and
instantly understood all the connections and ramifications.
Luckily, GiGi Mayfair would never let that show to anyone on
her doorstep. With one hand on her daughter's shoulder, GiGi
handily moved Lennon into the back mudroom and bypassed
her for her new boyfriend. In a second, she enveloped Gabe in a
hug as though he were a prodigal son returned. Even though he
was taller, she managed to engulf him.

"Gabriel Zemp, welcome to my home again." He had been
here at some point over the course of the years, Lennon knew,
just not for official Sunday Dinner. "Come on in. We're gonna
feed you right up. I'm so glad you could make it."

She let Lennon trail behind them, deviled egg plate still in
her hand. At least Bailey Ann had all the perfect dinnerware

pieces, and Lennon was able to keep the eggs in their individual wells. God forbid she show up and all her eggs slide onto the floor when her mother bypassed her for her boyfriend. Her mother always appreciated good, Southern manners, and having a real deviled egg plate was up there.

Heading into the dining room to set down the tray, Lennon encountered Jackson and his two little girls setting the table. Scarlet and Salem abandoned their work the moment they spotted Lennon. Running up, they threw their arms around her legs, squeezed her tight, almost toppling her. She was glad she'd already set down the eggs. "Hey, babies. How are you two doing?"

They did not appreciate being called babies, but it had become a running joke between them.

Scarlet, of course, put her hand flat on the top of her head and squished down her hair to the top of her scalp. She solemnly told Lennon, "I am this much bigger than last week."

"Yes. You are," Lennon exclaimed, though she could see no difference at all.

Trying to do so surreptitiously, she counted the seats at the table, making sure her mother had included an extra for Gabe. It was a stupid exercise. Of course Gigi had included the extra plate. No one would ever feel unwelcome at the Mayfair house.

Jackson, however, had not quite inherited his mama's charm. Lennon didn't know if it had never been there or if the police academy had beat it out of him, but he wasn't quite as welcoming. His eyes darted over Lennon's shoulder, watching what Lennon couldn't see and waiting until Gigi had dragged Gabe into the kitchen, so she could fix him a drink and get him some of the appetizers that were already out on the counter there.

"Well," Jackson dragged the word out over his daughters' heads, as he slowly pushed on their shoulders and turned them back to picking up the toys they'd managed to leave in their grandmother's living room. "Another Zemp?"

He had no love lost with the Zemp boys. Closer to Brodie's age, he'd warned her back in high school before she'd started dating the older brother. It turned out Jackson had been right, but she still hadn't quite admitted that to him. Not that everyone didn't know that it ended in an explosion, her leaving town, and eventually Brodie being dead, but all she could say now was a confident, "Yes."

What she wanted to say was, *Jackson, he's different. He's not like Brodie.*

She wanted to tell her brother how she felt this time around, but as she'd barely told Gabe her feelings, it didn't seem right to tell other people first. She was certainly uncomfortable telling anyone, maybe besides Emma Kate, what was going on. Maybe that was because she was leaving, and she didn't want to deal with their concern, their stares, and their condemnation for her getting so involved right before she turned around and left town.

She almost told Jackson, *He's just here for dinner.* But since she knew Jax wouldn't believe her anyway, she didn't try.

Gabe came out from the kitchen then, two glasses of sweet tea in his hands. He handed one to Lennon, because her Mama knew what she drank, and because—like every good, Southern girl—she drank sweet tea strong enough to stand the spoon up in.

Though Gabe, too, had seemed a bit nervous when they walked up the driveway, he seemed less so now. It was possible that GiGi Mayfair had simply used her charm on him, letting him know he was welcome and subtly making him understand that he would not be judged by the actions of his brother. It was equally possible her Mama had spiked his tea.

They managed a relatively normal, boisterous Sunday dinner. There was more food than the lot of them could possibly eat, and Lennon enjoyed having Jackson and the girls around, as she always did at Sunday dinners. Her brother was finally starting to open up after losing Shelle. It had been over three years and he'd been alternately depressed, bitter, and overwhelmed raising infant twins on his own. His smiles came more easily now, but Lennon wondered if he'd ever really heal.

Luckily, Gabe fit in at dinner just fine, despite Jax's mild but obvious distrust. Though Lennon could spot those moments where her Mama would normally ask a guest, "How's your mama doing?" her Mama knew Gabe had no family to reply about, and she'd held her tongue.

Everything headed on as normal, even though Gabe was a new presence. They asked Jackson about his job. Sometimes he told them what he'd done that week—what was going on around town that the regular folk didn't know about yet—but often just told funny stories, not wanting to say the stronger things in front of the girls. He'd already told Lennon and Gabe before dinner that he'd helped bust up a meth ring through a strip club earlier in the week, but he'd been careful that his girls were not around when he said it.

But then, it was Lennon's turn. Almost in unison, they faced her and asked what she'd found this week. She mentioned the large piece of clay, and the ensuing work it would require.

"Well, that's a good incentive to go all the way through and get your PhD!" her Mama smiled. "I always wanted a Dr. Mayfair in the family."

Lennon smiled. She knew that. Her Mama's wishes often kept her working when things were tough. But she couldn't make that decision on someone else's plans for her.

Her heart stuttered when her mother, father, and brother all turned and looked at Gabe expectantly.

It took him a moment to catch on, but he didn't falter when he looked up. "Oh, I would love to have her doing research here for a few more years. It's on my property. I'm in." He turned and smiled at her.

It was all she could do to smile back half-way convincingly. Because suddenly she was aware that her work *was* on Gabe's land. That was good for now, but all the reasons for not getting involved with him in the first place came flooding back. What if they broke up? He could ruin her PhD thesis if he pulled her use of his land. And if the way he'd acted when she first showed up was an indicator, he would.

He would also dump her so fast and pull his land right out from under her if she ever told him the truth about Brodie.

❄ 44 ❄

It was two days later before Gabe worked up the nerve to say what he'd been thinking since Sunday dinner at her parents' house.

Bracing his hands on the counter, he watched as Lennon stood at the stove top stirring a pot, her back to him. He liked the way she moved. He liked the way she joked with him. But he didn't like that she was hiding things from him. After Sunday dinner had passed, so had her unease. However, his had only grown. Still, he was here, making dinner and deciding if he should broach a sticky topic.

Neither of them were brilliant chefs, but they seemed to have done okay given that they were working together. He'd put pork chops in the oven and didn't have any cooking chore that required his immediate attention. Having the island in between them felt like a bit of a shield and having Lennon standing here with her back to him made this seem like the best opportunity. "Can I ask you something?"

"Sure," she said it with a light tone, but even he could hear that her voice was a little forced. He wondered then if she already knew what he was going to ask. Might as well say it, he thought. "What had you upset at Sunday dinner?"

"I wasn't upset." She said it quickly, too quickly. The added staccato of the words made it more than clear she wasn't quite being honest. He didn't know how he knew that, only that he knew *her*. Even though he really didn't.

"Can you tell me?" he asked. "I know there's something more here."

He knew, for example, that his father had paid for her entire undergraduate career. She had gotten an actual scholarship, but not for full tuition, and there was a matter of all the additional fees. Robert Zemp had taken care of the remainder of tuition, as well as room and board and paid that check each semester.

Gabe told himself that all he wanted was for her to admit that Robert had paid those things for her. To stop calling it a "Scholarship." Interestingly enough, that was not at all what came out of her mouth.

"You don't want to hear the other things I have to say." Her words were low, the tone soft, a hint of tears behind them though she didn't cry. His heart flipped. *Good Lord, there was more?* Had he not heard enough already? It was bad enough that she dated his brother, bad enough that she'd been pregnant. That his father had insisted on the abortion and so on, but how could she still have more to say that she'd already decided he wouldn't want to hear?

Had she blackmailed his father?

The possibility had not occurred to him until that exact moment.

When Gabe didn't say anything, she set the spoon into the ceramic rest his mother had left in the kitchen and turned around to look at him. "If I tell you, you'll hate me."

Gabe looked at her then, really looked at her. What he felt for her was far more intense than anything he'd ever known, and he didn't think that hating her was even possible for him. He was growing more certain that he already loved her.

He'd always loved her...on some level, but Sunday dinner had stirred a whole host of things in him. It reminded him of his mother's own big dinners. It reminded him of having his own family around. It told him that he'd made another step into Lennon's family, and that was huge. This whole thing between them was so fast, but really not fast at all.

This thing they had was years in the making. He'd felt like pieces were snapping into place, things between them that had been a long time coming. And then, Sunday dinner had told him there was something else under the surface, something awful. He almost asked, "Is this about the scholarship money?" using his fingers for air quotes, but he didn't.

She was looking at him, with a sadness on her face, that made him wonder if he wasn't already way off track. It wouldn't be the first time he'd been dead wrong about her.

She turned back to the pot and stirred some more, and for a few minutes he tried to let it go. He opened a bag of prepackaged salad and chopped carrots and bell peppers to add in. He pulled dressing from the door on the fridge and set it on the table, but the silence hung between them still. He couldn't stand it, so he tried something different.

Thinking that if he asked a small question, he would get a small answer and maybe that would be enough for now. Maybe they could work some part of it out and go to bed better for it. Next, they could tackle something bigger, work that out, too. Do the work piece by piece.

"So," he said, his tone overly casual, almost as if the question had come to him out of the blue, "can you at least tell me why you don't like Bobby's Pizza?"

She stiffened, almost dropping the spoon, it clanked against the edge of the pot, and she turned to look at him, "No."

Wow. He'd fucked that up, too. He couldn't ask her anything that didn't set her off. All he could think was *Really? She didn't like pizza, and she couldn't say why?*

Gabe frowned at her, "When and how are we going to get any further if we can't talk about these things? It's a company that I own. When I even discuss doing business there, you clam up."

"I told you, you don't want to know why I don't like it. You're happier not knowing!" She quelled her outburst as quickly as it had come on, though this time when she turned back to the food, she stirred the pot with added aggression.

Jesus, he thought, *this is not "the sauce is bad" or "I once got a moldy pepperoni there."* This was *big*, like the store had embezzled her family's savings (which Gabe knew now to be almost the opposite) or was built on her grandmother's grave site. And here he thought he'd asked a little question. "I don't know what to do if you can't tell me these things."

"Jesus, Gabe. Leave it alone!" But she threw the spoon into the pot, spattering the sauce out just a little and she turned to face him. Apparently, she'd decided to tell him anyway. "I don't like Bobby's Pizza because your brother always took me there."

It wasn't the whole story and both of them knew it. He made a motion with his hand and waved her on to continue the story. He wanted to hear this. It was more important than the half ready salad or the pot bubbling behind her, unstirred.

"Your brother took me there, and he fed me food he got for free, and then he acted as though I owed him."

"What do you mean 'owed him'?" Gabe asked. "Did he make you pay for dinner that he got for free?"

She stared at him, her expression incredulous, but he didn't understand. It took her a moment to see that she was going to have to spell it out for him. So she did. "No Gabe, he wanted sex."

Gabe's mouth fell open and he froze, every cell in his body lining up, rigid. His disbelief washed over him and he stared at her for a moment. He did not know how to process this, but finally he found some words. "Are you suggesting that my brother raped you... because of free pizza?"

"No." she said it calmly, but her eyes were glistening with forming tears. They didn't fall. She managed to hold them back, but her jaw was clenched. "That's not what it was. It was just what was expected of Brodie Zemp's girfriend. And I was young and way too naïve and I bought into it. I liked being seen with him. But the fact of the matter is, I never wanted to sleep with him."

❧ 45 ❧

Lennon stood there with Gabe staring at her. She felt the old walls go up around her. She had not felt them in a long time. She'd worked long and hard to bring them down.

She shouldn't have told him that. It wasn't his business. It was from a relationship literally dead and gone. But she'd blurted it out because she was irritated that he kept asking. Irritated that he thought they needed to work through some mythical barrier to higher ground. There was no higher ground for them. She was leaving. And they had too much past between them anyway.

She was irritated that he held the land on which her largest artifact had been found. She was irritated that she found herself thinking that she loved him. And she was irritated that he had asked, that he'd kept pushing and wouldn't let it go, and she'd said it. She'd held onto it for a decade, and now in the middle of making dinner, she'd thrown it out there like the grenade that it was. She could see he was stunned, and that he didn't really believe her.

"You're suggesting that my brother raped you." There. He'd *said* he didn't believe her, and that hurt. It was a sharp cut straight through to the core of her. It hurt now, but a slice that clean... the worst pain was yet to come. She knew it.

Lennon had known what would happen if she told him about Brodie. She'd said it anyway. Maybe she was trying to blow things up. But did it really matter? They couldn't go on very long with everything between them—all the past history that wasn't even theirs but sat squarely in the center of their relationship.

Maybe it was better to end it now. Maybe it was better to let the grenade blow everything up so when she walked away it was from wreckage and not something wonderful.

She turned back to the stove top and stirred the pot, as though nothing had happened, as though dinner were more important than the conversation. But even she couldn't make believe that was true. It was out there now. There was no cleaning it up. Her mouth got away from her.

"Now, the thing is, your brother was this town hero. Everyone loved him, and everyone thought he was amazing. So when he asked me out, I thought *I* must be amazing. No one had ever asked me out like that before. No town golden boy had ever been interested in me at all." Turning for a moment, she watched as Gabe somehow managed to stiffen even more, but she ignored it and turned back. She kept talking to the sauce. "I was so flattered that I went along with everything he suggested. I'm not innocent in this. I have never said such a thing about your brother. In fact, I never told anyone what happened between us."

That wasn't entirely true, she thought. She'd told Emma Kate most of it. And it had been so cathartic to get it out, but she didn't correct that. Now was not the time. "As his girlfriend, he expected certain things from me. Though he didn't lay it out for me, he clearly had a timeframe. Everything happened between us when Brodie decided we'd been together long enough that it was time. He knew at what point we would make each move further into our relationship." She looked to the side, then pushed her gaze back to the pot and her rhythmic stirring. "The truth is, even making out with him made me uncomfortable. It was never about me. I don't think it even mattered that it was me there. Just that he had a girlfriend and that she did what he said."

"Why didn't you just say no?" Gabe asked, as though her saying no might have stopped Brodie. She hadn't even tried. Everyone knew Brodie didn't take *no* for an answer. It made him a star. It made him the big guy on campus, but it also made her only "the girlfriend," and someone he thought he should control.

For a moment she only turned and looked at Gabe. "Did you ever try to say *no* to him?"

She waited until his eyes dropped and he stared at the counter. He didn't have to say it. He was the little brother. Brodie had possibly controlled Gabe as surely as he'd controlled her.

She didn't know what to say next. But she tried to find something. "I didn't say no. I never told him no," she said, "which is why I can't plausibly accuse your brother of *anything*, really, other than being pushy and a bit of an asshole who didn't understand his girlfriend. Now," she paused and gathered herself again. "It wasn't that he didn't understand me or didn't respect me. I didn't even rate that highly to him. He didn't care at all about my thoughts or ideas. I was something for him to *have*, like his sports car, and I needed to perform, like his sports car. Or I would be traded up for a working model."

Gabe was breathing heavily. She understood. This was a difficult conversation. Hell, it was one of the worst she'd ever had. It seemed all her worst times were with the Zemp men. Her eyes filled again, and she fought hard to keep tears from falling as she turned away. She should never have gotten involved with Gabe at all. *Look what she'd done.*

She could hear him shuffling around behind her, as though physically letting out the stress of what her words had put in him. Lennon waited until she had herself together to turn back around. When she did, he asked her "Why didn't you say no?"

It was half accusation, half whisper. The confident man she knew and was used to interacting with suddenly looking sallow.

"Look, Gabe, this is why I didn't want to tell you about any of it! You pushed and pushed. It's complicated. I was foolish and young, and I liked the benefits of being his girlfriend. I almost was homecoming queen. I was suddenly 'in' with the popular crowd. I don't know if you know what that's worth to a high school girl. So I was not innocent in any of this, either. But while I never told your brother no, I never said yes either.

"I spent three years in therapy working my shit out, Gabe." She sucked in a breath. "I sold my virginity for free fucking pizza! And I didn't realize then how much harm I was doing to myself. It took a long time to figure out that I wasn't worth as little as Brodie thought I was. Because I acted like I was. Back then, I was part of the problem."

She turned and went back to the pot, stirring it aggressively, thinking about the way the sauce had thickened at the bottom of the pan. It wasn't supposed to cook onto the bottom, because she was supposed to have been stirring it. She could feel Gabe staring at her back, but she didn't quite have it in her to turn around and face him again.

"What you're suggesting that Brodie did to you," he finally said, "is horrible."

"The whole relationship was horrible, Gabe!" She threw the spoon down again, splattering sauce as she turned to face him. "Brodie and I were terrible. We looked great on the outside. We looked happy and popular. Every girl wanted to be me for once, and I loved that! But *nothing* about that relationship was okay. I have spent years getting over it." She was almost exploding. She was vibrating with anger. She was angry at Gabe for making her tell, and she was angry at herself for still being upset about something that had happened and was done a decade ago.

"I don't like Bobby's Pizza. I don't like walking in there and eating the food that both of us knew he would use against me to make me put out later."

Another heavy silence fell with a thud between them, and she tried to focus on dinner. Tried to rescue the sauce. Tried to look over and see if he was finishing making the salad, though the idea of sitting down and eating a casual meal with him after this was beyond what she could imagine.

Finally, he spoke again, saying what she expected all along. "I'm just having a really hard time believing that Brodie would force himself on someone. That's not the Brodie I knew."

She nodded. She understood that. The Brodie people knew was different from the Brodie she knew, which is part of why she'd never said anything about it. She'd dealt with it quietly by herself over the years, and Brodie was dead. What else was there to do? But she didn't say that, she just stirred the pot. And she tried to quell the stirring in her soul that he simply didn't believe her.

"I'm having a hard time imagining someone as strong as yourself wouldn't have just told him no and broken up with him."

Lennon threw the spoon down again. "Gabe, I told you! I was not strong then. I was young, and I was stupid. I got a lot of benefits out of that relationship. Looking back, that's why I stayed in it. I don't know how many ways to tell you that. I never accused him of raping me."

Another pause, and then his voice was quiet again. "No, you just got pregnant with his child and tried to weasel your way into the family money."

"*I did not.*" Her jaw clenched and anger fused her cells together. *How could he suggest such a thing?*

"*Really?* Because you managed to get a full tuition '*scholarship*' out of my father."

Lennon felt her heart go cold.

❦ 46 ❧

I t took Lennon a moment to find her voice.

"I *never*. . ." But even then, she couldn't finish the sentence. She was too busy trying to sort everything else out in her head.

She'd had a partial scholarship to Cambridge from the beginning. She'd worried about how she and her parents would pay for it. They weren't poor, but they weren't Cambridge-University-out-of-pocket wealthy either. They'd signed up for loans and been ready to cover it. When she arrived at the bursar's office to pay her tuition, they told her it had been covered. When she asked, they said it was most likely a scholarship she'd gotten but had missed the notification of.

Her tuition and all her fees had been paid up every semester. And she'd not thought of it again.

Gabe was now suggesting that Robert Zemp had paid her way. Lennon couldn't fathom that.

She felt like she couldn't breathe. What Gabe said changed everything. She'd expected to throw things out tonight that would leave him stunned and angry at her. She'd not expected him to have anything to throw back at her.

He loved Brodie, and she knew it. She knew what she had to

say would be painful for him to hear. It was why she hadn't wanted to tell it in the first place! Brodie was the big brother Gabe had always looked up to. It was clear when she'd known them both in high school, and it was clear now when he spoke of his brother. She'd never wanted to mess that up, just because she'd had a terrible relationship with the man. But *this*? Robert Zemp had paid for her education at Cambridge?

The sauce pot was fully boiling now, and she was paying no attention.

Gabe came around the corner of the island, pushing into her small space as he reached out to hug her. For a moment she was too stunned to react, and she let him.

He murmured to her, "I'm sorry. I don't know what I was saying."

But that was a lie. He did know what he was saying. He'd said it. He'd been ready to throw it at her. It suddenly occurred to Lennon that was why he'd been acting the way he had Sunday night when her mother had commented on her scholarship.

The lie was too much. She'd never lied to him. So she burst out in anger, pushing at him, putting her hands flat against his chest, and shoving until he let go. She threw her arms out to the side, breaking out of his hold.

She'd run then, out of the kitchen, down the front hall and grabbed her purse from the entryway table where she'd thrown his shirt not that long ago. She looked briefly at the glossy wood flooring where her bra had lain—almost a week ago now—but she didn't stop. Lennon bolted out the door and down the steps to where she'd left her car parked in front of his garage. She grabbed her coat from the stand by the door on the way out. She'd started leaving it there when she came in, almost as though she belonged. *But she didn't belong, did she?*

Though she'd left the front door to the house wide open, she'd immediately pulled the door shut on her car. Apparently, she'd stunned Gabe with her flight, and she was starting the engine by the time he was there in the driveway, banging on the window. This was not what Robert Zemp had intended when he built such a grand house for everyone to see. Her own Mama would be ashamed at her making a scene in public, but she wouldn't be making a scene if Gabe wasn't banging on her window.

Lennon started the car and, without looking at Gabe, she backed out. She hoped she didn't roll over his foot. She hoped he was smart enough to get out of her way. After making a quick turn in the wide portion of the driveway, she gunned the engine and sped down to the bottom.

Taking her turn a little too sharply, she headed for home—home being Bailey Ann's house now. Lennon had considered going to her parents, as though for shelter, but she was not in any shape to face her Mama right now. God, Sunday dinner had seemed like such a good idea, but what a mess it had created.

She pulled into the back under the car port. Normally, she still parked to the left-hand side, as though she wasn't the only one who lived here, as if someone might join her. Gabe had. Once. But now she parked at an angle, using her one small car to block the entire space. With shaky hands, she used the key at the back door and let herself in, shoving it closed and bolting it with angry hands.

She hadn't turned on the lights and she was walking up the stairs when she tripped and bent her pinky toe. "Son of a bitch!" she yelled into the dark, before she turned and sat on the steps and began crying.

She hadn't told him everything about Brodie because she'd known he wouldn't believe her. Now that she thought about it—and she hated thinking about it—she'd had a whole relationship with a man who didn't trust her enough to believe her. Gabe simply didn't understand that she meant what she said. He didn't understand that she didn't lie to him, even when it would have been easier to do so.

She should have never gotten involved. She should have told him all of it right from the start, but now in the dark she saw the faint light of her stupid, stupid hope. The problem was, she'd thought he'd call her a liar and run screaming with the first thing she'd told him. Instead, he'd believed her about Robert. He'd understood about his father, about the baby, about all of it. Though she'd promised herself she wouldn't tell him the rest of it, she had held out some stupid little light in her chest that said if she did tell him, Gabe would believe, and everything would be okay.

That had been a fool's wish. And she shouldn't have bet anything on it, let alone her heart. Tears ran down her face as she cursed Gabe for being an ass. Then she cursed herself for being an idiot. She should have found a dig site somewhere else. Despite the friends and family she had here, there were too many bad memories in Breathless. She'd stupidly thought she was an adult and could get over her problems. Instead she'd taken the old problems and made them bigger.

She heard it then, the banging on the back door. His car had squealed into the driveway and she hadn't quite registered the noise. But now, now she could hear the glass rattle in the old door as he knocked like a hurricane trying to beat down her house.

She heard him yelling, "Lennon! Lennon, please!" And then, "Open the door," followed by, "Please! I'm so sorry."

But she didn't move. She sat on the dark staircase and stared straight ahead. He could be sorry all he wanted. It didn't change the fact that he didn't actually believe her. It didn't change that he'd known his father was responsible for her undergraduate payments, and he hadn't told her.

Tears ran down her face as she ignored the pounding on the door and the pounding of her heart.

How long had he known? she wondered. Had he discovered it recently, or had he known all along? Had Rob bragged about it? She had no idea. Her phone rang in her pocket, and she figured it was Gabe and pulled it out to see. No. Harper Rose's smiling face lit up the screen.

Shit, she thought, but holding it to her ear, Lennon did her best to answer it cleanly anyway. "Hey, Harper Rose."

Popping up, she ran into the bathroom, where she closed the door to keep out the noise of Gabe pounding on the house.

Even so, it didn't quite work. Given only the one greeting to work with, her cousin still picked up on the problems, asking right away, "Are you okay?"

"No," Better to admit to something than blatantly lie, Lennon decided. "I stubbed my toe."

"Well, I hope you're feeling better soon from whatever it is that hit you." Harper Rose offered a condolence that was far more than a toe warranted. Lennon had fooled no one. "Do you have a minute?"

In the background, Lennon heard Gabe, still calling for her at the back door. What must the neighbors think? "Yes." She just hoped her cousin couldn't hear the noise. "What do you need?"

"Well, I was planning on coming for Bailey Ann's wedding and then just staying. But things have gotten ugly here—"

"Ugly how?" She shouldn't have interrupted, but Lennon was grateful to have a worry that wasn't her own.

"The stupid shell corporation that owns my house keeps pushing the date up for when they want us out. We don't have much left in the way of furniture—they repossessed all the major pieces. I was trying to wait for fall break and not mess up school any more than I have too, but at this point I don't think I can mess anything up worse. This is getting depressing here. So I was hoping to come earlier. If that's okay with you?"

"Oh, Harper Rose! It's *your* house! You don't have to ask me." Lennon felt the tears rolling down her face and she told herself they were for her cousin and the awful situation she'd found herself in. Lennon consoled herself that she'd only lost something that didn't exist. She hadn't lost her husband and all her worldly goods. "I've been looking forward to having you all here. The house is too big for just me. Any time."

They talked a little longer. About the small U-haul that was all Harper Rose would need given the few possessions she had left. About an educational trek across the country rather than a straight up drive with three small children, and what day they were hoping to arrive. Lennon listened to all of it, happy for the distraction. Happy that she would have roommates soon. She would need them.

As she and Harper Rose said their goodbyes, she realized the knocking had stopped.

❧ 47 ❧

Four days later, Gabe was sitting in his office at the school. He was staring out the windows. All three had been replaced with the newer models, as the principal's office was on the backside of the building.

He couldn't escape her, even here. He'd left the office in the house because all he seemed to do was mope. He wasn't getting any actual work done sitting here. It made him think of her, made him think of her in that office, pregnant, young, and with Rob yelling at her that it was all her fault.

Sitting in the big chair, Gabe could now almost see the scene play out before him: Rob dictating her life for her and making her choices. Actually, refusing her the chance to live out her choices and making new ones. It didn't sound as though Lennon needed anyone to make those choices for her or even help. She'd known what she wanted, and Rob had taken that away from her. All because she'd made some stupid mistakes when she was a teenager.

Brodie had been older than her. Brodie was more responsible. Even if it hadn't gone down the way she said, even if it had been merely an accident with a broken condom or something equally unpredictable, then Brodie was still the more responsible one, or he should have been. Rob—as the actual adult—had the chance to make things better, but he'd only made them worse.

Gabe understood her anger. She was still angry at Brodie, though maybe not as much as she'd been years ago. She was still angry at Robert, and she had a right to be. But now she was angry at Gabe, too, and that was on him.

He'd spent too much time in that office, trying to figure out if Lennon was capable of bribing his father to pay for her school tuition. Bribery was the obvious answer: Give up the baby in exchange for college. If she couldn't get into the Zemp family via marriage, then at least she could get through Cambridge debt free. It had seemed a fitting second choice for someone who valued her education like Lennon did.

Except the problem was he had too many pictures in his head of what someone like Lennon was like. There was the Lennon he'd known before she dated Brodie, the sweet, shy girl who was nerdy and kind. Then, there was Lennon, Brodie's girl-friend, who was wonderful, Brodie said. Though Brodie had never gotten shiny-eyed and acted like he was gaga over her, he'd seemed to actually like her at the time. He'd always said positive things and when he told them, "Oh, I'm going out with Lennon," he seemed proud to be doing so. What Gabe remembered of her during that phase was a happy-go-lucky girl, pleased to be on his brother's arm, always doting on Brodie, something Gabe had always wished she would do to him.

But she didn't, or she hadn't then. Once she and Brodie had broken up, there'd been no Lennon that he knew of. There was only the Lennon Brodie spoke of, often in terms of "that bitch," and occasionally, the words from a bitter, angry man who'd been hurt. Gabe had recognized it even then and chalked all of it up to Lennon breaking Brodie's heart. Ironically, the tuition and room and board payments to Cambridge only further supported her story about the abortion, whether it was outright bribery or not.

Then there was the Lennon he knew now—driven, intelligent, and fiercely protective of her own past, until he'd forced her to tear it wide open. Unfortunately, she had been right: he hadn't liked what he'd heard. But in the end, it wasn't about her so much as it was about accusations she was making against people he loved. She'd put him in an untenable situation. It was either her or them. He couldn't have both, apparently.

So he'd left his home office and come to the school, figuring he would work out the kinks here, thinking he could forget about her. But he still couldn't.

He was listening to the cacophony of noises as the wood flooring was installed into the individual apartments, the planks the ones that had been torn up from the gymnasium. The shiny boards had random curved stripes and straight swaths in red and blue. But instead of putting the flooring down as an upgrade in just a few of the units, he'd followed Lennon's suggestion and had made it the kitchen and dining area flooring in as many units as possible. Her idea had been that more apartments would have unique features from the original design of the school building, like the teacher desks.

So while he watched the contractors install the flooring, he thought of Lennon. When he looked out the new, large, clear sheet windows, he thought of Lennon. And when Misty walked up behind him, he jolted, because he'd been thinking of Lennon.

"What crawled in your pants and died?" she asked.

He would have laughed if she hadn't been so spot-on, and Gabe swiveled the chair around to face her. Misty was managing the four new branches of Bobby's pizza that he'd put into two nearby towns, two in Alpharetta as a test market, two closer to Atlanta.

"What brings you here?" he asked.

"The fact that I sent you four emails and texts since this morning and you haven't returned any of them."

Sitting up straight, he immediately started tapping on his

laptop and saw that yes, she had in fact sent them. "Shit, Misty. I'm sorry. You need something quickly?"

"I do. I need a boss who's not mooning over a breakup."

He thought about it. Here he was, just like Brodie, an affair with Lennon having exploded in his face. Just like his brother, it left him thinking contradictory thoughts of "that bitch" and "How do I get her back?"

"It's that obvious?" he asked.

"Everyone in town seems to know," said Misty with a shrug of one shoulder. Misty was a shark. It was why he hired her and why he liked her work. However, she was not going to console him on his loss, or even say "better luck next time, boss."

Lovely, he thought. *Even Misty thought everyone knew.*

"What happened?"

He hadn't expected his assistant to ask that. She'd known he was dating Lennon, and he took just a moment to say, "I asked her some things, and I didn't like the answers."

"She apologized?" Misty asked.

"No. I've been texting her for four days and she won't reply."

"Well, if she's the one who said horrible things, why are you the one begging for an apology?"

"I wasn't so great myself," he admitted, though something about Misty's words rang true.

"Yeah, but if it was both of you, shouldn't she be apologizing too? Shouldn't she at least be taking your calls?"

Changing the subject, Gabe answered questions about repairs on one of the freestanding Bobby's locations. He authorized the expense and sent Misty on her way with an apology for making her come down here to get his approval.

"No worries, boss." She offered a small wave over her shoulder as she left. She had things to do, and she wouldn't sit around and coddle him. She was gone as fast as she'd arrived. But Gabe was left with the ideas she'd dropped in his lap.

Shouldn't Lennon be reaching out to him, too? Shouldn't she at least be sorry that she'd run from him? That she shut him out?

He'd wondered if she needed a few days to get her head together, since it seemed she hadn't known about the Cambridge money. But it had been four days and she wasn't replying to him at all. His olive branch should have been enough. Hell, he'd chopped a whole olive tree for her by now.

Maybe it was time to call it a loss and quit.

❧ 48 ❧

L ennon dug for the next several days straight, anxious to
finish up her work. The problem was, there was no finish
line. Her thesis was to find evidence, then take it back to school
—where she had equipment and experts—and analyze it. But her
drive made her dig and dig. She dug even though the weather
had hit a cold snap.

She dug because Gabe had eventually stopped calling and
texting, and she told herself repeatedly that it was for the best.
Though she'd found another small artifact that morning and
should have called it quits, she came back out the third day. She
was on her hands and knees, not paying attention to the cloud
cover when the rain began coming down.

Thinking she could still work, and needing desperately to
keep her thoughts on something other than her impending
depression, she headed inside the cave. With the lamp once
again on her head—who cared about her hair now?—she tucked
her tablet under her arm and walked through.

However, having been caught by surprise by the rain, she'd
gotten a bit wet before she entered the cave, and within
moments she found herself shivering and her teeth chattering.

It was time to give up, she thought, in more ways than one. . .

Lennon was angry—angry with herself and angry at the world. She was angry that she'd probably made herself sick, angry that she was here in the cave and so cold. She was even angry that she'd managed to dig up three more tiny pieces, and they were all on Gabe's side of the property flags. She was angry that no matter how many times she told herself to let it all go, she didn't seem to be able to actually do it. She found she was mad at Brodie all over again, though she'd believed she'd paid enough in therapy bills and hours on the couch to pay that debt long ago.

She tried to work for another hour denying her illness, denying the rain outside of the cave, denying that, with the clouds overhead, any natural light that had filtered in was long gone. She also denied to herself that she wasn't finding anything of value in here. Aside from a few scrapings, that could easily turn out to be mold or worse, the cave had yielded nothing so far.

There were enough forks and branches that she had far too much to explore. Even though she didn't think there would be anything in here, she couldn't declare it empty unless she explored the whole cave. And it was turning into a much bigger job than she'd anticipated. Lennon was considering simply noting that she'd found the cave and mostly leaving it out of her thesis. It was, after all, only a master's thesis, she told herself. It could be a pilot study. It didn't have to be perfect.

She hated leaving it, though, and the more she thought about it, the more she thought she was not going to be able to come back to Breathless and finish the dig as part of a PhD paper. It would likely sit here until some other graduate student got wind of her project and decided to come finish it up for their own master's or PhD thesis. But it wouldn't be her. Clearly, she couldn't live here. She had two more weeks, and then she was going back to Illinois.

Finally giving up, Lennon turned around and wound her way out of the depths of the cave, out to the entrance where she saw that the rain had picked up. No wonder she was getting sick. She really shouldn't be out in this. She should've been in the library doing research today. She should have checked the weather report before she came out and just stayed home. But she couldn't say that she was on her A-game these days. Not a good move for her thesis.

Her only consolation was that half the graduate students she knew spent three quarters of their time crying, so, well, if she was crying, at least it wasn't over her thesis. Wet and cold and ready to give up, Lennon told herself her dig was over. She could leave Breathless tonight if not for Bailey Ann and Finn's wedding.

She forced her thoughts away from the dig, away from the unfinished work out beyond the mouth of the cave, away from Gabe, who always seemed to linger at the back of her mind. Harper Rose was supposed to be coming in with the girls tomorrow.

Lightning cracked overhead and Lennon decided she just might go home, turn the heat up, and snuggle under the covers. She'd get up later—once she was warm again—and get the house ready for when the girls arrived.

But that work was at Bailey Ann's house. Heat was at Bailey Ann's. Lennon was still standing inside the cave, barely sheltered. She was going to have to make a break for the car and get wetter than she was. Surveying the distance between the cave and the car, she almost cursed herself out loud. She'd left some of her tools out on the ground. Since no one came around and she thought she'd be back to digging once the rain had passed, she'd saved herself but not her things.

Her tools had gotten wet in the sudden downpour. It didn't matter, it wouldn't damage them in any way. They were metal with plastic handles or wood. Water and dirt didn't hurt them if it was only a short period of time. They could easily be hosed off, but she probably shouldn't have left them lying around. And she would have to brave the rain to clean up her mess. It seemed a fitting analogy for her life right now. It was her last thought before she dashed from the cave.

Stopping in the middle of her site, Lennon went from wet to drenched as she gathered her things. Standing there with her arms full of wet, muddy tools, she made a full three-sixty turn, checking out everything, making sure she was leaving nothing behind. For a moment, she looked down the trail in the woods that led to Gabe's House, but she saw nothing.

Of course, he wasn't coming out. He wasn't walking out to meet her for lunch. The weather was terrible, and he'd not come out even on the nice days this week. She'd never returned his texts or phone calls and he'd eventually quit sending them.

Hugging her tools tightly, she ran to the car, opened the trunk, and slammed them inside. Then she jumped around to the driver's side and got in as quickly as she could though, once she was in, she didn't know why she'd run. She was drenched before she'd even reached the car.

Lennon turned the key and started the car, startled by cold air blasting at her from the vents, making her teeth chatter even more. She sat there, shivering until the heat came on.

She tried not to think about Gabe and how everything had blown up. She tried not to think that she was making herself physically sick. She tried to think warm thoughts, but eventually the air heated and her muscles unclenched and she headed for home.

She'd dashed in the back door, leaving wet footprints all the way to the upstairs bath. Peeling her clothes, she listened as each piece hit the floor with a wet slopping noise, but she left them there as she climbed into the tub.

After a far-too-long hot bath, she'd made tea from the stash Bailey Ann had left behind. She'd even hauled the electric blanket out of the closet and finally she was warm enough to go right to sleep. Lennon passed out, praying she didn't wake up sick.

She woke up much later that night, the room and the house

dark, except for a light that she saw at the end of the hallway. Though she was slow to wake she could have sworn she heard the chattering of voices.

She would have stayed in bed, given the choice, but it sounded like Bailey Ann's house had been invaded by fairies or birds or something else that twittered. Her brain still wasn't quite screwed in right, but she felt the need to get up and check.

Throwing off the blanket, she immediately regretted the lack of heat. Blinking, she checked that she was at least wearing pajamas, in case there was an intruder rather than the TV being on for some silly reason. Finally forming some decent thoughts, she ruled out Bailey Ann and Finn. Finn's voice was much deeper than what she was hearing. It wasn't Gabe, only because she would have felt it if it was.

She followed the light at the end of the hallway to find the kitchen full.

Harper Rose stood there with her three little girls in a circle around her.

✢ 49 ✢

A belle never lets anyone leave her house hungry.

LENNON TRAIPSED DOWNSTAIRS THE NEXT MORNING, GRATEFUL at least that she was feeling better. The rain had continued to pour outside all through the night and it looked like it had at least a full day to go.

If she hadn't already decided she was done with her dig, the weather would be making that decision for her. The good news was that she already had more than she'd expected. She had enough pieces to take back, get them to the lab, and get them carbon dated. She had a whole semester in the spring to analyze what she'd dug up, and she dug up a damn lot. The bad news was there was more to dig up and she was going to have to leave it in the ground for someone else. That particular spot was a gold mine and she'd barely scratched the surface of what was there.

None of that mattered now. She was ahead of most of her peers: she was done with the collection. She was done digging on Gabe's land. She was done walking through the cave. All she had to do now was wait out Bailey Ann's wedding, and then she could go home, because, Lord knew, Breathless was not her home. She might have thought otherwise for a short while, but that had been nothing but a pipe dream. Better it was revealed before she made plans.

As she turned the corner from the steps into the kitchen, she saw through to the newly opened dining area. Three little girls sat at the table, each eating a bowl of cereal. Apparently, each child had a different cereal and the boxes were arranged neatly in front of each girl as though they needed to see the pictures to know what they were chewing.

Harper Rose looked up as Lennon entered the room. "Good morning! We raided your cereal stash, I hope that's okay?"

Lennon waved her hand as though to brush it off. "Of course, it is. I bought extra boxes last week because I knew you guys were coming."

In fact, she'd stocked the fridge with milk, cereal, eggs, turkey bacon, bread, sandwich meats, cheese and more in the hopes of having a full family in the house soon. Already it felt warmer, and even that small change made her happier.

She'd felt better when the girls had bum-rushed her for a group hug last night. The chattering she'd initially heard had ratcheted up to actual words, but that didn't stop the speed. They'd told her about New Orleans and some restaurant in Texas. If Lennon hadn't already heard that Harper Rose had planned to take a scenic route and not drive more than four hours a day, she would have been hard pressed to figure out what the hell they were yammering about. Still it made her smile. They seemed more excited about a restaurant than the actual Alamo...but that was kids for you.

This morning, she didn't have the energy to join in, so she listened while she set herself up. Still not quite convinced that the rain yesterday wasn't going to eventually catch up with her, she made herself a cup of hot tea and offered some to Harper Rose. She'd even dug out Aunt Della's old tea pot to put it in and carefully pulled the tea cups down from the high cupboards where Bailey had stashed them.

Aunt Della had always kept them out on display, but Bailey had lived here for a while on her own and, though she hadn't changed anything while her father was still alive, once she'd inherited the house it seemed she'd done plenty. Nothing was the same color as Lennon remembered it from her childhood, but she liked this new version of the house better.

Harper Rose was looking around and saying the same kinds of things that Lennon was thinking. "Bailey Ann sent me pictures while she worked. Showed me the wall here coming out —" she motioned to the now open space between the dining room and kitchen. "She sent pictures of the colors, asked what I thought. She asked Em too, since the house technically belongs to all of us, but we basically gave her free range. I liked what she picked, but I had no idea it would be so gorgeous in person. She did great. If you want something decorated, Bailey Ann's your girl."

Lennon nodded as she looked around with fresh eyes. "I can't say that I miss the old green."

Harper Rose bust out a short laugh. "We always called it *booger green*. Bailey did everyone a service by getting rid of that. I don't know what Mama was thinking when she picked it. But I have to say, the old house is looking new and pretty." She pointed toward the kitchen and the new counter that jutted out into the space. "This counter is so much nicer than the tile and the wood flooring is gorgeous. And this open plan to the dining room just feels. . . Well it feels like a whole new house."

"I think we actually have Finn to thank for that." Lennon sat down next to Holland. The youngest, at two, she'd accidentally popped several Honey Nut Cheerios out of her bowl and Lennon absently picked them up and put them back in while she talked. "He helped remodel the upstairs bath, too. I'm assuming you liked that?"

Lennon had motioned Harper Rose into the master bedroom

the night before when she'd arrived with a suitcase in hand and three girls swarming her. Though her cousin had tried to apologize for arriving early while simultaneously declining the master room, Lennon had insisted. Besides, as she said, all of her things were already in the second bedroom.

She'd helped then, late though the hour was, to get the three little girls situated in the other room. The two youngest, Hayden and Holland, wound up sleeping with their heads at opposite ends of the one twin bed. Though they'd passed out quickly, even before the two women got the door closed, Lennon had felt guilty. Harper Rose basically insisted that she not worry about it, saying the girls would think it was fun and then demand to know why they couldn't sleep that way every night.

This morning Lennon saw that Harper Rose was right. They looked none the worse for wear. Still, she asked, "How did you two sleep?"

All three girls lit up with tales of their slumber party. It was impressive given that they'd basically fallen asleep the moment they hit the pillows.

Hannah, the oldest, looked up at Lennon and said, "I get your room when you move out."

"Hannah!" Harper Rose scolded her oldest daughter.

"That's what you said!"

"Yes, but you don't rub it in," her mother said, her eyes widening and her mouth grinning as she worked hard to appear stern and yet failed.

Lennon couldn't help but laugh. Harper Rose sounded much like her own mother had when she and her Mayfair cousins had been little. When they'd been scolded for saying what was on their mind rather than what was polite.

Lennon merely winked back at Hannah and told her, "I heard that, too. I can get out earlier if you want? I could sleep on the couch downstairs."

"Oh no," Hannah replied, this time like a true Southern Belle. "That's absolutely not necessary." In the sudden shift of manners and word-choice, Lennon saw the seven-year-old mimicking her mother's bearing and more.

It felt strange, Lennon thought, sitting and sipping tea like a grown up with her older cousin. Harper Rose was closer to Bailey Ann's age than to Lennon's and Em's. Em always said that she'd been an accident or, at best, an afterthought. Her parents already had their two children, and then obviously—*whoops!* —there had come the third.

Lennon was taking another sip of the tea getting ready to refill her tea cup and add a little more lemon when the back door rattled. Opening on its own, the space was filled with a familiar voice calling out, "Knock knock!"

Bailey Ann entered, Finn right on her heels. For a moment Lennon was self-conscious, sitting here at Bailey Ann's table in her pajamas. While Bailey Ann was awake, fully dressed, alert, and with her fiancé/husband in tow. Then Lennon realized Harper Rose was also in her pajamas—though hers were a matching set, flannel with champagne bottles on them. It figured, Harper Rose even did pajamas with more style than anyone. But her cousin popped up and hugged her older sister before anyone could say anything.

While the other two hugged, happy to be seeing each other for the first time in months, Finn turned to Lennon with a grin. "Good morning, future cousin."

"Um, Bailey Ann there let the cat out of the bag. So it's already cousin." She hugged him, feeling warm and happy with her family all around.

Until he asked, "Are you ready for the wedding? Have a date?"

No, she thought, *no date at all*. She'd had one lined up, but that had gone away.

❧ 50 ❧

Gabe had spent the day driving all over hell and back.
Actually, it was a normal day. It just felt like driving all
over hell because he had been in a remarkably sour mood for
several weeks now.

When she met with him, Misty had not hesitated to point it
out. "Should you even be making business decisions when you've
obviously got some stick up your ass?"

He'd almost snapped back at her, "No. Clearly, I shouldn't.
But I don't really have a choice, do I?" But he'd managed to bite
his tongue and just smile at her remark. It earned him one raised
eyebrow, but she didn't say more.

What could he do? It wasn't as if he could say, "You're right.
I'll just put this off 'till next week when I feel better," because he
wasn't going to feel better next week. He also probably wasn't
going to feel better the week after that. And he was beginning to
understand the sour mood Brodie had been in for months just
before he died, whether it had been over Lennon or not.

The only thing Gabe could say for certain was that he wasn't
going to drive his car into a tree. Though, to be fair, he wasn't
the best driver these days. He had moments where he decided
his brother's accident had been just that—an accident. Gabe was

feeling shitty enough to make that same kind of mistake it seemed. But he wasn't drinking and driving. And he was actively trying *not* to drive into a tree. He wasn't the reckless fool his brother had been.

Or maybe he was. Maybe he was far more like his brother than he wanted to admit. Gabe had also begun to believe that maybe his brother was much more like Lennon had said than he wanted to admit. Because here he was having fucked it up big-time. Over Lennon. Over Brodie. Over what she'd said that he hadn't wanted to believe.

Because of all that, *no one* had wanted to deal with him for the past week, which was a shame because the apartments were finally coming together. Once he'd figured out what to do, he'd lined up the contractors like Rockettes. Now that it was started, everything was going off like clockwork.

He was about to be able to make an announcement about when the apartments would be open for walk-throughs and available to begin renting. He had to start thinking about hiring staff, things like that. He should have been excited. Instead, he found he didn't care.

He'd driven out of town to visit the Bobby's Pizza building that Misty had requested the repairs for the week before. The free-standing building had been damaged in a storm, and Misty had handled all of it. So Gabe had gone and inspected the work since they needed his signature on it.

Once he'd seen that it was done, and done well, he thanked Misty for her always stellar work. Usually, seeing a shop repaired and back in business, seeing his employees back at work and the building making money again, gave him at least a satisfied feeling. Now, he discovered that, once again, he didn't give a shit.

Instead, as he and Misty left through the front entrance, they waved goodbye to the employees who'd smiled and waved at them as they'd come and gone. Though all of that was normal, his next move was anything but.

He turned to Misty there on the front step, and even as

patrons walked into the store, he looked at her and asked point blank, "Can you work up a price for me, for Bobby's?"

"What do you mean?"

"The whole chain," he said, "If I sold it, what would it be worth? Do we have any buyers who might be interested?"

"Are you fucking serious?" she'd retorted without thinking about it. Most people wouldn't talk to their boss that way. Misty was not most people. Her next words proved it. "Are you smoking crack? Had a psychogenic fugue? What the fuck, Gabe?"

"I just want to know. It's not about you and you don't have to worry. I'd make sure you still had the job, Misty. You're brilliant at this. So I'd write your position into the sale, or alternately I can bring you with me for whatever it is I decide to do next." He was waving his hands around, gesturing as though he knew what he was saying. The fact was, he didn't know what he would decide to do next. He didn't know what he was saying, and he hadn't thought about including Misty's job in the deal until he'd been standing there. But the idea had been brewing since the night before.

Misty was still staring at him, blue eyes wide, perfect mouth hanging open, and he wondered for a moment, *Why couldn't he have fallen for someone like her?* They seemed well-suited in every other aspect, but he wasn't attracted to her at all, and she wasn't attracted to him either.

Right now, she was staring at him like he was a blazing idiot. He knew Misty, and normally Misty was so straight-up logical that he could only conclude that she must be correct: he was a blazing idiot who'd gone right off the rails. But he didn't rescind his question.

Instead, he repeated it. "Work me up a price. What would it take to sell the whole chain?"

"Jesus, you're ridiculous, Gabe. Over a girl?"

"Woman," he corrected absently, as though it would make

any difference. And was it really over a woman? He didn't know. He did know Lennon hated the pizza chain. Was that why he was selling it? He couldn't deny that she was factoring into a lot of things she probably shouldn't be, but he couldn't help it.

No matter how he felt about her, or that she was part of the reason, she wasn't the whole reason. The breakup had turned things upside down for them. He'd seen things in a new light, not all of it good.

He'd taken a hard look at what he was doing. And, it turned out, he hated the pizza chain, too. It was something his father had left him—a responsibility his father had put *on* him, without asking if he wanted it. It seemed Gabe had never asked himself if he wanted it either.

The chain was a family legacy, the first business his father had started, with one pizza joint in a local strip mall. Robert Zemp had turned Bobby's into a local success. So he'd built another and another, until they dominated the town. His father had a fierce pride in that chain, but Gabe didn't feel the same way. It wasn't his. But he'd felt obligated to carry it on, even though he didn't like the work.

If there had been another family member, a cousin or something, he could have passed it off. But there was no one else in the family left. No one that his dad would have wanted him to give it to. He didn't even have young children to keep it going for. If he'd had toddlers, he might have stayed with it, just in case one of them wanted it someday. But that wasn't an issue. And the way Misty was staring at him, he could see he wasn't likely to woo anyone into giving him children any time in the next three decades.

"Yeah," he said again, reconfirming his crazy idea if only to himself and not to her, "See what it will take to sell it."

His father had been a workhorse, always in the business, only interacting with his kids to bat them back on course when they'd tried to fall off. It had been a heavy hand his father had used.

Neither Gabe nor Brodie had come out of that feeling like Rob was the gentle and loving father that they'd seen on TV, or even in other kids' houses.

No more. Gabe had no love lost for Bobby's Pizza. Just asking Misty to start the process of putting the business on the market lifted a huge weight off of his shoulders. Now, if only he could bribe some fool into buying it.

Thinking he'd feel better, and grateful he'd checked every box for the day, Gabe went home. They didn't need him at the school building. The contractors would work until dark and they knew what they were doing. The foreman had control and would contact Gabe if it was necessary. Gabe didn't expect that would happen, though.

So he'd headed back to the home office and begun his nightly ritual of going through his father's old papers and boxes. There was a glass-fronted armoire against one wall. The top held the liquor and cut crystal glasses, but the bottom hid drawers and paperwork and ledgers from decades gone by. Gabe was slowly pulling each one out and rifling through it. He held onto a hope that he would find out something about his father and the Cambridge money for Lennon. He just needed some reason that Robert had done it. There probably wasn't one, but still Gabe looked.

Though he'd searched through the papers, in the end, he'd been sitting at the desk, drinking his Gentleman Jack straight out of the crystal decanter his father had bought to replace the first one. It didn't look exactly like the original, but it was close enough. He tipped the decanter up for another drink and discovered it was empty.

Son of a bitch, he thought as he set it back on the desk none too gently. The empty decanter told him he'd polished off what was in there. *Should he refill it? Or quit?*

He almost reached for the bottle, but instead it was the decanter he reached for. It was empty, but it still held so much.

It held his father's plans. It seemed to be a vessel for everything Rob had thought Brodie would be, and the idea that it was so simply passed down to Gabe when Brodie wasn't available any more made him angry now.

He wasn't just another Brodie, whose only purpose was to step in and be the replacement when the first one was lost. But that was how his father had treated him. Even to the point of tapping out in a brutal way, when Gabe's mother had already been dying and Gabe was still learning the reins that had been looped around his neck.

He'd been too hurt at the time that his father had committed suicide to think about what it all meant. He'd just been trying to get through the days, to keep his mother upright, and when that was no longer possible, he'd fought to keep her comfortable. Then he'd fought to let her go. So he'd never examined—not until now, until Lennon made him—what his father had done to him.

He'd always thought of Rob as a hard man, a trustworthy businessman, and a decent person. Now? He didn't know. How decent was a man who *dictated* to his child and other people's children how they would live their lives?

Gabe was convinced now that Brodie was less despondent over Lennon than he was over being roped into the life their father had chosen for him. Gabe hadn't seen it until Brodie was gone and the mantle was far-too-readily passed to him. Brodie had worn it his whole life and struggled against it each day. Gabe saw that now. As he looked back, his past clicked into focus, scenes becoming clearer. His father and brother's constant arguments made more sense.

His father wasn't even here to argue with anymore, and Gabe had been on the losing end of it still.

He was done.

Picking up the decanter, he threw it, watching as it smashed against the wall and shattered much the same way the first one had. There was something satisfying in it. He didn't even get out of the chair.

He was probably half-drunk, but he made a second big decision for the day. He picked up the phone and dialed his real estate agent. . .

L ennon had spent her day out with her cousins. Emma Kate had flown in earlier and the two had squealed like school girls at seeing each other again.

Em stashed her bags at the house and then immediately began telling everyone how Lennon had finished her thesis.

Lennon laughed at having to correct her. "I only finished the dig," she told everyone. Then she had to correct herself. "Actually, 'finished' is a strong term, I could dig more. This site isn't fully excavated. Not by a long shot. But I have enough for my thesis."

"What is it, exactly?" Harper Rose asked for the first time. "I mean, I get the basics, but..."

At Emma Kate's insistence, Lennon explained her idea that it was plausible that there had been a nomadic society passing through the area almost twenty thousand years before the town of Breathless. "There's evidence from other nearby sites that it's possible. My dig won't prove anything, but I'm hoping to find some support one way or the other."

"Didn't you already find a lot of 'things'?" Em used air quotes to go along with her frown.

"Yes, but until I get them into the lab and test them and get the designs and ink types verified by higher level nerds than me, I don't have much *proof*. I have one semester to do that and also to write the whole thing up and defend it. No pressure." She grinned and was grateful when they hugged her and told her how proud they were of her. She wondered sometimes looking at Em if Em had wanted the same thing. No one doubted that Lennon would finish the thesis. No one asked Emma Kate about her own.

Once they'd gotten Em settled into the room with Lennon— the only place left to put her other than the pull out couch downstairs—they'd gone to the bridal shop en masse. Getting someone to look after Harper Rose's girls and Jane Copeland's small children separately had not been achievable apparently. So when Jane's sitter volunteered to add Harper Rose's girls to the mix, Lennon had looked at the babysitter as though she were bonkers. Lennon loved all those kids, but seven of them at once?

Though they all questioned the sitter's sanity, it hadn't stopped them from abandoning the young woman with the children and leaving to go to the bridal store, hopefully for the last time. While they were there, they all tried on their dresses, pleased to find, as Bailey Ann ooooohed and ahhhhhed and grinned, that they fit. It was quite the coup that everything went so well, since they were all standing around sipping from their champagne and getting a little bit tipsy with their excitement.

At last, the bride had come out in her gown while the brides-maids now all stood around in their coral dresses and matching dyed shoes. They returned the oohs and ahhs over Bailey Ann as she glowed.

Lennon, again, looked at her and thought, *sometimes it works out and sometimes it doesn't*, but she was happy for her cousin. She was happy, too, that pretty much as soon as the wedding was over she'd take only one day off then fly back to Illinois. Em would be heading back to UCLA and Harper Rose could have the house to herself and her girls.

Hannah could finally move into the big girl's bedroom,

leaving her two little sisters to share the other one. The setup worked well, after all it was the same one the three Mayfair girls had used growing up. It would be easier without Lennon in the house, and Lennon was glad to be leaving.

They'd taken the bride out for dinner and Lennon had been able to keep her mouth shut when Zeal was recommended as the go-to restaurant. It was Em who took one look at her and carefully steered the plan to a different place, one not owned by a Zemp.

"Thank you," Lennon had mouthed the words to Em and received a shrug said, "Of course."

They'd gone out, drunk margaritas, toasted Bailey more times than they could count, praised her on her choice of finally getting her head together and marrying Finn Malloy, and eventually they'd called a ride home as none of them were in any shape to drive.

Typical bachelorette party, Lennon thought, though it hadn't been an official one. Bailey Ann had asked that they not do it. And that if they did anything, it needed to be several days before the wedding. She was not going to have any bridesmaids looking hungover or groomsmen with black eyes. Lennon understood, she'd been to weddings with both. So they'd opted for this, holding their bride's gifts until the morning of the wedding.

The car had finally arrived to pick them up and proceeded to drop them off one by one. Harper Rose, Emma Kate, and Lennon were last. Jane Copeland's house was the stop just before theirs, so they could gather Harper Rose's girls from Jane's house.

Lennon was yawning and about ready to pass out. But much to Lennon's and Harper Rose's amazement the sitter still looked fresh and happy. All the girls were asleep except for Hannah, the oldest. Lennon watched as her older cousin slipped the sitter a twenty as a tip, though Jane had paid her earlier. There was no power in the universe, Lennon thought, that could have made her do that job, nor do it with any grace.

Hannah had helped them wake the younger girls up and the three Mayfair women had taken the next generation of Mayfairs —three sleepy little girls—home with them. It felt good, Lennon thought, to have a child curled up at her side, resting on her, and trusting her. Though it felt less good the next morning when she was yelled awake before eight a.m.

She'd wandered downstairs, eyes puffy, head groggy, vision blurry. Her hands lifted to the side of her head in reflex as she looked at Harper Rose through one eye. Harper Rose sat at the table, not looking much better than Lennon felt.

"Oh, dear God, it's way too early to be awake, especially after last night," Lennon said. "Weren't they up late too? Shouldn't they be sleeping in?"

Harper Rose shrugged.

The girls were happily eating cereal again, but Harper Rose sat at an empty seat and stared into space. It seemed she wasn't even up for the tea Lennon had learned she usually started her day with. She just sat there with her chin resting on a well-propped fist and looked at Lennon through semi-glazed eyes. "It's kids, man. You never get a morning to sleep in. Not unless you have a partner to give you a break."

"Oh," Lennon moaned. When what she had wanted to say was, "I'm so sorry," and "Oh, maybe we should find you one," and "Do you need a nanny?" Not that either she nor Harper Rose could afford such a thing.

Once she'd convinced herself she was actually awake, her day went better. However, Emma Kate had managed the sleep of the dead. The three children running through the house and maybe even jumping on the beds in the adjacent room hadn't woken her. Lennon wondered if it was because Em was still in undergraduate school. Or because she was in the dorm still. Had she simply learned to sleep through anything? Clearly, it was a skill Em had that Lennon had not fully developed.

Once her cousin had finally woken up, they'd headed out for lunch together, abandoning Harper Rose with her girls. Harper

Rose had not been open to any of Lennon's sympathy. "I appreciate your concern, but they aren't your kids. You don't owe me anything."

When Lennon had started to protest that she did—she was, after all, living in Harper Rose's house—her cousin had brushed her off again. "I know you and Em haven't seen each other in forever. You need some time out to catch up without me and elementary school kids in tow!"

After lunch, Lennon and Em had simply wandered around town. It was just like they'd done in high school; they would pick a neighborhood with low traffic and wander up and down the streets catching up on anything and everything. Only in high school, their choice of neighborhood had often depended on which hot guy lived where. The Zemps didn't have a 'neighborhood' just their own house by itself on the hill. For now, Lennon was glad Em couldn't make her walk by it. It didn't stop her cousin from grilling her about the now defunct relationship, though.

"Did you really give up on him?" Em asked.

"I did," Lennon said, before correcting herself. "I had to. I'm leaving. I'm going back to Chicago and he's here."

"He does practically own the town." She waved her hand around at the houses they were passing. Though Lennon was pretty sure he didn't own these houses per se, there was a Bobby's Pizza just one block over in the direction Em was waving. Though that might be true any direction she waved, Lennon thought sardonically.

"Yeah, he even owns one of the old schools now." She told Em about the project and Em frowned for a moment looking at her.

"Interestingly enough, you're excited about an apartment building. It doesn't have any buried Indian mounds under it, does it?"

"No. It doesn't," Lennon laughed, thinking that Em was right. Lennon had gotten excited because Gabe was excited.

Another thing to let go. She'd be glad to be back in Illinois. Hopefully, once she was in Chicago, this would fade away. But it couldn't quite fade yet. As much as she wanted to be, she wasn't done with Gabe Zemp. Or maybe he wasn't done with her.

She explained to Em the one thing she was afraid of. "I have to go see him. The contract says he gets to see everything I dug up off his land."

❧ 52 ❧

Lennon showed up, unannounced, at Gabe's house the next night. She'd come around dinner time, hoping to catch him in the middle of a meal of microwavable mac and cheese or something equally inane. She could admit she was afraid—just as she had been before—that he would be here with someone. That he would be eating well without her. That he would have moved on.

She didn't want him to be able to do those things, even though she knew that wish was wrong. Even though she wished all those things for herself.

She could do her job and leave, Lennon repeated in her head. She was capable of keeping this strictly professional. She'd taken a deep breath before she'd knocked on the door. Behind her, she pulled a wheeled crate that collapsed down to be easy to carry. Right now, it held smaller, cardboard boxes each with one of the artifacts she'd found carefully padded and protected within.

The contract he'd originally made her sign said she had to show all artifacts found on his property to him and so she was going to. She was going to open each box, show him each piece of broken clay pot, each artifact she had dug up, each picture of the foundation as it appeared on his side of the line. She was not going to be in violation of the contract in any way, shape, or form. Though she wasn't going to show him everything she'd found, only the things from his side of the property line. She was being petty and she knew it. However, that pettiness, that attention to detail was the only thing keeping her sane.

He didn't come to the door and she was beginning to believe she'd missed him. It appeared his car was in the garage which should mean he was home, but maybe she was wrong. She knocked again, getting ready to turn around, pick up her cart, and leave.

Just as she was ready to give up, the door pulled open. His eyes lit up for a moment before confusion clouded them again. His face looked a little haggard, dark circles smudged the skin under his eyes, and she wondered if she looked the same way.

She probably did.

"Lennon," he said, happiness almost permeated his tone, though there was an equal measure of suspicion. "You came."

She decided to clear up any confusion before it started. "I brought the artifacts. It's part of the contract we signed." As the words tumbled from her lips, she watched as his face fell. Why had she said that? Did he really want her back?

But he couldn't. Everything had exploded. There was no way he would want her back.

So she watched carefully as he looked at her and said, "I don't need to see them."

"I'm sorry, but you do," she countered his dismissal. "Until I have signed paperwork that says that you don't, I'm not violating any part of this contract. I'm leaving in less than a week. I've got Bailey Ann's wedding this weekend and then I'm gone. So I'm following our contract to the letter. I can't have anyone threaten any of the pieces."

She pushed past him, picking up the box to bring it over the threshold, because—despite the handy wheels—she couldn't pull it over the bump, not with the fragile artifacts inside it.

Even though he volunteered to help lift it, she shoved his hand away saying only, "It's delicate. I've got it."

Back on even ground, Lennon wheeled it carefully into the dining room then. The floor here was wondrously smooth, the fine workmanship showing through the whole house now that she was looking at it with cold eyes.

The dining room table was buffed to a glossy shine. *Probably by the maid*, she thought, as she began picking out the boxes one by one. Most of them were tiny, about the size jewelry would come in but she pushed that thought aside, as she laid them out neatly on the table top.

"Fine," he said, "Is there anything you need me to sign that I've seen them?"

"I wrote up a paper for each one," she added, their voices as monotone as the mood. The conversation followed a halting pattern. She started pulling the lids off and he looked inside the boxes as she laid out papers next to each one. He briefly read the first one and she pulled a pen out of her purse. She'd had it at the ready, to hand to him. *Fast and efficient*, she thought.

What she'd not been ready for were his fingers brushing hers as she handed him the pen. She almost visibly jolted, surprised at the arc that still sprung up between them. When he'd signed every last page, he still hadn't really examined any of the pieces. That's what Lennon thought he'd originally wanted—to see what was on his land, to know what kinds of things she'd removed and what it might mean. Now he wanted nothing to do with it. He didn't even ask to pick any of them up for a closer inspection.

"You can close them up now." Gabe turned away even as he said it, and Lennon began to put the boxes back. He said nothing until every box was back in her wheeled dolly, until she was turning and heading toward the hallway.

"Lennon." He drew her name out on a wistful sigh. "I'm sorry."

"Thank you."

"No, really. I'm sorry about the way things happened."

"Thank you." Was there anything else for her to say?

He asked the next question, incredulous. "*Is that it?* Is that *all* you have to say? Just 'thank you'?"

She shrugged. *Where could this possibly go if she said more?* "I don't need you to apologize," she said, not looking at him. Instead, she stood facing the door as it was much easier to talk to than the man she'd made love to last week. She wanted to let her head hang, but she refused to let him see it. When he didn't reply to that, she added, "I don't need your apology. I needed you to believe me."

"I do believe you."

"No," she said, "It doesn't matter if you believe me now. I needed you to believe me when I told you."

"I'm sorry for that. I can't change what I did. But I do believe you now. Is there any way to get past this?"

"I don't think so. I don't think there's a point to it. And I don't think you really even believe me now."

At least, with that, he conceded a little. "I believe you believe things happened that way." She tried not to show it as she seethed at his words. "But you're talking about someone I know. Someone I think I know better than you do, or ever did. And the person you talk about is not the Brodie I knew," Gabe said. It seemed he was still trying to plausibly defend his brother.

Lennon turned around and stared at him now, her gaze no longer sad but full of angry fire. "Of course, he's not! Why in hell would your older brother act toward you the way he acted toward his girlfriend? Why would *any* of that be the same? Why would you even think that the Brodie that you saw would be the same Brodie that I knew?"

Gabe pulled back, stunned at her outburst, and she wished she'd managed to keep her mouth shut. She wished she'd kept that all to herself. She should have stayed cold, closed off. She'd been so close to being out the door.

But now, his mouth hung open a little bit and he said nothing for a moment and then he replied, "I don't know. But the Brodie I knew went out of his way to be good to me."

"You were his *brother*. You meant something to him. He had to live with you for the rest of his life." She was waving one hand around now, no longer suppressing anything, now letting her anger run freely. She was angry that he still said this. Angry that she still felt the need to defend it. Angry that she felt anything at all when she'd been telling herself to let it go.

Finally, she forced herself to take a deep breath and try to find a little bit of calm. "What happened between me and Brodie doesn't mean that he didn't love you. It doesn't mean that he wasn't a good brother to you. Gabe, no one is all good or all evil."

This time he nodded. "Is that it? Are you going to leave?"

She nodded, because the answer was *yes*. That was it. If he didn't have anything more to say to her than to defend Brodie to her when Brodie was already dead and gone, then that was the very end of their story. Lennon turned and left, finally leaning down to pick up the box and carry it over the threshold and down the stairs. She could protect the delicate things in the boxes, even if she couldn't protect the delicate feelings in her chest.

She set it down when she reached the bottom of the staircase and felt like a chapter had closed.

❧ 53 ❧

B ailey Ann had taken them all to a salon that morning.
Though Lennon worried that they wouldn't know how to
handle her hair, they'd done a good job, and that was the end of
her concerns for the day—or so she thought.

She had her nails done in a nice French manicure, with a
white that wasn't shocking and pale tan that matched her skin
tone. Lennon had no idea how long that would last, but a girl
could dream.

Under her sweatpants and t-shirt—the way all of them had
arrived to have their hair and nails done—Lennon was wearing
the only strapless bra she owned. Though it was not her most
comfortable bra, mostly she was grateful that she wasn't in the
full corset contraption that Bailey Ann was in to get into her
wedding gown.

The group of bridesmaids and the bride eventually made
it to the church. All done up but still in their sweats. They
sat in the upstairs dressing room of the church, informally
handing Bailey Ann her bachelorette gifts one by one.
Lennon worried as she put the box she'd wrapped into her
cousin's hands. After all, she'd used the wrapping paper her
cousin, or maybe her aunt, had left in the closet to wrap it.

She was worried she might have gotten things completely incorrect.

After all, Jane had given the bride expensive, lacy lingerie. Emma Kate, in true fashion, had managed to produce both a sex toy and a framed photograph she'd had dug up from Bailey Ann's high school days and had printed on canvas like a painting. The photo was of Bailey Ann and Finn headed to the prom. Only Em could be so dichotomous in one gift, so Lennon handed her own over with a bit of nerves.

Bailey Ann gently peeled the paper and opened the tissue her piece was nested in. She took it out and looked at it for a moment. It was a clay disk with markings in black glaze on both sides. Lennon fought to hold back from blurting out what it was.

She managed to hold her tongue—still thinking she'd screwed it up—as they all sat and watched her cousin read the card that Lennon had neatly printed and included with the disc. She bought it from a craftsman who was native in heritage and owned a shop she'd stopped at several times on her travels between Chicago and Breathless. Lennon had bought this particular piece on the internet, but having seen his shop in person before, she'd been sure of the quality she was getting.

The clay had been made the same way the natives had made it for centuries. And the inscription on it was a symbol. It probably didn't mean anything to Bailey Ann until it was explained. Though it was simple, it was copied from ceremonial wear at weddings of native couples and was considered to be the equivalent of a prayer for a full, long successful life together.

Lennon was shaking her head as Bailey Ann read the card. "I don't know what you would do with it, but—"

Bailey Ann waved her hand, as though to dismiss Lennon's worries. As always, even as the bride, her cousin was the gracious hostess. "It's perfect, Lennon. I know exactly where it will go. And the even better part is that it's always clearly going to be from you. I love it. Thank you. I have a small round embroidery that my Mama did years ago. I'm going to frame both pieces and place them on either side of our wedding portrait when we get it."

Lennon felt her heart swell, and it was a good feeling, one she hadn't felt for a solid week. She'd been feeling cold and alone again until she'd put on her sweats this morning and become part of the group. She'd felt like part of the crowd at the salon, and then they'd come up here looking like fools, full faces of makeup, hair often partially done. The bride had half her hair professionally gathered and pinned, the other half still in curlers. They'd only just climbed into their wedding attire.

It was barely fifteen minutes now until the start of the ceremony. But Bailey Ann didn't look nervous at all.

Lennon turned her back to her cousin as she held the front of the dress in place. "Emma Kate, please zip me up."

But Emma Kate was already there. The two of them had been such good friends for so long they had the kind of short-hand married couples seemed to use. The women milled about, pulling out curlers and fluffing hair. Bending over and doing up the tiny buckles on their shoes. Even Sioban—Finn's sister—was part of the group.

She stepped forward now and offered a sincere hug to Bailey Ann. Something Lennon got the impression had not happened before. As she held Bailey Ann tightly, she whispered something in her ear.

But it was Bailey Ann who pulled back and said, "I win?"

Sioban nodded, though clearly, she had not intended the conversation to be shared with everyone around them. Still, she graciously repeated her words out loud, letting everyone hear. "You win. My brother is a prize and you've won him."

Bailey Ann nodded with a smile and even Lennon didn't know quite what to make of that statement. If she understood it as Bailey Ann had told it, Sioban had not been pleased with Bailey Ann being back in Finn's life.

But now, Sioban took both of Bailey Ann's hands in her own and looked at the bride, dressed wonderfully in white, her ankles crossed, perfect satin shoes just peeking out from under the flouncing hem.

"My brother is a prize, and you win. He is all I have left, and I'm so happy to be happy for him. . . You win because you're good for him."

"Stop it!" Bailey Ann demanded, on the verge of tears. "I cannot ruin my mascara today." But she popped up and engulfed Sioban in a huge hug.

Lennon felt another surge of hope. Sioban and Bailey Ann had been at odds for well over a decade. But weddings were good for making amends and stitching up old wounds.

A knock came at the door then, asking if they were ready. Finn was about to take his place at the front of the church, and so they headed down the stairs, careful in their dyed satin heels, ready to start the procession and get the wedding underway.

But as Lennon headed down around the curve toward the bottom few stairs, as she heard the music playing just before the flower girl headed down the aisle with her basket of petals, she remembered Gabe was sitting in the audience. He was supposed to have been her date.

❧ 54 ❧

G abe looked around the crowd at the wedding reception. By the end of the ceremony there had not been a dry eye in the house. But after a break for photos and a caravan of cars to the country club, he could see everyone had changed their mood from happy-to-the-point-of-tears to full party mode.

He had not made the transition himself and was now considering leaving. He'd put in his appearance, shook the hands he needed to, and got a check mark by his name for showing up. No one would even miss him, he thought. He was hanging out by the bar being anti-social and nursing a rum and coke, in which he'd told the bartender to hold the rum so that he didn't have to worry about driving.

When he'd originally replied as a yes, he'd checked the plus one box on his card. Instead, right now he was counting himself lucky that they hadn't made a formal place setting and had let the guests choose their seats for dinner. Otherwise he'd have had an empty seat next to him. He'd thought he'd have Lennon on his arm as his date, and that this reception was going to be the most fun he'd had in a long while. After all, Bailey Ann and Finn were having the wedding everyone had been waiting for. Especially since last spring, when the two had clearly hit it off again.

But the evening was not going the way he'd originally planned. Lennon was here, but she was on the other side of the room, ignoring him.

Though she'd danced once with a groomsman when asked, she'd otherwise only participated in the group dances, boogeying right alongside the bride and groom and jumping up and down to oldies that everyone knew. There had been no traditional father-daughter dance, nor mother-son dance, as neither the bride nor the groom had any parents left. But they had siblings, and they made the most of family.

The party had roared on around Gabe as though he were in a cylinder of plexiglass—able to see everything and hear it in muffled tones, but not able to feel any of it at all. Though he had been encouraged to dance, he'd not had it in him to get up and join the crowd, wave his arms around, and jump up and down like a fool. He wasn't feeling it, despite the good vibes of the wedding and his happiness for the couple involved.

At last, he saw Lennon sitting by herself and as the music changed, he decided, *why not?* After all, she was leaving. She'd told him she was heading back to Chicago right after the wedding. So if he was going to do anything, this was his last chance.

It was at a well-attended party, sure, full of people he knew, and he might crash and burn in front of all of them, but if he didn't? Well, if he didn't try, Lennon would be gone. So he'd set the coke down on the nearest tray and almost stalked across the room. Probably not his best foot forward, but he'd done it anyway.

She had begged off the next dance and sat down at a table with a handful of friends. Now by herself after her friends had gotten up, she'd watched them head to the dance floor, already paired off into couples. She was nursing a glass of ice water and looking just a little melancholy. Maybe she felt the same way he did. He could only hope. So he held his hand out to her.

"Lennon, come dance with me?" He watched as she started

to shake her head, but he tried to cut her off before she could actually refuse. "It's a wedding, Len. Just dance with me, that's all I'm asking."

When she still didn't decide, he tried one last time, playing the card he'd kept up his sleeve. "You were supposed to be my date. I thought I was going to be here with you. I thought I was going to be dancing every dance with you. Can I please just have this one?"

Then he watched as whatever wall she had built crumbled and she reached up, placing her hand carefully in his. But even as she did so, even as his hope surged, she told him, "Just this one."

He'd picked a slower song hoping for a close dance and a chance to get back into her graces. But he'd wasted a good thirty seconds of it crossing the room, convincing her to get up. He almost dragged her onto the dance floor, wanting to make the best use of every possible remaining note.

Pulling her into his arms, Gabe wrapped her up tight, holding her close as they swayed in step. He could smell her perfume or her shampoo or her soap. He didn't know what it was, but it was familiar, it was *Lennon*. And it triggered him back to mornings lying in bed with her, to nights hot and passionate, to cooking in the kitchen, and things as mundane as watching her dig up a rock from the earth and declare it special.

It felt good to have her in his arms again. More importantly, it felt *right*. But she was leaving, and there was nothing right about this.

When the song ended, he asked her, "Just one more?" And though she wanted to pull away, she was obviously torn. A little bit of pressure at her waist had her looping her arms around his neck again and giving in one more time as though she wanted this, too. So they danced another slow song, but she didn't say she loved him, or that she needed him, and when the music picked up tempo, she thanked him before disentangling herself from his hold. She managed it with a clinical efficiency that put a lie to her warmth in his arms.

As he watched, she walked away to the other side of the room, never once looking back.

✻ 55 ✻

Y*ou don't cross your mama. If she says jump, don't waste your breath asking, 'how high?' you'd better already know.*

LENNON LISTENED TO EMMA KATE AS HER COUSIN GRILLED her. "Where did he go? You were dancing with him."

"I don't know," Lennon replied, and she honestly didn't know, but only because she forced herself to walk away and not watch him.

"But it was perfect," her cousin protested. "You two looked wonderful together. What happened?" Emma Kate already knew every major bit of history between the two of them, so Lennon knew Em was referring only to the two of them dancing together.

Yet all she could say was, "I can't fix everything, and I can't change that I don't belong here in Breathless."

"No," Emma Kate protested, brooking no argument. "I know you guys have your problems, but no two people who danced together like that should be apart. You can fix it if you want to."

Lennon didn't really agree. Still, Lennon understood what Emma Kate had seen. Lord knew she'd felt it, but she replied to her cousin, "I can't help that. It doesn't change anything. How long can our relationship go on with me being angry at him? That kind of thing eats at any kind of chance. It's better to end it now rather than wait for it to collapse on me later."

Emma Kate was still shaking her head. Denying everything Lennon said, even though she knew the whole story, she still insisted it could work. "You figure out a way around it. You find a way to forgive each other."

But Lennon didn't think that way existed. Gabe didn't believe her, and she couldn't live with that between them. She was starting to say so, despite the fact that she knew it was silly and she didn't have to defend her position, when a voice behind her startled her.

"Honey," her Mama intoned with a heavy sound. "You looked great with that man on your arm. Better than I've ever seen you."

"It doesn't matter Mama. There's too many things between us." So now she was defending herself to two of her favorite people. *Way to be a bridesmaid!* she thought.

"I know," her Mama agreed. "I know you had problems with his brother, and I don't know exactly what it was, but I know it was bad. I know it was bad enough to make you leave town. And I know it was bad enough on Brodie's side that he spent the entire summer drunk until he ran his car into a tree."

She'd not expected her mother to be quite so blunt, but she couldn't deny the truth of any of it.

"But that's not enough," her mother said just when Lennon thought she'd finished. "It's not enough. That man is not his brother and you obviously have feelings for him. The kind that could go on and become something permanent."

"I live in Chicago now, Mama."

"Not good enough," her mother replied almost before Lennon even finished her sentence.

She couldn't quite believe it. GiGi Mayfair had never really meddled in either of her children's love lives before, but this time she seemed to be telling her daughter what to do. Lennon protested again and again until at last she looked around, glad the three women were being left alone in the corner of the reception tent. She pulled out her big guns and told her mother what she hadn't already told her. "Do you remember my scholarship to Cambridge?"

"You had several," her mother replied immediately with a proud smile.

"I know, it's what made it possible. But there was the one that we never figured out the name of, the one that paid up all the tuition?"

Her mother nodded, frowning, clearly not understanding where this was going.

"That money was from Robert Zemp," Lennon told her, watching as her mother's face opened wide from shock.

"Every semester it came," her mother said as though that was some evidence that Lennon was wrong.

"Yes. Every semester. Robert Zemp paid the remainder of my tuition, room and board at Cambridge University every semester for four years." She watched as her mother took a deep breath, her eyes drifting from one side of the room to the other. It was clear she wasn't looking at or for anyone, just thinking. *There*, Lennon thought, she'd finally thrown a boulder in the path big enough to make her understand, to make her mother understand that what she and Gabe had, though at times wonderful, was insurmountable.

Eventually her mother turned and looked at her. "Do you know why he did it?"

Lennon shook her head. She truly did not. Perhaps it was some kind of penance for forcing her to abort her baby. Perhaps it was something Brodie had demanded of him, if Brodie had truly felt about her the way Gabe insisted. It hadn't come from Gabe, of that much she was sure. He'd been far too surprised by any of it to have demanded at the time that Robert Zemp pay her tuition.

So she was shocked when her mother seemed to absorb the impact of the knowledge and once again aimed that laser focus at her, a hard but warm stare. "Honey, that man is not Robert Zemp either."

Lennon felt herself jerk in shock but watched as Emma Kate began to grin. Her mother leaned in a little closer. "You go after him. You can't give up the best thing you've ever found. I know it. I'm lucky. I still have your daddy after all these years. If you find something like that, you hold onto it and you don't let it go."

"Mama," she protested one more time. "You and daddy are not Gabe and me."

"No, we're not. You're different, but you're the same."

Emma Kate was wearing a full grin now and Lennon had only a moment to look sideways at her before her Mama said, "I told you to go get him. Why are you still standing here?"

❧ 56 ❧

The garage door was open when Lennon arrived at the Zemp home. She was standing on his doorstep in her pink bridesmaid's gown, her dyed-to-match shoes almost wobbling on the expensive flagstone of his front patio.

The dress was long and to get up the stairs she'd had to hold it up in front of her. She still held it gathered in one fist, to keep her hand busy, while the other reached up to knock on the front door.

She still had no idea what to say though she'd thought about it the whole way over. Could she just blurt out, *my Mama told me I had to come?*

The garage door was open, the light inside shown on his car, carefully parked in the middle of the space. So, she knew that he was home, but she also could tell that everything wasn't quite alright. Normally, he was meticulous in taking care of his things. The precisely parked car was evidence of that, but the open door wasn't.

When he didn't answer after her third knock, she became worried. She reached out and turned the knob herself, surprised that it gave way so easily under her fingers. It didn't mean anyone had broken in though. He had a full-scale alarm system and he could unlock the entire house with his code as he came in through the garage. So Lennon didn't think the unlocked door was a sign of intruders. Truly, she was only worried about Gabe.

"Gabe," she called out his name. She'd let the word drag out relatively softly, hoping that he would hear her, but also hoping it was not loud enough to startle him.

No answer came in return and she called out again. Turning to the right, she headed into the kitchen and then looked through to the dining room before heading back out into the central hallway. This time she aimed toward the living room.

Gabe was there, lying spread out on his mother's beautiful, upholstered couch. The pale color showed off his dark suit, one arm thrown across his face, one leg on the floor as if for balance. The room was clearly decorated for tea and small talk. Gabe, it turned out, was now using it for bottles of Jack and passing out.

This was not what her Mama had sent her here for. But she wasn't just going to walk out in a huff, though she wished she could.

Lennon frowned. Two bottles stood on the table in front of him—one empty, one partially full. Had he drunk one and a half bottles? She asked herself if he was medically okay drinking that much. So she headed toward him, pushing at his shoulder as she tried to rouse him. Though he didn't wake easily, she was grateful that he was still breathing. "Gabe, are you okay? *Gabe*."

At first, he started to bat her away but then seemed to recognize her voice.

"*Lennon?*" Somehow he managed to slur even the simple sounds of her name.

"Yes, it's me. Are you okay? Do I need to take you to the ER for alcohol poisoning?"

He frowned at her, though he seemed confused about the fact that she was asking him things at all. Honestly, it was probably a good sign. "Gabe, how much did you drink? Did you drink a whole bottle?"

At least he had the nerve to laugh at her. "Thah one wass

almost empty when I started." He pointed toward the coffee table though not toward a particular bottle. Clearly, at least he was indicating the empty one.

"How much have you had?" she asked.

"Not that much, juss enough. Juss enough to make-up for dancing with you and then having you walk away again." The words were drawn out, slurred enough that she couldn't quite put stock in what he was saying.

"Gabe," she sighed out his name. "You need to go to bed. You're drunk."

He sat up and looked at her then, his eyes clearer than she expected given the dismissive tone his words had had. "No," he replied, "*I'm not drunk enough.*"

This time he was angry. She turned to leave but he called out as she got close to the front door. "Lennon, wait! I love you."

But she didn't wait. She couldn't trust his words, not like this. So she closed the front door behind her as she headed down the front porch, probably for the last time. She fought hard against the tears that threatened to fall.

✌ 57 ☙

Lennon stood and looked out her apartment window, her brain not going much of anywhere these days. A foot of snow had fallen on Chicago overnight while she slept. Normally, it would make her feel colder, even though it had stopped snowing already, even though the wind and the air had been cold all along.

Winter in Chicago was not for the faint of heart, she thought. But the city, for the most part, knew what it was doing. The buses would run, at least relatively on time. Or, perhaps no worse than they ever did. The roads would be cleared. Unlike a snow in Breathless—which was rare—the citizens here would just go about their day and not freak out and buy all the milk and bread off grocery store shelves.

She'd considered going back home for Thanksgiving. Her Mama had made it clear she expected Lennon for the holiday. The drive wasn't too horrendous, though it wasn't easy. But, without classes and midterms, it was difficult to convince her mother that she needed to stay in Chicago. While she wanted to spend Thanksgiving with her parents, Jackson, and the girls, she did not want to be in Breathless. She did not want to possibly run into Gabe. She'd barely been back a week, but all at once it felt like years and like no time had passed at all.

She'd gotten dressed this morning—even put on makeup and sunscreen, despite the cold weather—and was ready to head out the door. Still, she hadn't quite brought herself to do it. Instead she'd stood at the window, telling herself she was enjoying the view, even though she wasn't really looking.

The apartment was really nowhere to spend the whole day. She and her roommates mostly survived by being gone. It had been a trade—to be close to the school, they had needed to give up space. Another option had been to pay more, but as graduate students, none of the three of them had it to spare. So square footage had been the thing they opted to let go. There were three of them in a two-bedroom apartment. Three beds in the large room. Three desks in the smaller one. And mostly, time spent out of the unit and at school.

She'd barely begun processing the things she'd dug up in Breathless. There was a long road ahead of her before she could defend this thesis. She reminded herself—and planned to remind her mother—she would definitely be going home for Christmas. But to make it to both Thanksgiving *and* Christmas? Lennon wondered if she could she just say she had too much work to do. Surely her parents would understand if it was for school.

A knock at her door startled her. It had never startled her when she was growing up in the small town in Georgia, but here, people rarely knocked on the door. And even more rarely did people knock on an internal door in an apartment building. Even packages were often delivered to the manager, and then left in front of her unit—usually right on her threshold for her to trip over as she left. So, the knock was startling, especially as she was in here alone.

She turned, and feeling suspicious, put her eye to the peephole. Her breath sucked in as she spotted Gabe Zemp standing there. Unable to do anything else, she turned the bolts, opened the door, and stared at him in stunned surprise.

"What are you doing here?" It was a terrible greeting, but it was what had come out and she couldn't take it back.

"I came to see you." His voice was soft, almost as though he'd been driving in the neighborhood and randomly wound up on her doorstep. In Chicago. Hands shoved down into his pockets, he rocked back on his heels and looked as though he understood she might not say anything in response.

She stared at him for a moment before waving her hand back toward the living area and welcoming him into the tiny space. She'd seen his home and knew hers paled in comparison. She didn't even have Emma Kate to give it a five-dollar makeover. He had to understand, this was the best that grad school money could buy, and it wasn't much.

"Why did you come?" She pressed the issue, but he didn't answer.

Instead, he held his hand out. "Come spend the day with me."

She didn't say anything, and he kept going. "Show me Chicago. Show me the city; show me why this is your home. Take me to the museums. Tell me where the best food is. It's all on me. I just want to see what's here."

She waited for him to say, "What's here that's so amazing it's keeping you away from Breathless?" But he didn't add the last part.

Lennon swallowed her thoughts and considered refusing him. But his request was relatively simple, and she'd always found it hard to say no to him. So instead, she asked, "Are you here on business?"

He shook his head. "I just came to see you."

Suddenly, it was even harder saying no to a man who had traveled all this way for her. So, she found herself standing in line to get inside the Pritzker Museum. The line was short because of the cold, but not short enough that they didn't have to wait outside for a little while. Once inside with the exhibits, she watched with stunned amazement as he went to each of the paintings, listing artists and styles.

He turned to her, a smile on his face. "This is a Cassatt. She has such a light touch with a brush and painted casual portraiture of mothers and children. It's what she's best known for, but her style is bright, and the subjects seem somewhere between alive and ethereal."

With his instruction and information, she tilted her head and saw what he did. Then she watched as he got his face in closer to another painting. "I don't know the artist, but half of this is painted with a palette brush. Look at the sharp lines and the heavy application of oil paint."

She remembered then, he'd originally gone to school in the arts, and she wondered what else she might have forgotten about him in the intervening years. She took him next to a Burger Shack. Excellent burgers and milkshakes. The food was served in waxed papers and disposable boats but for exorbitant prices. He'd not balked at any of it and appeared to have enjoyed the food immensely. As they tossed the trash, he thanked her for the meal he'd bought for her.

They walked around town for a little while, as long as the cold would allow. When he asked, she'd given him a tour of the school. When it fell dark, he invited her to the bar at his hotel for a few drinks and dinner. And afterward, when he'd paid the check, he stood up and held his hand out again.

"Come up with me, Lennon."

She balked almost out of habit. But then he leaned over close and whispered in her ear. "Give in to it. *Please*. Just this once. Let us be us again. If only for a little bit. I've missed you."

Lennon knew the wise thing was to say no. She'd left him, left Breathless, and understood there was nowhere this relationship could go. But he seemed to have found a loophole. He was here, and she could stay with him. Just one night. Just one chance to be loved by this man again. To feel what he made her feel.

He'd spent the day smiling at her, listening to her, and making her feel as though he'd be happy just following her around for the rest of their lives. But she knew she was here, and he was tied to Breathless in ways that could not be unbound. He waited patiently while she fought with herself.

At last she decided, losing him, losing *them* already hurt more than she was willing to admit. Probably more than she could handle. Tonight, she could ease that, a little. In the morning, it couldn't hurt worse than it already did—at least that's what she told herself.

Lennon only nodded at him, but she could see the tension drain out of him as he led her to the elevators. When the doors closed and they were lucky enough to be alone, he turned. His mouth was on hers and, before she could even think, she'd pressed herself fully to the length of him and was kissing him back.

Despite the fact that her brain knew better, her heart told her that this was where she belonged.

❧ 58 ❧

Southern Belles know some men are like a fine cabernet – a little bitter on the tongue at first but after a while you realize it's the best thing you've ever had.

LENNON WAS LYING IN BED NEXT TO GABE AT FOUR A.M. feeling sated and content. She was naked and more comfortable than she'd ever been, thinking about how he'd talked her into giving in. They were his words, but it felt like both of them had given in to whatever was between them. The red numbers on the hotel clock told her it was far too early—or too late—to be awake, but she could feel he was waking up, too.

As he came around, he didn't speak, but his fingers lightly traced across her shoulder, down her arm, and picked up at the curve of her hip. She felt the moment where her body moved towards his of its own volition. She wasn't in charge here, and she wasn't going to try to be. She'd given in, just as he asked, and she wasn't going to protest or get dressed and leave at least until the sun came up. Maybe not even then.

Gabe kissed her again, long and full, and she thought, *One more time.* Just one more time before she went back to her apartment and back to the life that didn't work with him in it. The life that didn't work in Breathless, Georgia. She curled into him, hoping she was showing him that she didn't have to forgive, but she was giving him everything she had anyway, because it was the last time.

Lennon had practically climbed naked on top of him, so she was surprised when he stopped kissing her and pulled back. Or he pulled back at least as far as he could. "Come here."

She was already as "here" as she could be. But he wanted to lie side by side, it seemed. He'd done that thing he always did, where he curled his arm up under his head and had her rest her head in the crook that his elbow made. With gentle touches, he guided her to nestle in beside him. It wasn't what she'd expected.

Though his fingers still traced her arm and lightly rasped against her skin, giving her shivers, his voice went in an entirely different direction. "Lennon, tell me. What's between us?"

She almost laughed. "Literally? Nothing," she answered.

They were naked. Skin to skin. The tips of her breasts brushing his chest, her thigh thrown over his.

"Right now, it's literally nothing," he said, running his finger along her collarbone and lulling her with his touch, "but tomorrow, what will it be? Because this is too good to give up."

She shook her head. Why was he doing this now? "Tomorrow it will be things bigger than what we have."

"What things?" He asked it sincerely. He understood, but he wanted specifics, probably so he could try to knock them down.

She hadn't agreed to that. Only to one night. "We have too much past." She stated it simply as though that were the end of it.

But it wasn't. Gabe was not finished. He was not operating on "one night" despite what he'd originally asked, and she felt the walls she'd built start to tremble, chips of clay and loose brick tumbling around her. He replied softly, "*We* don't. Other people have pasts that got in our way."

But she shook her head. "No. *We* do. We do *now*."

He nodded, understanding what she meant. "I'm sorry I didn't believe you when you first told me. I do believe you. But it took me a minute. Please forgive me for taking a minute when you came at everything I know and understand. Ultimately, you're absolutely right. There's no reason to think my brother would be the same for you as he was for me, nor my father. Nor anyone, really."

She nodded, finally feeling the loosening in her chest as she really accepted his apology. "I'm sorry. I wanted you to just believe me. And I should have understood that what I said would shake everything you believed about your family."

He nodded as though that was it, but his arms came around her and pulled her closer. Lennon didn't resist. She couldn't resist this man and the world he always managed to construct for her.

She felt the movements in his chest as he said, "What else, Lennon?"

But she didn't know. She only knew that it was there, and she figured he had let it go, but he didn't. He kept talking.

"I sold the chain."

"*What?*" She asked, suddenly startled.

"Bobby's pizza—I sold the whole chain. I mean, the paperwork isn't signed, but I found a buyer and Misty's writing up the contracts and—"

Lennon put her hand flat against his chest, almost smacking him to interrupt. "Why would you do that? I thought it was hugely profitable."

"It is," he said with a small, proud grin. "Which made it easy to sell."

"Then why would you do that?"

"Because I can't own a business that the woman I love justifiably hates."

She was startled, both by his sale of Bobby's and by his words that he loved her. "You don't have to do that for me."

"I do." He offered it up with a nonchalant shrug as though it both meant nothing and yet was inevitable. "I thought about it.

I thought about what we had and about everything in our way. I realized, Lennon, none of the rest of it matters. Not to me."

She felt her eyes well up with unshed tears as he spoke, but Gabe didn't stop. "I love you more than I love my brother, and I love you more than I love the memory of my brother. I love you more than I ever loved my father. I love you more than I like the life I lived. I never loved it. There were really great things about it, and there were things I didn't care about one way or the other. But when I thought about it—when I thought about living that life without you in it—none of the rest of it mattered."

A tear escaped her eye and rolled down her face. It landed on his arm so she knew he felt it, but she couldn't quite speak. Her breath caught in her throat and she saw a future she could now admit she desperately wanted even if it still wasn't quite within her grasp. Could she reach out and make it happen?

"Can you do it, Lennon?" Gabe asked it as if he could read her thoughts. "Can you let go of the past and help clear out the things in our way?"

She thought about it, about all of the anger she still held onto over Brodie, but she was angry at a dead man. She didn't get anything out of it anymore. It only kept her from Gabe. Brodie wasn't even still alive to hurt anyone else, nor was Robert Zemp. She was safe and there was no one she had to protect from them.

All she was protecting was herself, and in that moment, with Gabe there beside her, telling her what he was willing to do to keep them together, it was easier to let it go.

She nodded at him. "I can. But Gabe, I'm in Chicago. I have to live in Chicago—close to school—until I graduate in June. And you live in Breathless. You always have."

He laughed. His finger no longer tracing her arm but wrapping around her waist and pulling her closer. "I don't live in Breathless."

"What?"

279

"I'm selling the house."

"What?" She asked again, incredulously. "But that's your family home!"

"Lennon." His hand reached up and cupped her face, and he leaned in and kissed her full on the mouth. Full of promises of more to come. "Lennon, when you find the woman you want to spend the rest of your life with, everything else can be dealt with. Tell me you love me."

She didn't even wait a beat. "I love you, Gabe Zemp."

"Good," he said. "Then we live in Chicago until you finish your thesis. And after that, we live wherever we want."

She took a deep breath, and this time her tears did spill over. Though she tried to speak, she only gasped for air.

"Are you okay?" He was smiling at least, not horribly worried.

She smiled back at him through the tears, still trying to form words.

"I can get us an apartment here. Or I can get an apartment for myself, if you want to stay with your roommates, if you're not ready to move in with me yet."

Lennon was shaking her head, almost violently. "I'm ready. My half of the rent will be crap, but if you can handle that, I want us to be together."

His smile lit up the room. Or maybe that was the sun peeking through the heavy hotel drapes. She finally managed to get her tears under control and say what she needed to say. "I love you, Gabe Zemp. I want to spend the rest of my life with you."

At his answering smile, Lennon launched herself into the arms of the man she'd always belonged with.

EPILOGUE

E mma Kate could barely catch her breath.
Though she'd spent all day in the car with Keith, they'd
finally stopped for the night. This was their second night on the
road and they were making solid time. Only tonight, as Keith
headed into the bathroom to brush his teeth and wash his face,
Em started to have a small panic attack.

Take three slow, shallow breaths, she told herself and climbed
into the middle of one of the two queen beds. Crossing her legs
and closing her eyes, she walked through a mantra one of her
roommates used. Em was not prepared to use it herself. She had
no practice with talking herself out of a panic attack, and even
mentally the words didn't work.

I'm fine, I'm safe, I'm breathing. She let the breath push out
through pursed lips. Then she inhaled. Breath two. *I can do it. I've
got this.* Not her usual self pep talk, but it would work. Breath
three...

I'm going to do........Shit! She didn't know what she was going
to do.

Em started that last breath over again. On the slow inhale
she forced herself to think. *I'm going to go to Breathless and tell them
I fucked up.*

Nope. That was not acceptable. They could come to that conclusion on their own. She was not going to say it. She tried again.

And again.

Four breaths, and no reduction of anxiety later, she came up with an actionable step. *I'm going to call Lennon.*

Slowly, she forced that breath out, surprised to find the little exercise finally working. Lennon was who she wanted to talk to, and no matter what happened, Lennon would make her feel better.

Opening her eyes, she looked around. Nope, the room looked just as cheap as it had when she'd come in. But at least she had a plan.

Em wasn't sure why she was having an attack tonight. Why not the first night? Why not when she'd woken up and found him there?

It took a moment, but it came to her then. She was in full panic specifically because this cross-country plan *hadn't* blown up. If it had, she'd be free. Clearly, she must have, on some level expected it to. Or she wouldn't have panicked when it didn't.

Digging through her purse, she pulled out her phone and headed outside where the brisk January air hit her. She was just keyed up enough to not go back inside. Keith would be out any minute and she didn't want him to hear. He'd probably poke his head out the door and make sure she was okay, because he was just a decent guy. Or as decent as two days in the car could convince her he was. But Emma Kate believed.

She wasn't in danger, she was safe with him. Just not with herself. She had fucked up. Big time.

And the only one she could ask for help was Lennon.

The phone was ringing in her hand as she held it to her ear, praying for an answer. It was entirely possible that her cousin was naked in bed with that hot man of hers. Em was happy for her. Lennon and Gabe had been an inevitability from the start.

And Lennon deserved her happy ending. She'd done everything right, and that's what you got.

Em, on the other hand had done less than fifty percent of things right—and probably the bad fifty percent, if she was honest with herself—and this was what she got.

"Emma Kate?" The voice told her that she'd reached Lennon and that her cousin was a little surprised at the late call, but not put out.

Give me a minute, Em thought wryly. "Oh, Lennon, I did something."

"What did you do?" She loved that her cousin asked with only concern rather than ready to hear how she'd screwed up the next thing.

That didn't make it any easier to admit. "I got married."

AFTERWORD

Wow, I knew when I started that Lennon was as good at burying her own past as she was at digging up history. But, man, I have to confess even I did not know everything that would come out as Gabe pushed her to reveal what she was hiding. I put a lot on Gabe's plate, didn't I? And Lennon's, too.

I write romance because there wasn't enough of what I love to read...which is *real* characters. The struggle with what they both remember of Brody is such a normal one. He's different things to different people, but neither Gabe's nor Lennon's memories are wrong. That tore me up to write it. I'm not going to miss Brody Zemp, but I was definitely entangled in writing him. Gabe has come so far and my best wish is that you enjoyed the roller coaster I put you through! If you did, it would be fantastic if you're willing to leave a review. Reviews are gold to authors and I'll thank you in advance here: *Thank You!!!*

PREVIEW OF REBEL
(BREATHLESS, GA - BOOK 3)

A belle never shares an address with a man she isn't married to. Engaged doesn't count.

Em took a deep breath in and slowly let it out. Her head hurt. Vegas had managed to be both less and more than she expected. Her left hand felt weird, lying on something like a tutu. She was likely still in a weird dream.

Emma Kate had rolled in under the bright lights around five p.m., her U-Haul too big for the things she'd had in her dorm and they'd all been rattling around the whole drive. The rental shop had not had the small trailer she reserved and they acted as though they had been very nice giving her the larger one. The problem was, she didn't want the larger one. The excess space made it nearly impossible for her to keep her things safe. She'd packed her stuff in a two-foot layer on the floor of the trailer and hoped nothing broke. So, when she'd hit Vegas, she decided to call it a night, rented a cheap room, and grabbed a cab to the nearest luxury casino.

Now she lay on the bed, looking up as the ceiling came into focus. This ceiling was beautiful. If she could sit up, she could check it out. Emma Kate prodded at her brain and tried to figure out what she'd done last night.

She remembered playing the nickel slots and the guy next to her pointing out that drinks were free as long as you were feeding money into a game. Then she... well, she didn't really remember much after that.

Em took another deep breath in and out and only just then noticed the crown molding and the gold flecked wallpaper border. It was nice. Again she asked herself, how was a ceiling *nice*? But it certainly didn't look like what she expected from the cheap motel room she'd rented.

Wait, her brain stopped her. Frowning, she rolled her head to the left. The wall was very far away, the room much bigger than she remembered. She squinted. The wallpaper missing, the paint a peachy tan, beautiful and perfect. Not a peeling strip of tacky floral print in sight. She looked right.

Shit.

The curtains were barely open, revealing a slice of sky, but through that slit she could see daylight. She could also see that she was somewhere in the neighborhood of fifteen to twenty stories up in the sky. No, this was not the one-story motel room with one window and one door.

Where in hell was she?

Em knew that any normal person would have bolted upright just then, but Em also knew that she'd had too many free drinks the night before. Her head was pounding and spinning at the same time. She felt like a typical college student—though that might be a thing of the past. She cringed to herself and regretted that she remembered dropping out of school so clearly.

She wasn't generally one for doing really dumb stuff—she wasn't internet stupid—but she'd made more than her share of bad decisions. Emma Kate also wasn't one for freaking out. She'd had her freakouts earlier in the year when first her mother had died of cancer, and then her father had followed a few months later, apparently unable to go on without the love of his life.

Em was finished with freakouts. Now was not the time anyway. On the plus side, she was warm, comfortable, and clearly in a nice hotel room. She smiled to herself, pleased when that didn't make her brain protest. Maybe she'd won a lot of money and gotten herself a suite comped right here in the... No. She didn't remember which hotel she was in. It didn't matter anyway. The lamps were beautiful. The painting on the wall was much, much classier than the one in the room she'd rented.

She frowned. She was clearly in a different section of town from where she'd parked. She wouldn't have driven when she was drinking. She'd never done anything like that. So, her paid motel room, car, and trailer were probably still down the street. She'd gotten a ride to the casino because parking her trailer in the high-end parking lot would have made her look like she was coming to Vegas for the sole purpose of losing her shirt. She would look like Poor-down-on-her-luck-Emma-Kate, and that was not who she was. She'd made a decision to leave school. That was all.

After another deep breath, she slowly sat up, and that was when the troubles really began.

Though Em reminded herself that she wasn't one for freaking out, as she sat up, Emerson Kate Mayfair realized she had a serious problem on her hands.

For a moment, she thought the pounding in her head was also lying to her eyes. Surely, she was not seeing what she was seeing...

Being a smart cookie, she checked things out before flipping her lid. So she moved her hands around, feeling along the fabric, and realizing she had another sense confirming what she saw. *Well, shit.*

She did not remember how she'd gotten here, but the king size bed was softer than any she'd slept on in the past several years. Underneath her hands were yards and yards of white tulle. It looked like she'd slept on the puffy cloud.

Far too scared now to just look down at her clothing, she

touched the front of her chest. *Yup. That was lacework. And beading.*

When she did eventually look down, she saw a beautiful sweetheart neckline with cap sleeves, one of which had slid off her shoulder at some point in the night. The dress itself was gorgeous, but she had no idea why she was wearing it.

Damn. She looked amazing. Although, she reconsidered, there was every possibility her makeup had run down her face or smeared off onto the pillow. The dress might be amazing, but she might look like Frankenstein's monster was wearing it.

Reaching up to touch her hair, she instead felt the crisp reply of hairspray and curls. Clearly, it had been expertly coiffed and then slept on. Reaching around to touch the back, Em realized the hairspray wasn't as crunchy as she'd originally thought. That was more tulle... on her head. This did not bode well...

She found the tulle was trailing down her back from the tiara pinned into her hair. *A tiara. Of course, she was wearing a tiara.*

As she rolled her head to the side and looked down, she saw *him*. Dark hair, high cut cheekbones, long, inky lashes unmoving because he was out cold. Broad shoulders splayed across the bed on the other side.

She wouldn't have believed him being there was a problem, but he was wearing a tux, and Emma Kate was pretty sure she'd just gotten herself in a world of trouble.

Thank you for reading! I love romances with real love and believable characters, and I hope you found all that in these pages. I want to fall in love right along with the characters, and I do, while I'm writing it.

About Savannah

I started writing when I was eight—I hand wrote an 80-page novella that I believed to be (adult) romantic suspense. I'm proud to say, I've gotten a lot better since then. I've grown up to be a nerd at heart! I love neuroscience and people watching, and if you look, you'll find some of that in each Savannah Kade book. Most days you'll find me in my office, looking out my window at a handful of the neighbor's cows, or watching my dogs or my cat roam the backyard.

Follow me, find me, ask me questions! I would love to hear from you.
www.SavannahKade.com
Savannah@SavannahKade.com

www.ingramcontent.com/pod-product-compliance
Lightning Source LLC
Chambersburg PA
CBHW020948260626
47169CB00006B/1873

* 9 7 8 1 9 4 8 0 5 9 3 7 4 *